THE ICING ON THE CAKE

AN OTTER BLUFF ROMANCE

LINDA SEED

This is a work of fiction. Any characters, organizations, places, or events portrayed in this novel are either products of the author's imagination or are used fictitiously.

THE ICING ON THE CAKE
Copyright © 2020 by Linda Seed

ISBN: 978-1-7343453-3-9

The author is available for book signings, book club discussions, conferences, and other appearances.
Linda Seed may be contacted via e-mail at linda@lindaseed.com or on Facebook at www.facebook.com/LindaSeedAuthor. Learn more about Linda Seed's novels at www.lindaseed.com.

Cover design by Kari March.

❀ Created with Vellum

BY LINDA SEED

CHAPTER 1

*C*assie Jordan appreciated the merits of a good kitchen, and the one in which she stood was top-notch: acres of granite countertop, a double convection oven, a layout that made it easy to pivot from refrigerator to sink to stove, and a refrigerator big enough to accommodate a small restaurant.

She gloried in the luxury of it as she laid out flour, butter, sugar, and all of the other ingredients for her famous champagne cake.

Okay, maybe the cake wasn't famous.

And maybe she'd lose her job if anyone knew she was here.

The cake would be famous someday—she was sure of it. And nobody had to know about her illicit use of the kitchen at Otter Bluff.

Cassie preheated the oven and used the big KitchenAid mixer—another thing offered at Otter Bluff that she didn't have at home—and creamed together butter and sugar. She added three eggs, one at a time, then a teaspoon of vanilla. The batter whirred and blended in the stainless steel bowl.

Cassie usually wasn't one to flout the rules, especially when it threatened her livelihood. But she needed to get this cake done, and she was desperate.

It wasn't like she could bake, assemble, and decorate a three-tiered wedding cake in her Airstream trailer, and she didn't have anywhere else to do it. Her parents' kitchen was small, and worse than that, it was always packed with people—her siblings, her nieces and nephews, her mother's book group, and her father, who always seemed to be puttering around looking for snacks. That was fine when she was just whipping up a batch of cookies, but this cake was important.

This cake was going to launch her career as a baker.

At least, that was the plan.

She'd gotten the idea to use the kitchen at Otter Bluff when the family who'd been planning to rent the house for the month of April had canceled at the last minute. Cassie's boss, who ran Central Coast Escapes, was scrambling to find another renter, but until he did, the house was going to be empty.

Cassie had been in the house to clean it after the last guests had gone, and she'd had the idea of borrowing the place just long enough to get the cake done. Who would it harm? She would leave the house spotless, and no one would ever know she'd been here.

She'd done plenty of wedding cakes as favors for friends and family, but this was the first one she was actually being paid to bake. If all went well, the bride and groom's guests would be impressed, and they'd ask for referrals for their own events.

Wedding cakes weren't going to pay enough for her to quit her job cleaning and maintaining vacation rentals—at least, not at first—but eventually, who knew?

Carefully, Cassie combined flour, baking powder, and salt in a bowl and added them to the mixture. While the mixer whirred, she thought about Otter Bluff.

In the plus column were the location—perched atop a bluff overlooking the Pacific Ocean, with breathtaking views and the sounds of barking sea lions—and the newly renovated kitchen. In the minus column was the fact that only the kitchen had been renovated before the owner had either run out of money or had lost interest. The rest of the house hadn't been updated since it was built in the 1970s.

The harvest gold bathroom fixtures had been installed well before

Cassie was born, and there they still were, like some kind of museum exhibit of an earlier, more innocent America.

Then there was the shag carpeting in the master bedroom. Who knew what microbes lived there, even after a good shampooing?

The overall result was that Otter Bluff was a popular rental among people who were willing to put up with the shabby bathrooms, bedrooms, and living room in order to get the spectacular view at a relative bargain.

Cassie was mixing buttermilk and champagne in another bowl, preparing to add them to the batter, when her cell phone rang on the counter.

Her boss.

"Hi, Elliot." Cassie attempted to sound both perky and honest, like someone who would never use a house that wasn't hers.

"Cassie. Where are you?"

"Oh. I'm at my parents' place. Did you need something?" The lie fell out of her mouth with disturbing ease.

"Yes. The Taylors left Dolphin Dreams early, and I wondered if you could get over there and clean it."

Dolphin Dreams was a ridiculously named house in the Seaclift Estates neighborhood—four bedrooms, three bathrooms, partial ocean view. It was a nice place, but Cassie imagined some clients were put off by the name alone.

"But I have this afternoon off," Cassie protested.

"I know that, and I'm sorry, but the incoming renters want to arrive early, and now that the Taylors have left, there's no reason they can't—except that the house hasn't been cleaned yet."

Cassie had forgotten to turn off the mixer, and it was still whirring away in the background.

"What's that sound?" Elliot wanted to know.

Cassie switched off the machine. "Oh ... it's a mixer. I'm baking a cake."

"Weren't you just complaining yesterday that your mixer is broken?"

Oh, shit. Yes, she'd done that.

"I … got a new one." She closed her eyes tightly and prayed silently for forgiveness of her misdeeds.

"Ah. Well. Be that as it may." It was Elliot's favorite phrase: *Be that as it may.* She'd heard it from him so many times that it ceased to have any meaning—if it ever had meaning in the first place.

"It's my afternoon off, Elliot," she said again. Not that it would do any good. Elliot didn't respect days off, and he didn't respect people's personal lives. Come to think of it, he didn't seem to respect Cassie, either.

"If I have to call Rebecca in, I might just let her continue on full-time."

And there it was. The threat. Rebecca was their backup house-cleaner, and she'd been wanting to take over Cassie's job for months.

Cassie spent a happy moment imagining herself pushing Elliot down a flight of stairs, or perhaps off a cliff.

"Okay. I'll do it," she said.

"Wonderful. I've already told the new tenants they can check in at four."

Cassie looked at the time. It was just past one p.m. She could finish the batter, put it in the refrigerator, then go over to Seaclift Estates and clean Dolphin Dreams in time to get back here and finish baking the cake. She'd freeze the layers and begin decorating tomorrow. She still had three days until the wedding.

Irritated, she told Elliot, "You could at least thank me."

"I would think your paycheck is reward enough," Elliot said, and hung up.

BRIAN CAVANAUGH PEERED into the hole that had been cut into the drywall in his master bathroom, already certain that nothing inside there was going to be good. His black lab, Thor, sat at his side and whined in sympathy.

"See that?" Ray, his contractor, pointed a finger into the hole, his hand roughened by manual labor. "You've got a mold problem."

Brian squinted through his thick-framed glasses at the black substance that had been growing within his walls. "That doesn't look good."

"It's not. You want to know what else isn't good? You've also got termites."

"I do?"

Ray drew a cell phone out of his pocket and pulled up a photo of a wooden beam full of long, ragged holes. "I took this in the crawl space under your house. I figured you wouldn't want to go down there to see for yourself."

"Very thoughtful."

Brian had hired Ray to do some renovations in his bathroom because he was planning to sell the house, and his Realtor said he'd be leaving money on the table if he didn't fix it up a little. That was the Realtor's exact phrase: *leaving money on the table.*

Brian was getting the sense that he might have neither money nor a table when all of this played out.

"I assume neither of those things is going to be cheap," Brian said.

"You assume right," Ray said, then laughed. The bastard actually laughed.

At least somebody here was having a good time.

BY THE TIME RAY LEFT, Brian had the general outline of his situation. Not only were the repairs on his house going to be expensive, they were also going to take time. The place would have to be tented, the termite-damaged beams would have to be replaced, the leaky pipe that had caused the mold would have to be fixed, and it was likely the mold couldn't just be cleaned away—Ray would have to cut out and replace drywall, studs, and flooring.

Add to that the fact that Ray wasn't going to be able to start the job for another two weeks.

"Oh, my goodness, no. You can't just sell the house as is." Barbara, Brian's Realtor, scoffed at the very thought when he called and told her about Ray's findings. "Any offer that's made on your house is going to rescinded when they get the inspection. And I'll tell you something else: You can't stay there in the meantime. Black mold is no joke."

Yeah, Ray had said. So now Brian and Thor were facing temporary homelessness on top of the huge expense of making his house livable —and sellable.

He had savings. He wasn't broke. But he couldn't throw his money around like there would be an endless supply of it. His YouTube income was pretty good right now, but he couldn't count on that continuing forever. It wasn't as though he had job security. And he would need a healthy bank account to qualify for a mortgage on a new house.

Paying for the repairs would be bad enough. Now he had to pay rent on a temporary place to live, too.

Unless…

He could always ask his mother for help.

Brian had a vicious argument with himself after Ray had gone as he stared into the hole at the black mold.

I'm not going to call her. I am NOT going to call her.

Of course I'm going to call her. Why wouldn't I call her?

In the end, he called her.

"Otter Bluff?" Lisa asked, as though she owned dozens of beach-side rental houses and couldn't quite place the one Brian was talking about. "Well, yes, it's vacant at the moment. But I was hoping the rental agency would find me a tenant, because I rely on the income from that property."

Lisa Barlow did not rely on the income from Otter Bluff—she just wanted Brian to grovel and pledge his eternal gratitude if she let him use it. He weighed the pros and cons. Living in his car with his dog would be cramped and inconvenient, but the idea took on a certain appeal when he considered the hoops his mother was going to force him to jump through before she would agree to help him.

Screw it. He could crash on somebody's couch. He could take shelter under an overpass.

"Never mind then, Mom. I shouldn't have asked."

"Well, now, not so fast."

Brian closed his eyes and prayed for patience. "But you just said—"

"I said I was hoping the rental company could find a tenant. But they haven't yet, have they? I suppose you could use the house, just for the time being," Lisa said.

"Mom, thank you. I—"

"Of course, if they find someone, I'll need you to move out."

"But—"

"And maybe you can do some small repairs while you're there."

"Okay, but—"

"Though I don't know why I should do this for you at all, considering how seldom you call me or visit."

"Maybe because I'm your son and I have nowhere to live?" he suggested.

"Oh, Brian, dear, don't be dramatic," Lisa said. "You know where I keep the spare key."

CHAPTER 2

*B*y the time Cassie finished cleaning Dolphin Dreams, she was dirty and sweaty. She weighed the idea of going home to shower and change her clothes before returning to Otter Bluff to finish baking the cake, but that presented a number of problems.

For one thing, there was no way she'd be able to go into her Airstream in her parents' backyard, shower, change her clothes, and get out again without being noticed. Her mother would see her from the kitchen window, and once that happened, Cassie would get drawn into any number of conversations, household chores, bits of family drama, and obligations.

Her aunt and uncle were visiting from the Bay Area, and that meant even more peril than usual. Cassie's mother would insist that she go into the house, join them for dinner, then recount the details of her life for her relatives over olallieberry pie and ice cream.

The pie and ice cream had a certain appeal—as did spending time with her aunt and uncle, whom Cassie loved—but it would mean she would not get back to Otter Bluff that evening, and *that* meant the cake wouldn't get baked in time for her to begin decorating it tomorrow.

There was no way she would be able to apply hundreds of buttercream roses before Saturday if she didn't stay on track.

With that in mind, she opted to return to Otter Bluff and shower later.

But once she was there, Cassie lifted her arms over her head to get something out of a high cupboard in the kitchen, and she offended herself with her own aroma.

Okay, the shower wasn't optional.

She didn't have any spare clothes here, but that was okay. She could wrap herself in a towel and put her things into the washing machine while the cake was baking.

Cassie felt a twinge of guilt as she went into the master bathroom, stripped down, and got into the circa-1970s shower with its powder blue fixtures and cracked grout. It was one thing to use the kitchen in a house where she didn't belong—it was another to be naked in that house. But no one would ever know, would they? She would scrub the shower before she left. She would mop the water off the floor. She would leave things better than she'd found them, just as she always did as an employee of Central Coast Escapes.

The shower in her Airstream was the size of a phone booth, so using one that was big enough for her to turn around in was a luxury. She sang as she soaped up.

BRIAN DIDN'T PACK TOO many things for the move to his mother's rental place. After all, his own house was just a thirty-minute drive down the coast from Cambria, and he could always go back to get anything he'd forgotten.

He packed one suitcase with a few changes of clothes, some books, his laptop, and some basic grooming supplies. He also packed some things for Thor—kibble, a dog bed, a leash, and some chew toys. He brought the camera and tripod he used for his YouTube videos, because he couldn't stop working just because his house was being repaired.

On his way up the coast, he stopped at a grocery store and picked up some essentials: beer, Cheetos, frozen pizza, Cap'n Crunch, and milk.

Yes, the whole thing sucked. Yes, he hated having to ask his mother for help. But in the end, he had to admit that he'd probably survive. Otter Bluff had a stunning ocean view, and he was getting it for free—if you didn't count the list of chores his mother expected him to do.

He'd prefer to be home, of course, but things could be so much worse. The cost of rental housing on the Central Coast was astronomical, and he didn't want to spend that on top of what he'd already be putting into the repairs on his own place.

Avoiding that expense almost made it worth having to ask his mother for the favor.

He pulled up at Otter Bluff just after five p.m. as the sun was beginning its descent toward the water. The smell of salt air and seaweed hit him with its pleasant tang as soon as he opened the car door. Just beyond where the street ended, waves crashed into the bluffs and seagulls wheeled overhead.

He grabbed his suitcase and his bag of groceries and went up the front walk. Thor, happy to be out of the car, peed exuberantly on a bush.

His mother kept the spare key in a fake rock hidden amid an array of real rocks in the front garden. Brian hunted around for a rock that looked too perfect, found it, and grabbed the key from underneath.

He put the key in the door, opened it—and immediately sensed that something was wrong.

The first clue was that the lights were on. The kitchen, in particular, was ablaze with light from the overheads and the pendant lamps that hung over the granite-topped island.

The second clue was the array of round metal pans in graduated sizes lined up on the countertop.

The third and final clue was the sound of singing coming from down the hallway. "Like a Virgin," it sounded like, though the singer was off-pitch enough that he wasn't completely certain.

"Hello?" he called tentatively, putting his bags down on the floor as

Thor began sniffing the carpet, the sofa, and everything else he could reach.

The singing continued unabated.

He went down the hallway and poked his head into the master bedroom. The door was open, as was the door to the master bathroom. Steam billowed into the room from the bathroom, and Brian could smell the scent of shampoo and Dial soap.

As he stood there wondering who the hell was in his mother's house and whether there'd been some sort of mistake, the water turned off and he heard the shower door squeak open. Seconds later, a woman emerged, a towel wrapped around her head like a turban, another towel around her body, tucked in just over her breasts.

She was still singing.

"Like a vir—"

In the middle of the word, she looked up, saw him, and screamed. But she didn't just scream. She also leaped into the air, her feet scrabbling at nothing, her face a mask of horror and surprise.

"Wait. I didn't mean—"

"Shit! Shit! Oh my God! What are you doing? Who are you? Shit!"

The woman pulled the towel tighter around herself, as it had threatened to fall when she'd let go of it in surprise.

"I'm Brian."

"What are you doing here? Get the hell out! I don't have any money! I don't have any valuables! I'm calling the police! I have a gun!"

She obviously didn't have a gun—at least, not on her. Where would she have concealed it?

"I think there's been some kind of misunderstanding. This is my mother's house. Are you a renter? She said the place was empty. Did she get her dates mixed up?"

CASSIE HAD BEEN SO terror-struck by the man in the bedroom doorway that she'd immediately assumed a fight-or-flight posture, preparing to hit him with a lamp or flee through the bathroom window.

But now that his words were sinking in, she began to understand what was happening.

She was the intruder here, not him.

"Your mother's house? Your mother is Lisa Barlow?"

"Yeah. She told me there was no one here. But here you are. Are you a renter?" he asked again.

The simplest thing would be to tell him yes, she was one of Lisa's tenants. Then he would blame himself for the mistake and leave.

And then call his mother and tell her exactly what had happened.

No. She couldn't have that.

"Uh … I'll just step out of the room while you get dressed," he offered.

"I don't have any clothes," she said. "Well, I do, but they're in the washing machine."

He blinked at her. "All of them?"

"Yes."

He looked confused. She didn't blame him.

"Well … my mother keeps some things in the closet in the spare bedroom. It's locked, but …" He pulled the house keys from his pocket and dangled them.

"Oh. That would be great." Cassie nearly wept with relief.

TEN MINUTES LATER, Cassie was sitting on the sofa in the living room wearing an expensive pair of linen pants that were too long for her and a black cotton crop top that bared an inch of flesh at her midriff. Cassie had never met Lisa Barlow, but judging from Brian's age, she had to be in her fifties, at least. The crop top was unexpected.

Cassie had taken the towel off her head, and her blond hair, still wet from the shower, hung over her shoulders, creating damp spots on the T-shirt. Thor had climbed up onto the sofa next to her, and she scratched behind his ears.

"Okay, so you're not a renter." Brian sat on a chair across the coffee table from her. "You're … a baker?" He gestured toward where the pans were still lined up on the counter.

"Yes. I was just …. I was using the kitchen here because I have to make a wedding cake by this weekend, and I live in a trailer with a countertop the size of a breadboard, and the house here was just sitting empty, and I didn't think it would hurt anything…." She recognized that she was rambling, and she forced herself to stop. She wasn't wearing a bra under the T-shirt—hers was in the laundry—so she folded her arms over her chest to hide the fact that she was feeling a little chilly.

"So you, what, broke in?"

"No! No, no. Let me back up. See, I work for Central Coast Escapes."

"The property management company."

"Right! I do the cleaning and some of the maintenance—odd jobs and such—and my boss told me there were no renters here this month. And I had a key, and I thought … Oh, God, please don't call the police and have me arrested. Though you could. You really could. I'm so sorry. I didn't mean any harm. It will never happen again."

She watched him as he took all of this in, and as she did, she thought that she'd seen him somewhere before. Had she met him when he'd been to the house on some earlier occasion? Had she seen him around town?

"You thought the house was empty, and you needed a good kitchen, and Otter Bluff has one. So you just thought you'd pop in and bake a wedding cake," he summarized.

"Well, it sounds weird when you say it like that."

Brian was utterly mesmerized.

When he'd come to Otter Bluff, he had hoped that maybe, if he was lucky, the former renters might have left some Cokes in the refrigerator.

Never in his wildest dreams had he imagined he'd get here and find a naked woman in the bedroom.

And a damned cute one, at that.

What she was doing wasn't cool, obviously. It was a serious breach of her responsibilities as an employee of the property management company. And yes, he could get her fired in a heartbeat if he told her boss—or his mother—what had happened.

But somehow, he didn't want to get her fired. He didn't even particularly want her to leave. The sight of her sitting there all fresh and dewy from the shower, wearing his mother's clothes and petting his dog, made him smile in a way he hadn't smiled in quite some time.

"Okay," he said after she'd finished her story. Just *okay*.

"What does that mean?" she asked. "What does 'okay' mean?"

"It means, I acknowledge that you're not here to steal the TV and the silverware. You're just here to use the kitchen."

Until now, she'd looked mortified. Now, for the first time since he'd gotten here, she looked hopeful.

"Does that mean you're not going to tell your mother?"

"For the time being."

"Meaning, you might tell her at some point."

"I might. I mean, if I go through the house and find that you've stripped the light fixtures or something."

"I didn't. I swear to God, I—"

"Then I won't tell her." He didn't know why he'd made that particular promise. He should tell his mother. He should also call Central Coast Escapes and tell whoever was in charge over there. Clearly, it wasn't okay that some random person was using his mother's house for her own purposes.

But if he did that, this very cute, formerly naked woman would be mad at him. And that prospect didn't seem appealing.

"But ... why not?" she wanted to know.

"Maybe you'd better quit while you're ahead," he suggested.

Cassie had already transferred her clothes to the dryer, and now they heard the ding that indicated the cycle was done.

"I guess I'd better get dressed," she said. "In my own clothes, I mean."

Regretfully, he agreed. The crop top looked a hell of a lot better on her than it did on his mother.

THE ENTIRE TIME Cassie was in the bedroom getting dressed, she racked her brain to remember where she'd seen this guy before. Because she knew she had. Did they go to the same coffeehouse? Had she seen him at the gym?

When she came out in her jeans and sweater, her damp hair pulled back into a ponytail, she gave him the clothes she'd borrowed, now neatly folded. "Thanks for letting me use these."

"No problem." He adjusted the glasses on his nose. "Not that any of this is her fault, but my mom should have told the property management company that I was coming. It was a last-minute thing. My house is being tented for termites." He grimaced ruefully. "If this had happened six months ago, I'd have just stayed at my friend Ike's place, but he moved, so …"

That was what did it. The name Ike. That was when it clicked in Cassie's mind where she'd seen him.

"Ike. Your friend Ike. As in Ike and Brian."

"Well … yeah."

Oh, shit. Ike and Brian. She'd watched their show on YouTube. He was a celebrity. An actual celebrity had seen her in nothing but a towel while she was illicitly using a house that wasn't hers.

She was horrified.

"Oh, God. Oh, God. You're Brian Cavanaugh. From YouTube. Shit. Shit. I knew I knew you from somewhere. Oh, God."

He looked at her with furrowed brows. "How does that make this situation any worse?"

"I don't know, it just does." She hurried into the kitchen and started gathering up her cake pans. "I just … This is … I'd better go." She hurried out of the house with her arms full of pans.

When she was gone, he felt the loss of her. She shouldn't have been here, it was true. But she'd filled the house with noise and light and color. Now that she was gone, it was just ... a house.

He fed Thor and set about the job of unpacking his things. When he opened the refrigerator to put in his groceries, he noticed a large bowl covered in plastic wrap. He lifted the wrap and peered at the contents, taking a sniff.

Cake batter.

Interesting.

CHAPTER 3

assie thought about concealing what had happened, as it didn't show her in the best light, but once she got home, she thought, *screw it*. Lacy, one of her sisters, was sitting at the kitchen table in their parents' house, and Cassie couldn't resist spilling everything.

Why not? It wasn't as though Lacy would judge her. Their mother? Yes. Their oldest sister, Jess? Certainly. But Lacy would find the story amusing and would probably have a nugget or two of useful advice to offer.

When Cassie came in through the back door, having dropped her stuff in the trailer, Lacy looked up and smiled.

"Hey, you. You missed dinner, but there are still some leftovers in the fridge."

That was one nice thing about living in her parents' backyard— any time she didn't want to fend for herself, all she had to do was cross the lawn to get a home-cooked meal. She went to the refrigerator and peered inside.

"How was your day?" Lacy asked.

"I'm glad you asked. It's a story."

"Ooh. I love stories."

Cassie pulled a casserole dish out of the refrigerator, put it on the counter, and got a plate out of a cabinet. "Are Daniel and the kids here?"

"He took Danny and Caleb to the movies. Some Pixar thing. Mom's in the living room with Trevor. She can't get enough of him." Lacy had been married for five years, and in that time, she'd managed to have three kids—all boys. The youngest, Trevor, was just eight months old.

"Ooh, I've got to go in there and pinch those cheeks," Cassie said.

"Whose? Trevor's or Mom's?"

"Very funny."

"Anyway, you're not going anywhere until you tell me the story. I need a good story. All I ever hear about these days is Minecraft and SpongeBob. I'm tired of SpongeBob."

"All right, all right. Keep your pants on. Just let me get this heated up first. I'm starving."

Cassie spooned some casserole onto her plate and put it in the microwave. When it came out, she grabbed a fork and brought her plate to the table. She sat down across from Lacy and took a bite—her mother's ground beef and cheesy pasta bake. It had always been one of Cassie's favorites.

"Okay," she said, finally ready to launch into it. "First off, I have to tell you that I did a thing. A thing that wasn't strictly ... well, you know. Legal."

Lacy's eyes grew round. "What illegal thing did you do?"

"I might have just ... you know. Used one of the rental houses without permission. Otter Bluff. You know the one on Marine Terrace with the blue siding and white trim?"

"What do you mean you've been using it? Have you been sleeping there?" Lacy sounded horrified.

"No! No, no. I've just been using the kitchen." She explained her situation—she had a wedding cake to produce by Saturday and no kitchen to bake or decorate it in. She described the wonders of the kitchen at Otter Bluff, which had just been sitting there, empty.

"It was the perfect plan!" Cassie threw her hands into the air for

18

emphasis. "I was going to clean up, leave the place spotless, and leave before anyone knew I was there!"

"But …?" Lacy asked.

"But, a guy showed up. In the bedroom. When I was getting out of the shower wearing nothing but a towel."

Lacy let out a guffaw. "Okay, wait. Who was the guy? And why were you taking a shower if you were only there to use the kitchen?"

Fair questions.

"The guy was the owner's son. She told him he could use the house, but she didn't tell Central Coast Escapes, so our records showed that it was empty. And I was in the shower because Elliot, my asshole boss, made me go clean one of the houses in Seaclift Estates, even though it was supposed to be my afternoon off, and I got dirty and sweaty, and I stank." Cassie ate some more of the excellent casserole as Lacy absorbed the information.

"Well, that must have been awkward."

"And," Cassie added, "the guy? He's kind of famous. I watch him on YouTube."

"Oh, jeez. That's—"

"And," Cassie went on, "I was washing my clothes, so I didn't have anything to put on. Other than the towel. I told you it was a story."

"You did," Lacy acknowledged. "You did say that."

"So, to summarize," Cassie said, "a famous guy saw me almost naked and has my future in his hands, because if he tells anyone what I did, I'm going to get fired and maybe arrested. And—oh, damn it, I just realized. I left my cake batter at Otter Bluff."

" 'I left my cake batter at Otter Bluff.' Someone could make a country-western song out of that," Lacy observed.

"It's not funny! Now I've got to start all over on the cake, and I'm never going to finish it by Saturday. Especially since I don't have a kitchen. I can't do it here. You know how chaotic it gets with everyone coming and going. A wedding cake takes concentration. Jeez. This is bad. This cake was supposed to launch my new career."

"You can use our kitchen," Lacy said.

"You've got three kids under five."

"Fair point."

"Thanks, though. I'll have to figure something out."

"You could go over there and ask for the cake batter," Lacy said. "At least then you wouldn't have to start from scratch."

She also wouldn't have to waste the ingredients. On the money she made, paying for another batch of groceries was no small thing—especially when one of the key ingredients she needed was champagne. Okay, sparkling wine. By either name, it was still expensive.

"I would be mortified," she concluded. "If I have to go over there and ask for the batter …"

"Well, better for you to be mortified than for the bride and groom to get married without a cake."

BRIAN THOUGHT about what to do with the giant bowl of cake batter sitting in his refrigerator.

He could throw it out. He could bake some cake.

He was a big fan of cake.

Or, he could get in touch with Cute Towel Girl and arrange for her to come and get her batter.

The more he thought about it, the more that plan sounded good to him. The way she'd told it, she was really pressed for time with the cake. Without the batter, she would have to start over, which she probably would rather not do.

Also, it would be a waste to throw it out, especially when he could earn some serious points with a seriously cute girl if he returned the batter to its rightful owner.

Brian had found that whenever it was possible to earn points with a seriously cute girl, it paid to take advantage of the opportunity.

For the karma, if nothing else.

He resolved to call her and arrange for her to come and get her batter.

When she did, there might even be some flirting—on his part, at least.

CASSIE WAS at work the next day, doing paperwork in the Central Coast Escapes office on Main Street, when Brian called.

"Central Coast Escapes, this is Cassie."

"Hi, Cassie. This is the guy who caught you in my mother's house last night wearing nothing but a towel. Oh, wait. The way I said that, it could be interpreted that I was the one wearing the towel. But I hardly think there's any room for confusion about who was wearing the towel."

Cassie felt her face heat up with what was certainly a fierce red blush. "Oh. Ha. No, I remember who was wearing the towel. Did you call to tell Elliot about what I did? Because, yes, that would be well within your rights, but I would like to point out how good it can make a person feel when they show mercy toward someone who really can't afford to lose their job...."

"I didn't call to tell your boss. I called to ask if you want your cake batter back."

Cassie froze in disbelief. She'd been trying to work up the nerve to call him to ask for it, but so far, she hadn't been able to bring herself to do it. Could it really be this easy? Could he really be letting her off the hook?

"Cassie?"

"Uh ... I would really like to have my cake batter back. Yes. Yes. Oh, my God. So much."

THAT LAST PART—THE *yes, yes, oh my God, so much*—distracted Brian to the point where he forgot what they were talking about. Was it his fault if he'd involuntarily imagined her saying those same words to him under other circumstances?

Fortunately, he got it together quickly enough that he probably hadn't embarrassed himself too severely.

"Ah ... all right. Do you want to come get it after work?"

"Yes. Thank you. I mean it. Thank you. I really appreciate—"

"And you might as well bring your pans and bake it here. I mean, you said you don't have a good kitchen, right?" He hadn't planned to say that last part. That hadn't been what he'd rehearsed when he'd made the call—and yes, he had rehearsed. His intention had been to offer her the batter and get off the phone before he could say something stupid, as he often did when pretty women were involved. Instead, the last part had just … slipped out.

Now that it had, he couldn't believe his own genius.

"You would really let me do that?"

"Sure, why not? I've got two ovens just sitting here."

"Thank you. That's … just, thank you. I can get my pans and be over there by six, if that works for you."

With that out of the way, Brian had to formulate a plan for what he would do once she got here.

Make a move on her?

Play it cool and act like it was perfectly normal for women he didn't know to come into his house and bake cakes?

He was pretty sure the last one was the way to go. He hadn't had a date in a while, and the thought of sharing space in the house with a lovely woman was attractive on its own, even if nothing happened between them. Even if they only, for a little while, breathed the same air.

"Hey, Thor," he told the dog, who was looking up at him. "A girl's coming over."

Thor wagged his tail hopefully.

CHAPTER 4

*A*fter Central Coast Escapes closed at five, Cassie went home, got her cake pans, and drove to Otter Bluff with a combination of excitement and uneasiness in her belly.

Excitement, because she really might get this cake done on time, and also because it wasn't every day that you got to share a kitchen with a guy you regularly watched doing comedy bits on YouTube.

Uneasiness, because he still could decide at any time to tell Elliot what she'd done.

She was still pondering that when Lacy called. Cassie took the call on her car's Bluetooth as she drove.

"So, what happened with the guy and the cake?" Lacy wanted to know. "Did you call and ask for it back?"

"No. He called and asked if I wanted it. And he offered me his kitchen. Can you believe it?"

"Wow. That's ... really great, Cass."

Cassie frowned. "You don't sound like it's great. You sound hesitant."

"I'm not hesitant."

"Yes, you are."

Cassie heard Lacy's breathy sigh over her car's speakers. "Okay. It's just … you don't know this guy. And you're going to be alone with him in his house. And he's got something on you. I mean, he could make one call and get you fired. It doesn't sound like the safest situation for you to be walking into."

The thought had occurred to Cassie, but she pretended it hadn't, mostly because she didn't want to be talked out of using the Otter Bluff kitchen.

"What are you talking about? That's just silly. If he wanted to get me fired, he already would have."

"Unless he wants to use what you did as leverage."

She shook her head impatiently. "Look. I know this guy from YouTube. He's … he's a harmless goofball. He and his partner make a living out of shoving things up each other's noses and running races while wearing five pairs of pants. Or, he used to do all that with his partner. Now he does it alone. The point is, he's not exactly someone I'm afraid of."

"Cassie. That's his public image." Lacy sounded patient but serious —a tone she often took with her children. "That's not necessarily who he really is. You don't *know* who he really is. He could be a predator. He could be luring you over there in order to take advantage of you."

Cassie wanted to shrug it off—wanted to ignore what Lacy was saying. But, damn it, she was right. Maybe Brian was the silly, fun-loving guy she knew from the Internet, but maybe he wasn't. He wouldn't be the first person whose public image was at odds with his private behavior.

"Okay. Okay. Shit. Fine." Cassie blew out a puff of air. "But I really need that kitchen, Lacy. I need to finish this cake."

"Well, maybe I can help out."

"What do you have in mind?"

"Come by and pick me up," Lacy said. "I can be ready in ten minutes."

WHEN BRIAN OPENED his front door in response to the doorbell—

Thor by his side, quivering expectantly—he expected to find an attractive blond on his doorstep. He didn't expect to find two of them —one of whom was toting a baby on her hip.

"Oh. Hi." He tried to keep the disappointment out of his tone. Not that he was disappointed about a visit by two attractive blondes. The baby, though, added a certain Good Housekeeping Seal of Approval to the whole thing that he hadn't been anticipating.

"Brian, this is my sister Lacy and her son Trevor. She's here to help me with the cakes. I hope you don't mind. Hi, Thor." She leaned down and gave the dog a vigorous rub.

"Oh," he said again. "Ah ... of course not. Come in."

As Lacy passed, Brian grinned at the baby, who really was pretty damned cute. "Is he here to help with the cakes, too?"

"No, he's here because he's still nursing, so I couldn't really leave him with his father."

The mention of nursing necessarily roused the thought of breasts —specifically, the breasts that were right in front of him—and he felt himself blush a little. Breasts were great—he loved breasts—but these were motherly breasts, soon to be used for motherly purposes, and that was an entirely different ballgame.

He cleared his throat.

"Can I get you two anything? Beer? Cheez-Its?"

"No, no." Cassie waved him off. "Don't lift a finger for us. We're just going to bake the cakes and be out of your hair. Did I mention that I really appreciate you letting me do this? And also that I appreciate you not getting me fired?"

"You did mention it, yeah. Well, I guess I'll just ..." He motioned to the sofa, where he'd been sitting and watching a show on Netflix when they'd arrived. He went back to his seat. Thor jumped up onto the sofa and curled up next to him, and Brian reached out to scratch the dog's ears.

He pretended to be watching TV, but he was really watching the women through his peripheral vision. Cassie was arranging pans on the countertop, greasing them and doing whatever one did with cake pans before pouring the batter into them, and her sister was just standing there holding the baby.

It occurred to him that a person didn't need assistance just to pour cake batter into pans and put those pans into the oven. And a person really didn't need assistance to wait however long it took for the cakes to bake.

The only possible conclusion was that Lacy was here to chaperone.

He considered how he felt about that, and decided it was sensible. One might even think it was cute.

Useful, even.

If Brian hoped to ask Cassie out on a date—which he did—then it might be to his advantage to get to know her a little in a context where she felt safe. If she'd felt intimidated, she'd be more likely to say no—or, at least, that was one possible scenario. This way, though? He wasn't a threat. He was just a charming and handsome man.

At least, he hoped he would come off as charming and handsome.

Okay, maybe just charming. The handsome would be open to interpretation.

Of course, he wasn't going to be charming if he was sitting here staring at a TV screen. He grabbed the remote, turned off the television, and turned to look at the women.

"Anything I can do? You need anything?" Being helpful was always good.

"No, no." Cassie was using a rubber spatula to scrape batter out of the bowl and into a large round pan. "Thanks, though. I've got it under control. These are about to go in the oven."

He got up and wandered to the kitchen to see what she was doing. As he watched, she reached into her bag and produced strips of cloth that looked like they had been cut from a towel. She wet the strips at the sink, wrung them out, then began fastening them around the cake pans with safety pins.

Interesting.

"Why are you doing that?" he asked.

"Oh. It's to make the cakes rise evenly. You know how you bake a cake and you get this bump in the middle?"

"Sure." In fact, he had never baked a cake, but he didn't want to say that.

"Well, that happens partly because the edges cook first. The wet towels slow that down so the cake will rise without the bump."

He watched what she was doing with interest.

"Cool. Does that work?"

"Mostly. It might still be a little bit higher in the middle, but if it is, I'll cut it to make it even."

"Huh."

She had a lot of cake pans and what seemed like gallons of batter. But he supposed wedding cakes had to be big.

"What kind of cake are you making? Do you have a picture?"

She smiled—a radiant smile that showed her even, white teeth— and reached for her purse. She dug around in there, in the mysterious and unknowable depths, and produced a folded page that had been torn from a magazine. She handed him the page, and he unfolded it and spread it out on the counter.

The cake depicted in the photo had three tiers, right on top of each other—none of those froufrou posts holding them apart—with white frosting and a veritable garden of sugary roses cascading from the top to the bottom in a pink, flowery swirl.

"You're going to make this?"

"I'm going to try."

"Wow. I mean … wow. Really?"

"You sound doubtful," Lacy observed. Her son grabbed a hank of her hair, and Lacy gently pried his fingers off of it.

"Not doubtful, just impressed."

"Let's hope you'll be equally impressed when I'm done," Cassie said.

"If you can do this"—he pointed at the photo—"then why are you cleaning houses for Central Coast Escapes?"

"Cassie's going to be a professional wedding baker," Lacy said, looking at her sister fondly. "It's what she's working toward. This cake —if all goes well—is going to be her professional debut."

"Really."

"That's the plan," Cassie said. She opened the ovens—both of them —and slid cake pans onto the racks. There were too many pans to put them all in at once, even with two ovens. He supposed she planned to do them in shifts.

"I can't wait to see how it comes out." To his surprise, he meant it.

CASSIE SUPPOSED it was obvious that she hadn't really brought Lacy to help. Help with what? All Cassie had to do was pour batter into pans and put the pans in the oven. Okay, yes, there were the towel strips, but that was hardly a two-person job.

Well, it didn't matter. So what if he knew why Lacy was here? It was only reasonable for a single woman to protect herself. It was only sensible to take precautions.

When the cakes were in the ovens, Cassie told Brian, "If you want, we can leave and come back in half an hour when it's time to take them out. We don't want to impose on you, so …"

"You're not imposing. Have a seat. Relax. I was just about to put on a movie. I'll even let the two of you choose."

Cassie and Lacy exchanged a look.

"All right," Lacy said. "If you really don't mind."

"I really don't. Make yourselves comfortable."

So they did. Cassie sat on the sofa with Brian and Thor, and Lacy took a reclining chair with Trevor in her lap. Brian didn't even protest when the sisters chose a rom-com instead of the action flick he'd had in mind.

"THIS IS REALLY NICE OF YOU," Cassie said again as the movie started and the smell of cake began to waft through the air.

"No problem. I don't mind." Brian pushed his glasses up on his nose and leaned back on the sofa, propping his feet up on the coffee table.

The truth was, he really didn't mind. It was nice having attractive women in the house, even if one of them was a wife and mother. It had been nice having attractive women working in the kitchen, though he knew better than to say that.

It wasn't that he had some kind of male fantasy of women cooking for him. It was more the feeling it created to have them bustling around with their mixing bowls and their spatulas.

It felt like home.

Not like any home Brian had ever known, but like the one he imagined in his fondest fantasies. It felt like warmth and nurturing. It felt like some elusive thing he'd always wanted but had never had.

It was even nice having the baby in the house, he thought—until he glanced over and saw that Lacy was nursing her son under a light blanket she'd brought out of her diaper bag.

He felt himself blush but pretended he hadn't seen what she was doing.

He put his eyes back on the screen.

CHAPTER 5

When the timer went off, Cassie paused the movie, got up, and used a wooden toothpick to check the cakes for doneness. The toothpick came out clean, so she removed the cakes from the ovens and put them on cooling racks she'd brought with her.

"Okay, I have to wait a few minutes for them to cool, then I can turn them out of the pans and onto the racks," she explained to Brian. "Then I can put in the rest of the cakes. The whole thing is going to take another"—she mentally calculated—"forty minutes or so. You sure it's okay?"

"We've come this far," Brian said. "Might as well see it through."

By the time the next batch of cakes was in the oven, Trevor was asleep on Lacy's shoulder. Cassie came back to the sofa, and Brian started the movie again.

"I wouldn't have chosen this movie," he said, "but it's not bad."

"You mean you've never seen it?" Lacy asked in surprise.

"No. Should I have?"

"It's *When Harry Met Sally*!" Cassie said, as though the very title of the movie were all the answer that was necessary.

"Well … I know that. But, no, I haven't seen it."

"It's a classic!" Cassie put her hands on her hips, glaring at him in indignation.

"Still ..."

"I'll bet you've seen every movie Adam Sandler has ever made, though," Cassie observed.

Brian blinked, uncertain whether he was being insulted. "You say that like it's a bad thing."

Cassie shook her head and rolled her eyes to assure him that he was, in fact, being insulted. "Just watch the movie," she said.

BY THE TIME the last cake had come out of the oven and was cooling on a wire rack, it was around nine p.m. Lacy was yawning and Trevor was beginning to fuss. The movie wasn't over yet, but she got up and stretched, saying she needed to get her son home and get back to her other kids before they plotted a coup against her husband.

"Okay. I still need to wrap up the cakes and get them into the freezer," Cassie said. "But they need to cool completely first. How about if I drive you home and come back in a bit to finish up?" She looked at Brian, who was still lounging on the sofa. "Is that okay with you?"

"Sure." He waved from where he was sitting. "Bye, Lacy. Trevor. Good to meet both of you."

"You too." Lacy, weighed down with her child and her diaper bag, waved back with two fingers, which were the only parts of either hand she had free.

When Cassie and Lacy were in the car, with Trevor strapped into his car seat in the back, Lacy shifted in the passenger seat to face Cassie more fully. "I think you're right about the harmless goofball thing. I'm not worried about you coming back later."

"Neither am I." Cassie pulled away from the curb and started the short drive to Lacy's house. "He's fine. He's actually pretty nice."

"And cute," Lacy said. "Don't forget cute."

"You think?" Cassie wrinkled her nose.

"Why? You don't?"

"I don't know. Maybe." She considered it. "The thing is, I've always known him as one of the two knuckleheads on the Ike and Brian show. Now I've got to think of him as a real person. I'm still making the transition."

"I get that. But, I've got to tell you, as someone who's never seen the Ike and Brian show? He's cute. Objectively, actually cute. For what that's worth."

"What, are you trying to fix us up now?"

"No. I'm just saying."

As Cassie drove, she considered Brian's objective cuteness. Dark, wavy hair. Blue eyes. Thick-framed glasses that were kind of geek chic. And his smile. The smile was vaguely mischievous, as though whatever amusing thing he might be thinking was also a little bit scandalous.

"Yeah, okay. He's objectively cute," she agreed.

"I didn't see any evidence of a girlfriend," Lacy said. "It's something to think about."

ONCE THE WOMEN had left and Brian was alone in his house, Thor's head resting heavily on his thigh, he was feeling pretty good about how things had gone. He'd enjoyed watching the movie with Cassie and Lacy, had liked being helpful, and was optimistic about his chances for getting Cassie to go out with him.

Hell, he'd liked learning about cake baking, too. It wasn't anything he'd ever given any thought to, but now that he had, it was interesting.

It might not reflect well on his manliness that he was looking forward to watching her decorate it. But, to hell with his manliness. He had an abundance of that, he assured himself. He could spare a little.

He gently nudged Thor's head off of his leg, got up, and stretched.

Then he went into the kitchen and looked at the cakes with some satisfaction. Three tiers, two layers per tier. Some of the cakes were cooling on the kitchen counter, and three more were on the dining room table. They smelled fragrant and comforting.

He yawned and decided he had time for a quick shower before Cassie got back. He went into the master bedroom, stripped down, and stepped under the hot spray.

He was just pulling on his clothes when the doorbell rang. Perfect timing.

He went straight from the bedroom to the front door, without detour, and opened up for her.

"Hey. That didn't take long." He smiled, happy to see her.

Together, they walked into the house and toward the kitchen.

"I'll just get the cakes wrapped up and—" Cassie gasped and slapped both hands over her mouth.

Brian spun around to see what had alarmed her—and his own mouth fell open in speechless horror.

In front of them, Thor was standing on top of the dining room table, his tail wagging. His front paws had disappeared into one of the cakes as he gleefully ate another. The third one clearly had been stepped on—the center bore the distinct and deep impression of paw prints.

From the look of things, Thor had used one of the dining room chairs to get up there. Had Brian forgotten to push them in? Oh, shit. Had he?

"Oh my God," Cassie gasped when she could finally form speech.

Then she burst into tears.

"Shit. Shit. Thor! Bad dog. Bad, bad dog!" Brian ran over to the table, grabbed Thor around his midsection, and lifted the dog off the table, putting him down on the floor. Then he grabbed Thor by the collar, led him into the bedroom, and closed him in. Thor whined and scratched at the door a little, but that didn't last.

The dog wasn't a fool. He knew what he'd done wrong.

With Thor neutralized, Brian rushed back to where Cassie was standing in the dining room looking at the devastated cakes and sobbing into her hands.

"Don't cry." He patted her shoulder ineffectually.

"It's ruined! The cake is ruined! The wedding is on Saturday! What am I going to *dooo*? It's never going to get done in time! I'm going to ruin the bride's wedding! They're going to have to get married with ... with a sheet cake from Costco!"

"I love sheet cakes from Costco."

"Don't!" she yelled at him. "Don't make jokes! This isn't funny!"

In fact, he hadn't been joking. He really did love sheet cakes from Costco. Who didn't? But this hardly seemed like the time to defend himself.

"Okay, let's think." It sounded to him like a good, helpful thing to say. "Today's only Thursday."

"Nobody can bake and decorate a three-tiered wedding cake for one hundred in a day!" Cassie wailed.

"Well ... what time is the wedding?" Brian asked.

"Two o'clock."

"Okay. The way I see it, that gives us one and a half days, not one."

"What do you mean 'us'?" Cassie said.

THE WAY SHE SAW IT, her aspirations to bake wedding cakes professionally were lost in Thor's digestive tract along with her cake. And they were going to end the same way—in a steaming pile of shit.

That was bad enough. Disappointing a bride who'd been counting on her was worse.

The bride—a friend of Cassie's sister Jess—had been reluctant to hire Cassie, knowing she was a hobbyist and that she didn't have the experience of an established baker. Cassie had sworn that she was up to the job. She'd sworn it. And now Deandra's greatest fears would be proved true.

My God, Cassie might not even be able to get a Costco sheet cake at this late date. They might have to settle for Walmart. Cassie would be disgraced. Word would get around, and that would be the end of her dreams.

"I'm sorry," Brian was saying. "I'm so sorry."

She wanted to scream at him. She wanted to demand to know why he'd left a dog alone with several tantalizing cakes. Why hadn't he kept an eye on Thor? Why had he left the dining room chairs situated in such a way that Thor was able to get up there? Why, why, why?

But that wouldn't be fair. The cakes were her responsibility, not his. She hadn't thought about the dog, either. She hadn't moved the chairs, either. He'd only been trying to help. He'd had no obligation to let her use his kitchen, but he'd done it.

She wasn't going to punish him for that.

Cassie wanted to tell him all of that—that it wasn't his fault and that he shouldn't blame himself. But she was too choked with emotion to get out any words.

"Oh, God. Here. Sit down." Brian pulled over one of the dining room chairs Thor had used to get onto the table, and she sat. He went to the kitchen and pulled some paper towels off the roll and brought them to her.

She wiped her eyes and blew her nose loudly into the towels.

"You've got a day and a half," he said. "You can't give up."

"I can't … I can't give up," she repeated.

"You've got to try."

"I've got to try." He was right. She did have to try. It wasn't just her reputation at stake—it was someone's wedding.

She nodded and dried her eyes one more time. "All right."

"We can do this," Brian said encouragingly.

"We?" she asked.

"I can help," he said.

Maybe he could.

In any event, she had to do something. She had to come up with some kind of cake for the wedding, and it had to look like a wedding cake. She couldn't just grab a Disney Princess cake from the refrigerator section at Albertsons.

"You'll help?" she looked at him hopefully, sniffling a little.

35

"Of course I will."

"But … why?" Why would he do this? Why wouldn't he just send her on her way with a handshake and a few empty words of encouragement?

"It was my dog," he said. "Besides. It could be fun."

CHAPTER 6

*I*t was already late, so Cassie decided there was nothing they could do that evening. She still had three cakes that hadn't been violated by Thor, so she wrapped those up and put them in Brian's freezer.

They agreed that she would return to Otter Bluff at eight a.m., when the Cookie Crock opened, so she could get more ingredients and dive into the task of baking the replacement cakes.

Cassie barely slept that night, tossing restlessly in her bed in the Airstream. When she did sleep, she had nightmares of ruined weddings, angry brides, collapsed cakes, and possible lawsuits.

She got up early, showered, and drank a cup of strong coffee, trying to create a plan for the day that could plausibly result in a finished cake by tomorrow at two p.m.

She was still thinking about it when her sister Jess called.

"How's the cake coming along?" Deandra was Jess's friend, and Jess had been the one to recommend Cassie for the job. Of course she couldn't admit it was all going to hell.

"Fine." Cassie squeezed her eyes shut, as though the lie might not count if she couldn't see herself telling it. "I baked the layers yesterday." That, at least, was not a lie. She'd baked them. She had no obligation to reveal what had happened after that.

"Okay. You're sure you'll have enough time to decorate it? You only allowed yourself one day, and it's a pretty elaborate cake, so ..."

"I have a day and a half," she said. Another not-lie.

"Yes, but—"

"Jess. I'm telling you I've got this under control."

"But it's your first wedding cake for an actual paying client, and—"

"I'm hanging up now."

"Fine. Do you need help? Is there anything I can do to help?"

"No, thanks. I've got this."

She didn't have it, but Cassie would call on just about anyone other than Jess if she needed help with this—or anything, really. Jess, the big sister, had always seen Cassie as the family's adorable screwup. The immature one. The one who lacked ambition, lacked direction, lacked everything except their father's favor. (The fact that Cassie did seem to be Vince's favorite made Jess even more likely to point out her faults whenever she found them—which was often.)

"I swear, Cassie, if you mess this up—"

"God, Jess. I won't. Can't you just have a little faith in me for a change?" Cassie was so involved in her own righteous indignation that she forgot how justified Jess's lack of confidence was.

"I'm just saying."

"I'm hanging up."

And she did.

By the time Cassie showed up at Otter Bluff, Brian had a plan. He liked having a plan for this situation or any other—he was, after all, an idea man. Brian's ideas had been the driving force behind the Ike and Brian show, and he hoped they'd be equally useful here.

"Give me a list and send me to the grocery store," he offered. "While I'm doing that, you can start making the flowers. You already have the ingredients for that, right? I looked it up on Google—you can make them ahead."

"You looked it up on Google? You really researched cake decorating?"

"Of course."

"Well … yeah. I can. But—"

"I mean, from what I can figure from the articles I read, making the flowers will be the most time-consuming part. The earlier you get on that, the easier it's going to be to get caught up."

She frowned—not in an unhappy way, he was glad to see, but in a thoughtful one.

"Yeah. That is the most time-intensive part. So … that could work."

"Great." Brian clapped his hands once, as though he were giving a pep talk to a sports team. "Give me that list, and let's get going."

There was the expected argument about who would pay. Brian offered, as it had been his dog who'd destroyed the cakes. Cassie tried to refuse, because Brian wouldn't be in this in the first place if she hadn't appropriated the use of his kitchen without permission.

In the end, Brian won. List in hand, he rushed out the door and to the Cookie Crock. When he got there, he scanned the aisles for flour, sugar, eggs, butter, and the various other things Cassie needed.

This was good. This was useful.

He liked to be useful.

It didn't feel good just because he was buttering up an attractive woman, either. It felt good because he loved a nice project. He enjoyed having something to sink his teeth into—metaphorically—and this was as good as anything.

He didn't know if one brand of flour was better than another, but he assumed the brand mattered. He bought the big-name stuff instead of the generic, just in case.

He wanted to get this right.

AT OTTER BLUFF, Cassie mixed up a batch of buttercream frosting, using the big mixer to blend butter, powdered sugar, a touch of cream, and food coloring to get a cloud of frosting the color of a faint blush.

She made up a pastry bag out of parchment, fitted it with a rose petal tip, then used a rubber spatula to spoon frosting into the bag. She cut out squares of parchment, used a dot of frosting to glue one of them to the head of a flower nail—a gizmo that looked like a stainless steel thumbtack blown up to ten times its normal size—then took a deep breath and blew a lock of hair out of her eyes.

She'd been practicing roses for weeks. She knew how to do this.

She closed her eyes, took a moment to center herself, then opened them and began shaping her first rose.

Brian got back to Otter Bluff with two bags of groceries and a fresh sense of purpose.

He'd given Thor an extra-long walk this morning and had settled the dog into a bedroom with his bed and a fresh chew toy.

There would be no more ruined cakes today—not on his watch.

He came into the kitchen in triumph, a bag under each arm.

Then stopped and marveled at what she'd done.

Already, there were dozens of flowers. Roses in various stages of opening and in varied colors of pink. Dark ones, fully bloomed. Light ones in tightly coiled buds. Some in between, their petals just beginning to open, as if to welcome the spring.

Every damned one of them looked like it had been freshly plucked from some perfect garden tended by forest sprites.

"Wow." That was all he seemed to be able to say. He hadn't even put the grocery bags down yet. He was too busy staring at the sugary bouquet.

"Wow good, or wow, how can I expect someone to actually pay for that?" Cassie looked at him, her brows furrowed.

"Wow, those are works of art."

She smiled, and her smile filled his chest with warmth and light. "Really?"

"Really. You've got a gift for this."

"God, I hope so. Put that stuff down, and I'll get to work on the batter."

CASSIE HAD BARELY STARTED on the roses—she had a few dozen finished, and she needed hundreds—but Brian's reaction pleased her and gave her a much-needed boost of optimism that she might actually pull this off.

She transferred the finished roses to the refrigerator to set, then started mixing ingredients for the next batch of cakes.

"What can I do?" Brian asked. "I want to help."

She glanced at him and saw that he meant it—he really did want to be involved.

"How about you start cracking eggs? I'm going to need the whole dozen."

"I'm on it." He rooted around in a cabinet for a bowl, then began cracking eggs with a level of concentration that was both amusing and adorable.

"Do you cook?" she asked as she measured butter into the bowl of the KitchenAid.

"*Mmm?*" He was focusing so completely on his task that he didn't seem to hear her at first. "No, not really. Unless you consider putting a frozen pizza in the oven to be cooking."

"I don't."

"I make a mean bowl of cereal," he added.

"I don't think that counts."

"Don't be so sure. Getting the perfect ratio of cereal to milk isn't something most people master."

She glanced at him, smiling. "No, I suppose it's not."

They worked side by side companionably. When he'd finished with the eggs, she put him to work cutting rounds of parchment to line the bottoms of the cake pans. While he did that, she creamed butter and sugar together, then added the eggs and vanilla, watching as the mixture turned into a smooth, creamy blend.

"How's this?" He held up a parchment round.

"Perfect. Keep going on those. I need two more."

Cassie wondered if this was what it would be like to rise in her profession to the point where she could eventually hire an assistant— even two. She imagined herself barking orders, assessing cakes for quality, insisting that substandard decorations be redone.

She'd be harsh but admired for her commitment to excellence.

"Where'd you go?" Brian asked after a while. "Seems like you were off in your own special world somewhere."

"Oh … I was just thinking about cakes. And business." He didn't need to know about her desire to be the baking equivalent of Gordon Ramsay. "Would you mind preheating the ovens? Put them at 350."

"Got it."

She'd never thought about working with someone else—she'd enjoyed the solitude of baking—but now, with Brian enthusiastically responding to her every request, she had to admit it was nice.

Fun, even.

She sifted flour, added baking powder, salt.

The whir of the mixer blended with the soft snick of the scissors as Brian cut more parchment rounds.

Before long, Cassie had the next batch of cakes in the oven, strips of wet toweling wrapped around each pan like little scarves.

"All right. What's next?" Brian asked.

"More roses. But I'm not sure you can help me with that."

"*Hmm.* Probably not. But I can keep you company while you do them."

She wanted to tell him that he didn't have to—that she'd already taken up too much of his time. But another part of her thought it would be pleasant to have someone to talk to while she crafted one buttercream rose after another.

"Okay. That would be nice."

∾

BRIAN WAS FASCINATED, watching Cassie make roses out of frosting.

He leaned his forearms on the countertop and watched as she squeezed out one perfect petal after another.

"You sure you don't mind me talking to you while you do that?" he asked.

"Not at all. Go ahead."

"Okay. How did you learn to do this?"

She told him the story of her first cake decorating class at the Michaels in Paso Robles a couple of years before. Her mother had bought her the classes for her birthday after Cassie had mentioned that she wanted to learn a craft.

"I complained at first. 'This isn't a craft. This is cooking.'" She laughed at her own remembered foolishness. "Just try it, she told me. So I did. You should have seen how crappy my first cakes came out. My flowers looked like little blobs of unicorn poop."

"Colorfully put."

"But I got to eat a lot of cake, and I like cake." She formed another rose on the nail, then slid it, on its parchment, onto the counter.

"Hey, could you cut me some more of these?" she indicated the parchment squares she was using for the roses.

"Sure. I'm on it."

She continued her story about cake decorating—how she'd gotten progressively better with practice, using her new skills on her siblings' birthday cakes, her sister's baby shower cake, her parents' anniversary cake.

"That was the one that did it. The anniversary cake. I made it look like a wedding cake, with two tiers, lots of flowers, fondant lace. It came out better than I ever could have expected. That's when my mom suggested I make wedding cakes professionally. As soon as the idea came out of her mouth, I knew it was the right thing for me. I knew if I could make that work, I'd finally know what to do with my life. I'd be doing something I loved. And it shows when you love what you do, don't you think?"

"I do think that, yes."

She paused in her work, stretched her neck, and looked at him. "Well, you must love what you do, right? The YouTube show?"

"I do love it, yes. When Ike and I were doing the show together, it was—well, it was my dream. I still love it, and I still make a good living. But it's not the same without Ike."

"So what happened? Why did he quit?"

Brian shrugged, focusing on his parchment squares. "Ike just didn't want to do it anymore. He wanted to go back to law school and get married. I was so happy doing the show, I didn't realize he wasn't having as much fun as I was."

"The show's still good with just you," she pointed out. "I know, because I watch."

"Yeah, but …" He shrugged again. "It isn't the same. Now it's a job. With Ike, I was just playing and getting paid for it. I miss him."

"So, what are you going to do to get the magic back?"

He looked up from what he was doing and smiled, hoping the smile didn't look as wistful and sad as he felt. "That's the question, isn't it? Maybe I'll get a new partner. Or maybe I'll quit the show and take up cake baking with you."

CHAPTER 7

For Cassie, the rest of the morning was nothing but cakes.

She finished baking the new layers, then turned them out of the pans and onto the racks to cool—being sure to check Thor's location before she did it.

When they were cool, she wrapped them and put them in the freezer because it would make them more stable and control the crumb when she was ready to frost them. She crafted an entire garden, a veritable greenhouse, of flowers. Then she made a batch of white fondant and set it aside for later.

Through it all, she issued orders to Brian and answered questions about why she was doing one thing or another. That last part could have been annoying, given how hard she was working, but it wasn't. She enjoyed the why and how of it, and his interest reminded her of just how cool it all was.

It wasn't just a cake she was making—it was art. Art that would be devoured by the bride and groom's one hundred closest friends, but still.

She was creating something beautiful, and that had value, however fleeting it might be.

By early afternoon, Cassie was ready to frost the tiers and

assemble them. A twelve-inch double-layer round tier for the base, a ten-inch tier in the middle, and a six-inch round on top. She frosted them from a giant bowl of cloudlike buttercream, inserted dowels for stability, then stacked one cake on top of another.

With that done, she stretched her neck, which was starting to cramp.

"Almost there," Brian commented, and Cassie laughed at him.

"Yeah, right. I've got another six hours to go, easy."

His eyes widened. "Seriously?"

"Yes, seriously. If this were a sculpture, we'd be at the big-lump-of-clay part."

"Oh. Jeez."

"Yeah."

"You're gonna get it done in time, though, right?"

She propped one fist on her hip and considered it. "I should. But if one more thing goes wrong, I'm screwed."

As if on cue, her cell phone rang. She looked at the phone as though it were a rattlesnake or a ticking bomb.

"It's Elliot. This can't be good." She picked up the phone, reasoning that she couldn't just ignore him. "Hi, Elliot. What can I do for you on my day off?"

Elliot launched right into it without an apology for disturbing her and without any polite chitchat. "The new renters at Dolphin Dreams say you did an inadequate job vacuuming the master bedroom, and you didn't leave them enough towels. I need you to go over there and fix it."

Cassie suddenly felt sick with stress, and she pressed one hand to her middle. "Elliot, I can't. It's my day off, and I'm in the middle of something."

"Well, you should have thought of that before you did a shoddy job on Dolphin Dreams."

"I did not do a shoddy job. The renters are ..." It was on the tip of her tongue to say the renters were assholes—they'd been clients before, and it was an accurate assessment—but at the last moment, she remembered her professionalism and amended her word choice.

"They're overly particular. You know that. You've dealt with them before."

"Well. Be that as it may."

Cassie gritted her teeth to keep from throwing the phone. "You'll need to send someone else."

"But you were the one who cleaned that house in the first place. And I'm using the word *cleaned* loosely. Ha ha."

If it were possible to strangle someone through a cell phone, Cassie would have done it. She wished there were an iPhone app for that.

"It's. My. Day. Off," she repeated.

"Well, we all make sacrifices," Elliot said. "I'll tell them to expect you." He hung up before she could respond.

OH, shit. Cassie was starting to cry, and Brian hated it when women cried. It was messy, for one thing—all that leaking. For another, it was a mystery to him what one could do to make a woman stop crying once she'd started.

He wanted to help, wanted to make things better for her, but who knew the mysteries of a woman's emotions?

Thor seemed concerned, too; he sat down at Cassie's feet and whined a little.

"Elliot is such a dick." Cassie grabbed a tissue from a box on the counter and blew her nose. "Shit. Shit. Well, that's it, then. I'm never going to get this done. It was stupid to think I could. It was stupid to think anything's ever going to change for me. I'm going to be working for Elliot forever, cleaning people's vacation houses and delivering towels, running around at their beck and call."

The *beck and call* part gave Brian an idea. He pulled out his own cell phone, Googled Central Coast Escapes, and dialed.

"What are you doing?" Cassie asked.

Brian held up a finger to quiet her.

When Elliot answered, he said, "This is Brian Cavanaugh—Lisa Barlow's son."

"Oh. Hello, Mr. Cavanaugh. How's your mother?"

They made polite conversation for a minute before Brian got to the point. "Did my mother tell you I'm staying at Otter Bluff for the rest of the month?"

"Oh. No. I had no idea you—"

"Well, I'm sorry she didn't let you know, but that's what's going on. You can call her if you like." He listened while Elliot made a few murmurings about having looked for renters and how it was inconvenient for him not to have been informed.

"I'm calling because the heat isn't working," Brian went on, ignoring Elliot's complaints. Even as he said it, he felt a blast of cozy heat coming up from a register in the floor.

"Well, that's not our responsibility," Elliot began. "As the homeowner, you and your mother—"

"I realize that," Brian said. "But I wondered if you could send over the woman who did maintenance for us here before. What's the name? Callie something?"

"Do you mean Cassie?"

"That's it." Brian grinned at Cassie, who looked amused. "Cassie. She fixed our heating once before when it wasn't working right, and I thought you could send her over."

"But—"

"I'll pay her, of course. I don't expect you to foot the bill."

Elliot's tone softened at that. "Well, that's fine, but—"

"I wouldn't ask, but I've tried to get a heating guy over here, and they're all booked up for the next week, and it would be so much simpler if Cassie could come over, since she's dealt with it before, and I'm sure she'll know right away what the problem is."

"I'm sorry," Elliot said. "I wish I could help you, but Cassie is on another job, and I can't just reschedule her on such short notice."

"On a totally unrelated note," Brian said, "has my mother mentioned that we're looking at another property management company? Lower rates, and everybody says their service is top-notch." Brian waited while Elliot silently seethed.

"She'll be there within the hour," he said.

Less than a minute later, a text message came in for Cassie, telling her to go to Otter Bluff rather than Dolphin Dreams. She picked up her phone, sent a response, then grinned at Brian.

"That was masterful," she said.

"I have a few tricks."

"You clearly do."

Brian was a little stunned by the smile—the sheer voltage of it. Being useful to Cassie could get to be a habit.

CASSIE WORKED on the cake late into the night. Her estimate of having six more hours of work, it turned out, had been wildly optimistic.

She lost herself in the job, though—in the art of it. She lost track of time, of her surroundings, of everything as she rolled fondant and laid it over the frosted cakes so it resembled ivory silk carelessly draped over the tiers. Then she applied the roses she'd so painstakingly made: a lush bouquet on top, cascading down the sides and pooling at the base in a riotous tribute to the bounty of nature.

If she hadn't been so worried about finishing on time—and if her back and shoulders hadn't ached as much as they did—she'd have been having a wonderful time.

Hell, she was having a wonderful time anyway.

After the last rose had been placed, she stepped back to look at the finished cake.

"Brian. Come take a look." Brian had been on the sofa with Thor watching a movie—something involving martial arts and a band of crooked cops.

"Is it done?" He blinked a few times, and she suspected he'd fallen asleep.

"It is. What do you think?"

He came over and stood beside her. Then his eyes widened. "Holy shit."

"Again, I have to ask: is that 'holy shit' good, or 'holy shit, what an epic disaster'?"

"It's holy shit, I can't believe you made that. I can't even believe it's cake."

Cassie smiled, pleased with his reaction. "It'll do."

"It's … it's perfect."

"You're damned right it is." Cassie was exhilarated, thrilled with the way it had come out, the way her vision had been perfectly replicated in the confection standing proudly on Brian's countertop.

She'd practiced, sure. But practice was one thing. Producing something as a professional—knowing she'd be paid for her work and that her cake would be the centerpiece of the biggest day of a couple's lives —made her feel positively giddy.

She bounced on her toes, ignoring the exhaustion, the sore muscles, the anxiety she'd felt not knowing how this would go.

"It's good, Brian. It's actually good."

"It's amazing," he said. "Now how are you going to get it to the reception without ruining it?"

BRIAN WAS surprised by the simplicity of the answer.

Cassie was going to put the cake in a box.

She'd be delivering it as though it were a package from Amazon or a carton of dishes being transported during a move from one apartment to another. He watched as she laid a non-slip pad on the bottom of the big box she'd brought with her, carefully placed the cake on top of the pad, then closed the carton around it.

She pulled a roll of packing tape out of her bag.

"What's that for?"

"Keeps the moisture out. Otherwise, the fondant will sweat, which would really suck." Cassie carefully sealed all of the seams of the box, then stood back with her hands on her hips.

Once that was done, she looked into his refrigerator and frowned.

He peered inside with her and saw the problem. There was no vertical space high enough to accommodate the cake.

Working together, they moved Brian's stuff to one side of the refrigerator, removed some shelves, and slid the cake in.

Cassie shut the refrigerator door, leaned back against it, and closed her eyes.

"There. Done. *Finito*. Now all I have to do is get it to the reception in one piece."

"Too bad I won't get to taste it."

Cassie opened her eyes and grinned. "Who says you won't? I'm going to the wedding. You want to be my plus-one?"

CHAPTER 8

*B*rian had never liked weddings. But it wasn't the weddings themselves he didn't like. The problem tended to be the people getting married and their guests—most of whom were his relatives.

He liked champagne, cake, music, and dancing. He just didn't like them well enough to have to put up with the family drama that came with them.

The benefit of Cassie's invitation was that all of the family drama would be someone else's. He could have the champagne and the cake and the music and the dancing without any of the emotional baggage.

He would also get to see Cassie in a pretty dress, which was a significant bonus.

"Are you sure this is okay?" he asked the next morning when she called him to make sure Thor hadn't somehow eaten this cake, too. "I mean, don't people usually want some notice before an extra guest comes to their wedding?"

"It's fine," she told him. "I RSVP'd with a plus-one just in case I found a date. I didn't find one. That is, until I found you."

"*Hmm.* That's interesting. Who did you try?" Not that he would know any of them. He'd asked because he found it hard to imagine anyone turning down Cassie Jordan for a date.

"Nobody," she said. "I didn't try anybody. Weddings are tricky, you know? If you're dating somebody and you ask them to go to a wedding, it sounds like you're taking a step. All of that talk about marriage and the future. So, to avoid making them think you're taking a step, you have to specify to them that you *absolutely are not taking a step*. But what if you do want to take a step with them at some point? Now you've already told them you're not doing that. You've ruined it."

"You've given this a lot of thought."

"Of course I have, I'm a girl."

She certainly was—in all of the best ways.

"But," she went on, "you and I aren't even dating. You're the guy who helped me with the cake. So there's no thought of what steps we might be taking. It's just about the dessert."

"Which makes me kind of perfect," he added.

"It does."

Except for the fact that he'd been friend-zoned before they even walked in the door of the reception hall.

Well, he'd see what he could do about that.

"What about this one?" Cassie turned in front of the mirror mounted to the closet door, modeling a dress for Lacy.

They were upstairs at the Jordan house, using Cassie's childhood room. The bed was littered with dresses, including a couple of Cassie's, some from Lacy's wardrobe, and one—which she was wearing now—that she'd borrowed from her sister Whitney.

Lacy wrinkled her nose. "No. I mean, it's fine. It's pretty. But basic black is Whitney. It's not you. You're colorful.'"

Cassie smiled, liking that her sister thought of her as colorful. Colorful was so much better than boring—which Whitney's dress was. She turned her back to Lacy to be unzipped and grabbed a hot pink dress from the pile on the bed. Cassie had bought it for herself when she'd been invited to the wedding, but she hadn't been sure she'd have the nerve to wear it.

"Let me just try this one," she said.

FIVE MINUTES LATER, Cassie was standing in front of the mirror in a confection of fuchsia satin and Lacy was giving her a long, slow whistle.

"That's the one," Lacy said. "That's the dress."

"Are you sure?" Cassie turned to one side and then the other, inspecting her reflection.

"Yes, I'm sure. It's fabulous. Plus, it's the one you originally picked out for yourself. Why are you waffling?"

"I'm not waffling." But she was. She was waffling.

Lacy was right, the dress was fabulous. But it was so flirty. So pink. So flouncy. So emphatically *there.*

The other thing that was emphatically *there* was Cassie's skin. The dress was strapless with a plunging neckline, and the skirt, a ruffly pouf of pink satin, ended at mid-thigh.

"You don't think it's too slutty?" Cassie asked.

"It's fun. It's young. You've got great legs, and it shows them off. It's perfect with your coloring."

"You didn't answer the question about whether it's too slutty," Cassie reminded her.

"It's exactly the right amount of slutty."

Cassie spun around to face Lacy. "Also …"

"What?"

"Did I mention that Brian is coming?"

"To the wedding?"

"Yeah. He's my plus-one."

"Oh." Lacy looked thoughtful. "So, we have to reevaluate the dress in light of the question of whether you want to come on to him or not."

"You see? This is why I'm asking you for advice and not Whitney or Jess. You get it. You get the exact dynamic. Is the dress the right amount of slutty in light of the fact that Brian will be there?"

Lacy's eyebrows rose, and she sat back on the bed, propping herself up on her arms. "That depends on your intentions. Are you interested in him?"

Was she? Cassie hadn't had time to think about that while she'd been frantically trying to finish the cake. She'd had a laser-like focus on her work, and she'd only thought of Brian in terms of how helpful he'd been.

But now she was going to go out with him. Yes, he'd said it was just because he wanted to try the cake. And maybe that was true. Nonetheless, they'd be dressed up. Eating. Maybe even dancing.

It sort of seemed like a date.

"He's cute," Cassie offered, though it didn't directly answer the question.

"He's very cute, in a geeky smart-boy kind of way."

"Geeky smart boys can be hot," Cassie observed.

"They really can."

"Plus, he was so *nice*. About the cake, I mean. And the fact that I illegally set up shop in his mother's house. He even bought ingredients for me."

She liked him, she had to admit. She'd liked him when he was just a funny guy on YouTube, and now, in person, she liked him even more. What harm would there be in seeing where things went? What was the downside in having fun and letting things develop however they developed?

"Of course," Lacy said, "you do have to take into account the power imbalance. The fact that he could get you fired with one phone call does affect the whole dynamic."

It did. But he'd shown no indication yet that he intended to take advantage of that.

He deserved the benefit of the doubt.

Plus, *cute*.

Cassie finally answered Lacy's question. "If something should happen between us, either at the wedding or as a result of it, that probably wouldn't be the worst thing in the world."

Lacy nodded. "Then this is the dress. Now, let's talk accessories."

BRIAN HAD OFFERED to pick Cassie up for the wedding, which made it seem like a real date. Except there was the cake to think of, so her coming to him made more sense.

She had to get to the venue early to set up the cake, so she got to Brian's house at noon for the two o'clock event.

She was so used to seeing him on YouTube in jeans or shorts and a T-shirt that the sight of him in a suit left her momentarily speechless. The suit was expensive and well-cut, his hair was newly trimmed and combed neatly away from his face, and the layer of stubble she'd seen on him the day before was gone. So were the thick-framed glasses that had given him that oddly appealing nerdy look.

The overall result was that he didn't look cute anymore.

He looked damned hot.

If she was surprised by his appearance, he seemed positively stunned by hers.

"Wow," he said.

"Do you like it?" She did a little twirl on his front porch.

"You look even better in that than you did in the towel. Which is saying something."

Oh, crap. She was blushing. She could feel the heat in her cheeks.

"And," he said, "that was a really crude remark. Right? I'm sorry. It's just … the way you look right now has shaved about twenty points off my IQ. Can we start over?"

Cassie grinned at him and walked past him to come into the house. "You don't have to start over. You're doing fine."

BRIAN TOLD himself to get his shit together.

First, he'd made a crude remark about Cassie. That was bad enough. Now, he was having a hard time focusing on the task of transferring the cake from the house to Cassie's car. The last thing he needed was to trip and drop the damned thing on the floor.

"Careful. Keep it level," Cassie said. She was holding one end of the box and he had the other as they walked together across the foyer and toward the front door. Brian had already walked Thor, and he'd put him in the bedroom so the dog wouldn't get underfoot while they were carrying the cake.

The finished cake was damned heavy, but the weight wasn't the issue. If they shifted slightly and tipped the cake, it was going to come out of the box smashed on one side. And, by God, if that happened, it wasn't going to be Brian's fault.

"Sorry." He leveled out his side. "Sorry. I've got it."

They went outside and down the front walk, then they carefully slid the box into the back of Cassie's hatchback.

Once it was in, Brian looked at her, pleased. "We're home free."

"Sure," Cassie said. "Now all we've got to do is drive it across town, get the box into the reception hall, and get the cake out of the box without tipping it, dropping it, or letting the top tier collapse onto the table."

"Okay, so not home free yet," he said.

FORTUNATELY, they didn't have far to drive. Cambria was a small town, and nothing was very far from anything else. The wedding and reception were at Cambria Pines Lodge, barely a five-minute drive from Otter Bluff.

Cassie drove well below the speed limit, easing over speed bumps and through intersections. A couple of cars had stacked up behind her, and a Ford Explorer riding her bumper honked.

"Keep your pants on, I've got a wedding cake in here!" Cassie yelled out her window.

Brian found that cute, but he didn't want her to think he was being patronizing, so he hid his grin by looking out the passenger side window.

"Where the hell do they have to be in such a hurry?" Cassie said. "I doubt Ford Explorer guy is on his way to do brain surgery."

"I think we just got passed by a ninety-year-old pedestrian. With a walker," Brian added, unable to help himself.

"That's enough out of you." But she was grinning, and that made him happy.

Maybe weddings weren't so bad.

CHAPTER 9

*C*assie felt such a sense of buoyant relief as the ceremony started that she barely heard a word the minister was saying. The cake had gotten to its appointed spot in the reception hall without incident, and the bride had loved it. She'd *loved* it. Deandra had squealed with happiness, grabbing Cassie in a tight, impulsive hug.

After that the ground beneath her could have been swallowed in a massive earthquake and Cassie wouldn't have minded.

She'd been validated.

She had the talent, had the skills. She could do this. She could bring her chosen career into being through the sheer force of her will.

It didn't even matter that the bride and groom were likely to smash her work of art into each other's faces a couple of hours from now. She'd done what she'd set out to do—what she'd promised to do —and that felt freaking fantastic.

"You're practically glowing," Brian whispered to her during a quiet moment in the service, which was being held in the garden at the lodge. They sat on white folding chairs on a manicured lawn, what seemed like a hundred kinds of spring flowers blooming around them.

"My cake looked awesome," she whispered back to him. "Did you see it? It was fucking flawless."

"It really was."

It didn't even matter that Deandra had paid her a fraction of what a cake like that usually went for. Cassie had accepted the lower price because she was a relative novice. She was unproven. She'd needed this gig to establish her credentials as an experienced wedding baker.

Well, now she had one unqualified success under her belt, and that would lead to more.

Who knew how many people here were planning weddings of their own? Who knew how many clients she might find because of this?

Okay, true, her business was technically illegal at this point, as she didn't have a license from the health department for her kitchen. Mainly because she didn't have a kitchen. But those things could be worked out. She would save money, find a space with a kitchen, get the necessary inspections and permits, then maybe expand, hire an assistant, attend bridal shows....

She was mentally rehearsing her future Food Network show when Brian nudged her. Everyone except Cassie was standing for the bride's entrance. She jumped up, still imagining her bright and impossibly sweet future.

IT WAS ALMOST like there were two Cassies, Brian thought. The stressed, frantic one he'd gotten to know while she was trying to produce the cake under intense time pressure, and the happy, bubbly one who was currently sitting next to him.

The frantic one had been appealing. But the happy one was downright luminous.

That wasn't a word he would often use—*luminous*—but it seemed apt here. The victory of her cake triumph was practically shining out her pores.

Had he thought she was cute before? Such a small word for what she was. Beautiful was closer. But even that didn't quite hit the mark.

While she watched the bride walk down the aisle, Brian watched Cassie. Flawless ivory skin. Golden blond hair swept up into some kind of complicated bun, with wispy tendrils framing her face. And that dress.

But what really captivated him about her was her smile. It wasn't just a pretty smile—though it was that—it was mischievous, as though she were thinking something scandalous at any given moment.

That thought made him wonder what the scandalous thing might be, which led him to indulge in any number of happy fantasies.

As the bride passed them, they all turned forward toward the gazebo where the groom and the wedding party waited. From here, Brian had an excellent view of the back of Cassie's neck and her bare shoulders in the strapless dress. Her skin was right there, close enough for him to touch it.

He didn't have permission to touch it, but maybe later, when they danced, with the music and the low lighting ...

Brian scowled at his own train of thought. When, exactly, had he gotten to be romantic? When had he turned into that kind of wuss?

The minister was talking about love, and the bride and groom were gazing at each other, and women in the crowd were quietly crying into tissues they'd pulled from their purses. So, it wasn't entirely his fault if he was getting swept up in the thing.

It wasn't as though a wedding ensured a life of married bliss.

His own parents had taught him not to believe in the fairy tale.

Still. Cassie did look like some kind of Disney Princess—if the Disney movies were R-rated.

Now, that would be something worth watching.

WHEN THEY GOT to the reception, the cake was still standing—a development Cassie hadn't completely taken for granted. The bride was still happy, and the petals on Cassie's buttercream roses still looked as though they'd come straight from a florist.

Not only that, but Cassie had a check for three hundred dollars tucked into her purse.

She was home free.

"God, yes," she said when Brian offered her a flute of champagne. They hadn't taken their seats yet and were standing beside a large floral arrangement near the bar. "I earned this."

"You sure did." Brian grinned at her. "Did you get pictures of the cake?"

"Only about a thousand of them. Plus, Deandra has promised to give me some from her photographer. This was a complete success." She felt close to levitation, she was so elated with what she'd accomplished.

"Thor might have to admit otherwise," he said.

She laughed—a carefree guffaw that, under other circumstances, she might have worried was unladylike. "The challenge just made the victory sweeter."

"Good. I'll tell him you're not mad at him."

"He's too cute to be mad at." The dog was adorable—that furry, innocent face—but in truth, Cassie doubted she could be mad at anyone right now, even if she gave it her best effort.

"Here's to a gorgeous cake." Brian raised his glass, and she clinked it to hers.

"Here's to you," Cassie said. "I mean it, Brian. You could have thrown me out of Otter Bluff and gotten me fired with one phone call. You don't even know me, and you let me take over your kitchen. Seriously, I could not have done this without you." She reached up on her toes and kissed him on the cheek.

"I didn't know you then, but I do now, and I think I made a good call," he said.

BRIAN HAD BEEN TRYING to keep himself in check, but now he had alcohol in his hand, and that was going to make it harder.

Even if she hadn't kissed him.

Yes, it was just a kiss on the cheek. A thank-you kiss. The kind of kiss you'd give your brother. But he hadn't reacted to it like her brother. He'd reacted to it like a guy who was starting to get loopy for a beautiful woman.

He couldn't afford to get loopy. He had a lot on his mind: a house that needed serious work, a career that required his constant attention, and a problematic mother who was almost certainly going to be on his ass now more than ever, just because he'd been forced to ask her for a favor.

All that, and his best friend had recently moved away.

He had shit to deal with, and he couldn't get all caught up with a woman, even if the woman smelled good and inexplicably—at least for the moment—made him feel like all of his problems had somehow magically disappeared.

Her lips were soft on his cheek, and her perfume lingered in the air for just a moment after she'd pulled away from him.

And there was the dress. And the champagne.

"Everybody take your seats so your meal service can begin," the DJ said from his station at the other side of the room.

"Shall we?" Brian swept an arm in front of him, gesturing for Cassie to precede him.

GOD, Brian looked good. Also, who knew that when you put a nice suit on him, he transformed from this goofy guy into a gentleman with impeccable manners and a smooth way with women?

Maybe she was imagining that. Maybe it was the romantic music, or the champagne, or the high she was riding due to her cake triumph. Whatever it was, she found herself scooting her chair a little closer to his. She also found herself openly flirting, laughing too loud at his jokes, and taking any opportunity to lay her hand on his arm.

Cassie heard her cell phone buzz in her purse, and she pulled it out to find a text message from Lacy. She checked it discreetly, keeping the phone below the level of the table for the benefit of the other eight people—random friends and relatives of Deandra—who were sitting with them.

How's the reception going? Was the cake okay?

Cassie texted her response—*The cake is fabulous, thank you very much*—and attached a photo as proof.

Oh, my God. You're an artist! Lacy texted back with a string of emoticons to indicate enthusiasm.

I am. I really am.

And how are things with Brian?

"Lacy wants to know how you're doing," Cassie told Brian. She leaned in next to him, took a selfie of the two of them, and sent it to Lacy.

Zowie. He cleans up really well, Lacy answered.

Keep your eyes off of him, I saw him first.

Cassie sent the text and slipped her phone back into her purse before Brian could catch a glimpse of what she'd written.

BRIAN HAD KNOWN they might dance at the reception, and if they did, he might develop a thing for Cassie even more than he already had.

Plus, he didn't really know how to dance.

So, when the time came, he was more than a little nervous about it.

"Do you want to?" Cassie asked when the DJ had invited the guests to take the dance floor and many of the other occupants of their table were out there spinning each other around.

As far as he was concerned, he had already lost at least one point by waiting long enough that Cassie had been forced to be the asker. Nothing to do about that now—the proverbial ship had sailed. But now he was hesitating, and that threatened to make it even worse—a loss of two points, maybe, or even three.

He got up from his seat, maybe a little too fast. "Of course. Yes. We should ... Right. Let's dance."

It wasn't like Brian to be tongue-tied. After all, he spoke on camera for a living. But that was different. When he'd had a partner, he'd done the show with Ike. If Ike had been a long-legged, beautiful blond, he suspected he'd have had trouble with that, too.

The song that was playing was halfway between fast and slow—a person could reasonably go either way on the dance style. Which presented a problem. Should he hold her in his arms or assume they would be freestyling separately the way people did to a more upbeat tempo?

He wanted to hold her in his arms, of course, but he didn't want to assume.…

Cassie put her arms around his neck and stepped in close, and his hands went to her waist without consulting him about it. The subtle scent of her perfume—something floral and spicy—drifted to him, making it hard to think.

But did he really need to think right now?

IT WASN'T AS though Cassie had planned to snuggle in close to Brian while they danced. They barely knew each other, and snuggling sent a message. At this point, she wasn't sure what message she wanted to send, if any, or how she wanted to send it. FedEx? Pony Express? Carrier pigeon?

The thing was, she felt so happy. And her happiness relaxed her, and relaxation naturally segued into snuggling.

So, that was how she ended up with her arms around his neck and her head resting on his shoulder as she gently swayed to wedding music.

And now that she was here, she felt very little desire to leave.

He looked good, he smelled good, he'd been nice to her about the cake, and—oh—the hands he'd had on her waist were shifting to her back as he brought her in closer.

She closed her eyes and let out a sigh.

THE SIGH—THAT was what did it. That was the moment when Brian went from interested and intrigued to captivated. That wasn't a word he would normally use, as it sounded like something from a 1940s movie. But who the hell was he kidding?

He was captivated.

The sigh ran straight through him like a gentle hum of electricity. And, of course, it made him wonder what kinds of sounds she might make when she was carried away by sexual pleasure.

Not that he'd be lucky enough to experience that firsthand.

His own eyes were slipping closed and he was lost in the moment, feeling her body tucked close against his, enjoying the rise and lull of the music, when somewhere nearby, a female teen voice said, "Ohmygod. Is that the guy from Ike and Brian?"

He was grateful for his viewers, he really was. But right now, the timing kind of sucked.

He pulled away from Cassie, apologized to her, and went for a round of autographs and selfies.

CHAPTER 10

"*A*nd then, before I even knew what was happening, he was off doing selfies with Deandra's fifteen-year-old niece. Which I get. I mean, he didn't get his show to where it is by ignoring the listeners. But damn it, I was enjoying that dance!"

Cassie was at home in her trailer, lying on her back on the bed. She was wearing her bathrobe, her dress hung up in her tiny closet, her shoes discarded on the floor. Lacy had called to find out how it went, and Cassie was giving her sister the recap.

"Well ... what about after that, though? Did you dance again?"

Cassie blew out a puff of air. "After that, the spell was broken. You know? We had a moment, then the moment was gone."

"Oh." Lacy sounded disappointed. "How was the cake, though? Did you get to try a piece?"

That subject, at least, helped Cassie to perk up. "The cake was perfect. Sublime. A miraculous fantasy of sugar and flour."

"That good, huh?"

"Brian had two pieces, and I think he'd have had a third if he weren't trying to be polite."

"What about at the end of the night?" Lacy asked.

"Was the cake still good at the end of the night? Well, most of it was gone, so ..."

"No, you jerk. I meant, what happened between you and Brian at the end of the night? Did he kiss you? Did you kiss him? Was there any talk of a second date?"

"I don't even know if this qualified as a first date," Cassie said. "And, no, he didn't kiss me. And I didn't kiss him."

"But you wanted to," Lacy said, for clarification.

"God, yes. I wanted to. But maybe it's better that we didn't."

"But why?" Lacy said it in a way that indicated she disagreed —strongly.

"Because with the wedding, and the cake, and the music, and the flowers ... I wasn't in my right mind."

"Huh." Lacy was quiet for a moment, considering it. "What if he were to call you when you are in your right mind? Say, tomorrow or the next day? Would you go out with him again?"

"Oh ... that's probably not going to happen."

BRIAN HAD NEVER MUCH ENJOYED DATING. It wasn't the dating itself that disagreed with him—it was more the inevitable self-doubt the next day.

Right now, the self-doubt was kicking his ass.

Everything had been going so well until the fan had recognized him. Then ... he'd lost his mojo. He'd wanted to get it back, but it seemed like the magic spell that had enveloped him and Cassie during their dance had broken.

Shit.

They'd danced again, but they'd been faster dances, displaying his awkward lack of rhythm. They'd talked, but people kept interrupting them, either to compliment Cassie's cake or to find out more about Brian, given what had happened with his teenage viewer.

But none of that was the problem, really.

The problem was that Cassie was way out of his league.

He hadn't thought so before, when she'd been frantically rushing around the kitchen at Otter Bluff trying to avert a cake disaster. At the time, he'd thought they were roughly matched in their potential appeal to the opposite sex.

But then she'd gotten dressed up for the wedding, and that premise had been shot to hell.

She wasn't cute the way he'd thought she was. She was gorgeous. And she had a kind of grace, a kind of inner light, that Brian couldn't hope to match, let alone deserve.

She looked too good. She had too much beauty, too much ... everything. Her overall magnificence had thrown his confidence.

And that's why he hadn't tried to kiss her at the end of the night, which, in retrospect, he probably should have done.

"Dude. I was kidding myself," he said to Ike on the phone the next day, while he was rooting around in the refrigerator for a Mountain Dew. It was early still—not yet ten a.m.—and he had the living room window blinds raised so he could take in the ocean view. Waves crashed against the bluffs, throwing a spray into the air, and off in the distance, a boat passed by near the horizon. Thor, anticipating that Brian might be getting something to eat, sat at his feet and whined softly.

"What do you mean, you were kidding yourself?" Ike asked.

"She's too hot. The Principle of Equivalent Hotness says it would never work." Brian had formulated the Principle of Equivalent Hotness—which said a relationship worked best if both parties had generally the same physical appeal—back in college, and he hadn't strayed from his rock-solid belief in its soundness.

"I've told you before, that theory is bullshit. Mainly because you can't quantify hotness. It's all based on the perceptions of the parties involved, and you can't know another person's perception." Ike, whose superior IQ often interfered with discussions of this sort, clearly didn't agree with Brian's own view that there were certain aspects of hotness that weren't relative. They were laws of nature.

Brian launched into the laws of nature argument—which Ike had heard before—when his friend stopped him.

"So, you're making up a crap argument to justify not kissing her. Which is fine, I guess, if you want to spend the rest of your life growing old with your dog, watching Netflix and eating frozen pizza."

"You know … that doesn't sound so bad," Brian said.

Ike laughed as though Brian had been kidding (he wasn't). "There's only one thing to do now."

"Get another dog so at least Thor won't be as pathetically lonely as I am?" Brian said.

"No. Ask her out on another date, then man up and kiss her at the end of it."

It was a thought. He just wasn't sure he was ready for such a drastic step.

THE SOLUTION to Brian's problem came the next day, when Cassie called him.

"I have good news, and I have a problem," she said.

The good news, it turned out, was that she already had another gig booked. One of the guests at the wedding had her own wedding coming up, and her baker had flaked at the last minute. She was so impressed with Deandra's cake that she wanted Cassie to do hers.

"And she's going to pay me extra for the rush job," Cassie said, excitement in her voice.

"Well, that's great." Brian was genuinely pleased for her. "But what's the problem?"

"The problem is that I still don't have a decent kitchen."

To Brian, that didn't sound like a problem at all.

It sounded like a solution.

"When do you want to come over?" he said.

THE WEDDING WASN'T for a couple of weeks yet, but Cassie wanted to do a trial run of a design before she committed to it. The idea was to do a much smaller and simpler version of the cake she had in mind just to see if it was viable. Then, if it worked, she could show it to the bride-to-be to get her final approval before Cassie started work on the real thing.

Of course, she still had her day job to think about. She had two houses to clean in the morning, then she had to cover the office for a few hours in the afternoon. By the time she got to Brian's house with two paper bags full of cake ingredients, it was after four p.m. She greeted Thor with a tummy rub and a vigorous scratch behind his ears, then got down to business.

"So, here's what I'm going to do." She took two folded pieces of paper out of her purse and smoothed them out on the countertop to show Brian. "This is a sketch of my concept for the final cake. And this one is the miniature sample cake I want to start today." She pointed with one finger, which, he noted, had a nail painted the color of Bazooka bubble gum.

"Cool." He bobbed his head a few times. "So, you got this job from the last one?"

"Yes!" Cassie bounced on her toes in excitement. "One of the guests at Deandra's wedding loved the cake, and her wedding is in two weeks, and her baker had a family emergency and had to cancel, so she called me."

Brian nodded sagely. "What other marketing have you done?"

"None. With the last cake, I was just trying to get a portfolio started. I don't even have a kitchen."

Brian had a degree in marketing, and that had always been his specialty on the Ike and Brian show—it had been the reason they'd done as well as they had. If anyone asked, he'd have said it was his chemistry with Ike, or the upbeat mood of the thing in uncertain times, or maybe Ike's comic timing. But really, it all came down to marketing. Almost everything in business did.

Unbidden, ideas about how to market Cassie's business began moving around in his brain. Most of those involved social media—his particular strong point.

"You're on Instagram, of course," he said.

She blinked a few times. "Why? Should I be?"

"God, yes. And how does your website look?"

Her shoulders fell. "I guess I need one of those, too."

He wanted to roll his eyes and ask her how it was that she'd missed the advent of technology, ask her if she still used a rotary phone. But he didn't want to make her feel bad, so he downplayed his horror.

"You know what? I can help you with those things. I mean … if you want."

"Really? That would be great. That would be really great. But …"

He raised his eyebrows, waiting.

"Marketing isn't even my biggest problem. I'm not licensed. This whole operation is illegal. Which is okay, I guess, as long as I stay under the radar. Do cakes for friends of friends. But as soon as I start really getting my name out there …"

She left the rest of the thought unspoken, but Brian got it: she'd be screwed.

"Tell me more about what you need," he said.

As Cassie told Brian everything she needed—starting with a commercial kitchen space that could pass a health department inspection—she began to see the impossibility of it all. And that made her earlier excitement begin to deflate like a leaky pool toy.

"I make barely more than minimum wage." She shook her head. "I mean, that's okay. I get by because I don't have to pay rent on the Airstream. But I don't make enough money that I can save any. Where am I going to get enough to rent a space and renovate it the way I'd need to?" She sank down onto a barstool, being careful not to step on Thor, who'd barely left her side. "I don't know why I'm kidding myself. This is never going to happen."

"*Hmm.*"

"… And I'm boring you. You're bored. I'll just get to work and let you get back to … whatever it was you were doing."

"I'm not bored." A vertical line appeared between Brian's eyebrows. "I'm thinking."

"About what?"

"About how you can get your kitchen space."

"You might as well think about how I can get to Mars. Same likelihood." She sighed. "Okay. I'd better get this batter started."

CHAPTER 11

The next day, Brian went down to San Luis Obispo to check on his house. He didn't know anything about construction, so he probably wouldn't even know what he was looking at once he got there. But he felt like he should be there anyway. It seemed right—manly, even—to peer at exposed studs while nodding thoughtfully as the contractor explained things to him.

So he walked Thor, fed him, then left the dog at Otter Bluff while he made the forty-minute drive south.

When he arrived, there were no studs to peer at. No contractor, either. His house stood alone and forlorn, mold and termites violating it even as he stood on the sidewalk.

He went up the front walk, let himself in, and pulled out his phone to call the contractor.

"Hi, Ray." He tucked his free hand into an armpit as he talked. "I'm here at the house, and there's nobody here. I thought work was supposed to start today."

Ray, whose name he'd gotten from a neighbor who'd had work done, explained about flexible schedules and an emergency roofing job, and some guy across town who'd had a kitchen fire.

"Well, but ... I can't use my house. I would think that's an emergency, too."

"You can stay there if you want to—there's nothing stopping you. Unless you've got a problem with allergies."

He did, in fact, have a problem with allergies. Throughout elementary school, Brian had been that kid with an EpiPen in his backpack, a list of food intolerances, and a constant stuffy nose during hay fever season. He'd thought he'd had a persistent low-grade cold for the past month—symptoms that had promptly cleared up as soon as he'd vacated his house for Otter Bluff.

He rubbed his forehead. "Look. Can you just ... maybe get to it as soon as you can?"

"You bet," Ray said. "But it all depends on the availability of my subcontractors, so ..."

A world of potential inconvenience and expense lay in that one little *so*.

Brian couldn't stop his YouTube schedule just because he'd been put out of his house. He sat at the patio table at Otter Bluff, brainstorming ideas with a notebook and pen in his hands and Thor stretched out on the patio at his side.

Beyond him, so close that he could feel the spray, the ocean pounded against the bluffs below the house.

The whole thing had been a lot easier when he'd done the show with Ike.

The height of the Ike and Brian show hadn't been that long ago. In fact, the income from those episodes was still coming in, sustaining them both. They'd been riding high, their subscriber numbers and views at an astounding peak, when Ike had decided to leave the show.

Ike hadn't liked acting like a doofus on camera, it turned out, and had opted for law school instead. That was fine. Brian had been pissed and hurt at first, but he'd gotten over it. Ike was his best friend, and he always would be. Brian wanted him to be happy.

But Ike's departure had hurt Brian's viewer numbers. He still had enough to make a comfortable living, but he wanted to win those fans back—he just hadn't figured out how to do it.

It was the chemistry. He and Ike had chemistry that came from a lifetime of being as close as brothers. Without him, Brian's solo videos had an entirely different dynamic. Maybe the key wasn't to win back the old viewers. Maybe the key was to attract new ones.

He jotted a few ideas into his notebook, but nothing jumped out at him. Brian had a kind of sixth sense that told him when a video was going to take off—when it was going to go viral—and his gut told him nothing here had that kind of potential.

Shit.

He took off his glasses and rubbed at his forehead, willing the inspiration to come.

He was still thinking when his cell phone rang, and his avatar for his mother—an image of Godzilla devouring Tokyo—showed on his screen.

As usual when she called, Brian had a momentary fight-or-flight response as he tried to decide whether to pick up or let it go to voice mail.

If he ignored the call, he would just have to call her back later, creating the kind of anticipation one usually felt before a colonoscopy or a root canal.

He picked up the call.

"Hi, Mom."

"Brian, I expected to hear from you by now. My goodness, I thought that since you're staying in my house, you would at least call me more often. I thought my generosity would have bought at least that."

He closed his eyes, feeling the headache beginning to stir behind his eyebrows.

"Well, we're talking now. How are you?"

She launched into a tirade about her dealer—the woman was spending too much time promoting another artist over Lisa—and Brian found himself hoping that he'd get off easy. Maybe if he just let her complain while he made soothing sounds, the phone call might be relatively painless.

But then she got to the real purpose of her call.

"I've got an empty weekend, dear, so I'll be coming to Otter Bluff on Friday afternoon."

"You ... what?" Brian tried to convince himself he'd misheard.

"I said, I'll be arriving at Otter Bluff on Friday."

Had he issued an invitation he didn't remember? If he had, it would surely be some indication of a serious condition that had impaired his mental function. That would be the only possible explanation.

"But ... Mom, I've got a lot of stuff going on this weekend, and I don't think—"

"Brian Julian Cavanaugh, I can't seem to get you to visit me in Los Angeles for any reason short of my imminent death. So, I'll simply have to visit you. I hope you're not saying I can't do that. I hope you're not suggesting that I can't visit my own property, which I've been so kind as to let you use while you're having housing issues."

He fell silent until the silence itself became at least as oppressive as his mother was.

"No. I'm not suggesting that."

"Excellent. I'll see you on Friday afternoon."

Unless he could find a plausible excuse to move to Thailand by then.

CASSIE HAD BAKED the layers of her sample cake at Brian's place the day before. Today, she was planning to go over there to start decorating it.

But first, she had to finish all of the various tasks Elliot had scheduled for her.

"The renters at Cabin in the Pines just checked out, and I'm afraid they left it in quite a state. I'm counting on you to get it back in shape." Elliot peered at her over his glasses as she came in that morning.

"What does 'quite a state' involve?"

He sighed. "It means that, by all appearances, they are not members of Mensa. I've withheld their security deposit, of course, but it's going to take a little extra effort on your part."

Oh, crap.

"How much extra effort are we looking at?"

He grinned slightly, and she couldn't help thinking of the grin as sadistic and self-satisfied.

"You'll need some rubber boots and a Shop-Vac."

CASSIE WOULD HAVE THOUGHT that by now, everyone in the United States of America knew it was a bad idea to put regular dishwashing detergent in a dishwasher.

She'd have been wrong.

When she opened the front door of Cabin in the Pines, she didn't notice anything amiss. The place looked reasonably tidy, in fact, as though the renters had made some effort to clean things up before they left.

Had Elliot been joking about the boots and the Shop-Vac?

Then she turned a corner into the kitchen and gasped.

Before her on the kitchen floor were enough white, fluffy suds to accommodate dozens of bubble baths. And the dishwasher was still running, churning out more.

"Oh ... God."

Fortunately, she'd worn the boots. She sloshed across the kitchen to the dishwasher and turned it off. On the kitchen counter, she found a note.

We ran out of Cascade, so we used Dawn. Didn't know you weren't supposed to do that, ha ha! The rental agreement said to leave the dishwasher running when we left, so that's what we did. Sorry for the mess!

Cassie closed her eyes, took a deep breath, and tried to control her exasperation. Not Mensa members, indeed.

Her cell phone pinged in her pocket, and she took it out. A text message: Elliot.

How bad is it?

At least the renters had told Elliot what they'd done—if they hadn't, the water might have been here for hours, causing unknown damage, until Cassie got here later in the day.

She snapped a picture of the suds on the floor and sent it to Elliot with a message.

The rental agreement said they were supposed to leave the dishwasher running when they left. So they did. Apparently it never occurred to them to turn it off when bubbles started pouring out of it.

In a moment Elliot messaged back.

Oh, dear.

No doubt, Elliot was even now adding a line to the rental agreement specifying that dishwashing liquid was not to be used in automatic dishwashers. People always thought the Central Coast Escapes rental agreement included ridiculous and oddly specific clauses, such as the one prohibiting the use of a blow dryer while sleeping and the one strictly forbidding the use of a barbecue grill indoors.

In fact, those weird, obvious clauses were the result of somebody actually using a blow dryer while sleeping (Dolphin Dreams, 2019) and firing up a barbecue grill in the living room (Seaside Stunner, 2005). At least the Dawn debacle now spreading out in front of Cassie hadn't put lives at risk the way the other two incidents had.

Cassie opened the dishwasher, causing more soap suds to pour onto the kitchen floor, and carefully made her way through the bubbles to remove the dishes from the inside of the appliance. Then she plugged in the Shop-Vac and went to work.

"I swear to God, Elliot. You need to give people some kind of test of their common sense before you let them rent." Cassie had spent all morning on the mess at Cabin in the Pines, and she was just dragging herself into the office after stowing the boots and the Shop-Vac in a storage shed behind the building.

"Don't think I haven't considered it." Elliot was sitting behind his desk, his reading glasses low on his nose as he pecked at his computer keyboard with his index fingers. "Any damage?"

"It looked okay." Cassie sank into the chair behind her own desk. "I disconnected the dishwasher and pulled it out so I could dry the floor underneath. It's a good thing the owner had laminate flooring put in last year, because if it had been wood ..." She left the thought out there. Wood floors and standing water did not mix.

"All right."

She waited for Elliot to thank her for her hard work, but she'd be waiting forever. Once, when renters had let their dog pee and crap all over the house, leaving Cassie to clean it up, she'd reminded Elliot to thank her. She still remembered his response: *Oh. Apparently, you're not sufficiently rewarded by a job well done.*

Cassie sighed and turned on her computer.

"Oh. Are you planning to work like ..." He gestured vaguely toward her. "Like that?"

She looked down at herself. "What's wrong with how I look?"

"Cassie, mirrors are your friends."

She got up, went into the bathroom, and looked at herself in the mirror over the sink.

Good God. Her hair was askew and partly wet from the dishwasher mess, she had splotches of water on her shirt, and her makeup was smudged from the moisture she'd been immersed in.

She went back out into the office. "I see what you mean. I'll just run home and clean up a little."

"Of course. We'll just take it out of your lunch hour."

"But Elliot, I need my lunch hour so I can eat lunch."

"Be that as it may." He waved vaguely, as though shooing her away.

CHAPTER 12

*B*rian didn't know what Cassie was so pissed off about when she arrived at Otter Bluff that afternoon to continue working on her cake. He only knew that she was damned cute when she was mad.

"Shit. Shit!" she muttered as he let her in.

"Hello to you, too."

She looked at him as though she wanted to punch him. Or punch something, at any rate. Thor took the opportunity to sniff Cassie's shoes, wagging his tail in a wide arc.

She squeezed her eyes shut and pressed two fingers to her forehead. Then she looked at him and started again. "Okay. You're right. That was rude of me. How was your day?"

"Well, I—"

"That's nice. You want to know how mine was?" She dropped her bag onto the floor and jammed her hands onto her hips, spinning to face him. "I spent all morning vacuuming up soap suds, then mopping floors, then rerunning a damned dishwasher over and over again until the foam was gone, then hand-washing the dishes that should have been in the damned dishwasher. Then, when I got to the office, Elliot —who sent me to clean up the mess in the first place—got into a snit about how I looked. And I did look like crap, so, yes, I can admit that —but then I had to spend my entire lunch hour changing my clothes and drying my hair and reapplying my makeup, so I haven't eaten anything but a granola bar since eight a.m." She blew out some air that caused her bangs to flip up. "I really need a new job."

"Okay." Brian nodded a few times. "I can't do anything about the job, but I have food."

Cassie winced in guilt. "Ah, jeez. I'm sorry. I didn't mean you had to feed me. I'll just go out and—"

Ignoring her protests, he went to the refrigerator and peered in. "Leftover pizza okay? Plus, I have beer."

She tilted her head to the side, and he might have seen the slightest whisper of a smile. "Leftover pizza and beer sounds perfect."

"Great." He pulled the pizza and the beer out of the refrigerator. He opened a bottle and handed it to her, then grabbed a plate for the pizza.

As a couple of slices were heating in the microwave, she took a long drink from the beer—something from a local craft brewery— took a moment to rub Thor, then grinned at Brian.

"You know, you really are a lifesaver. First, letting me use your kitchen. Now this."

"Hold that thought while I tell you something."

"What?"

"My mother's coming."

Cassie's eyebrows rose. "Coming here?"

"Yes."

"When?"

He checked the clock on the top of the stove. "Oh ... maybe an hour. Maybe less. Depends on how many times she stopped on the way for espresso."

Cassie's mouth opened, then closed. "Should I leave? Is this awkward? I mean, I'm using her kitchen without her permission, so ..."

"No, no. You've got my permission, so it's fine. Really. It's fine."

For some reason, Cassie thought the second *it's fine* indicated that it wasn't actually fine. Generally speaking, when a person said that phrase one time, it tended to be true. When they said it a second time, they were trying to convince themselves as much as whoever they were telling it to.

"Okay," she said. "What's the story? You can tell me while I'm eating my pizza."

"Why does there have to be a story?" Brian was standing in the kitchen with his hands shoved into his pockets, trying to look convincing.

He was failing.

"I guess I can just ask her when she gets here." Cassie was playing with him, trying to tease it out of him.

"Oh, God no."

"Why? Does she have secrets?"

"No. Exactly the opposite. She has *no* secrets and no filter."

"That sounds like fun," Cassie said. "Oh, good. The pizza's ready."

Half an hour later, as Cassie was beating a bowl of buttercream frosting in the kitchen, Thor standing by in case she dropped anything edible, Brian considered his conflicting emotions about his mother's impending arrival.

The fact that she would be meeting Cassie could be either a good thing or a bad thing.

On one hand, it would distract his mother from all of Brian's various failings, one of which, horrifyingly, was her belief that he wasn't having enough adventurous sex. If his mother thought he and Cassie were a couple, that might make her ease up on him.

On the other hand, it would be awkward for Cassie, who was just trying to get her cake finished and who wasn't having any kind of sex —adventurous or otherwise—with Brian. Also, his mother was ... a lot. If Cassie thought she was entirely too much, and if she assumed Brian got the bulk of Lisa's genes, it would hamper Brian's ambitions to get Cassie to go out with him on a real date. One that didn't involve her thanking him for use of his double oven.

Honestly, it could go either way.

Cassie was just about finished with the buttercream when the front door opened.

Here we go.

CASSIE DIDN'T KNOW what she'd expected from Brian's mother. She'd dealt with the woman on the phone a few times in relation to Otter Bluff, but they'd never met.

Whatever she'd expected, the reality of Lisa Barlow was nothing she'd been prepared for.

"Hello!" Lisa came into the room carrying two bags—one in each hand. She set them down just inside the front door and put her arms out to Brian. "Sweetheart. For God's sake, get over here and hug me. I haven't seen you in years."

"It's been four months," Brian said.

"Well, it feels like years."

Lisa's tall, slim body was clothed in a long, flowing wrap skirt in moss green and a close-fitting white sleeveless top with a plunging neckline. The top showed an inch of tight, fit midriff above the waistband of the skirt. A chunky silver and turquoise necklace hung just below her collarbone, and stacks of silver bracelets jangled on her wrists. Her hair, which had gone gray, was in a short buzz cut—as though she were maybe a week past having shaved it entirely. A tattoo of some flowering vine crept down her left shoulder, the vine reaching down her arm and toward her hand.

"And who's this?" Lisa released Brian and turned her attention toward Cassie.

"I'm Cassie Jordan, Mrs. Barlow. From Central Coast Escapes. We've spoken on the phone a few times." Cassie wiped powdered sugar off her hands with a dish towel and offered a hand to Lisa, who took it in both of hers.

"My dear, it's not *Mrs.* and it hasn't been for a long time. I'd prefer that you call me Lisa."

"All right. Lisa, then."

Lisa's delicate brows rose as she regarded Cassie. "I seem to have interrupted you in the middle of some kind of food preparation, so I assume you're not here on Central Coast Escapes business."

"Ah ... no."

"Cassie's a baker," Brian cut in. "She needs to decorate a wedding cake—a sample of a wedding cake, really—and she doesn't have an adequate kitchen, so ..."

"I can go," Cassie said. "I can ... You know, I really should. This is your house, and I'm intruding, so ..."

"Darling, don't even think of it. My son doesn't cook, and the last time I tried to use a kitchen I set the drapes on fire. No one but you will be using that particular room, I assure you. And cake decorating? I'm fascinated."

"Well, if you're sure." Cassie smiled in what she hoped was a winning way.

"I'm always sure."

"That's no joke. She is," Brian said.

CASSIE DID a quick series of calculations. On the fly, she had to balance Brian's obvious discomfort against Lisa's lack of it, multiplied by Cassie's lack of a kitchen and her need to get this cake sample done.

There was an additional factor, as well: Cassie's curiosity about Brian's family dynamic.

This woman with her high cheekbones and her innate, quirky elegance contrasted so sharply with Brian's man-child persona that Cassie had to wonder whether Brian was adopted—or if he was maybe playing some kind of trick on her in claiming Lisa was his mother.

"Okay. I'm just gonna work on this, if that's all right." Cassie gestured toward her bowl of frosting. She'd come straight from work, so she was dressed respectably, but Lisa's presence made her feel as though she were hopelessly lacking in style.

"Of course. I can't wait to see what you'll do." Lisa smiled warmly, her lips done in a bronze color Cassie had never seen before—at least, not on lips. Thor came up to Lisa, wagging his tail and pressing his wet nose against her hand. She patted his head a few times in acknowledgment.

Cassie noticed that Brian had said very little since his mother's arrival. Lisa had apparently taken over as head of the household, as she was the one making the call on whether Cassie would stay or go. She sneaked a look at Brian, and his sheepish, forlorn expression gave her the sense that he'd looked exactly this way as a child.

What was going on here, exactly? Was it simply a power imbalance between parent and child? Or was there more at play than the obvious?

Cassie whipped her frosting and thought, *Interesting.*

CHAPTER 13

"*S*o ... what's happening with this?" Lisa gestured vaguely toward the kitchen where Cassie was working. She and Brian were standing on the back patio, where Lisa had brought him on the pretense of taking in the view. Thor, who'd spotted a rabbit, was growling and whining at the bush where the rabbit had taken shelter.

"By *this*, do you mean Cassie?"

"Well, of course I do. I show up to find a woman—a girl, really—in your kitchen and you expect me not to ask about her?"

Brian let out a sigh. "She's a woman, not a girl. And there's nothing happening except that I offered her the kitchen to bake her cake."

Lisa's eyebrows rose. "You're not sleeping with her, then? That's a pity."

"Mom—"

"What? A young man has to have his needs met." She turned to face the ocean and the limitless horizon. "Does that mean the two of you are not even seeing each other?"

"Well ... I don't know," he admitted. "We went to a wedding together, which I suppose was a date. And ... I might ask her out again. If I do, it'll be because I want to get to know her, not because

I want my 'needs met'. Thor, leave that rabbit alone." He retrieved Thor, led him to the sliding glass door, and put him inside the house.

"*Hmm.*" Lisa looked out at the waves crashing against the bluffs instead of looking at her son.

"Does that sound mean you wouldn't approve if we … you know. Became a thing? A thing that was more than just sex?"

Surprise registered on her features. "It doesn't mean any such thing. She's darling."

Brian knew his mother well enough to know that *darling* was not a compliment. *Darling* was the word she'd have used to describe a Pomeranian in a sweater.

"All right, what?" Brian folded his arms over his chest. "What's the issue?"

"I don't have an issue. Though I do wonder why she doesn't have her own kitchen."

"She doesn't have a kitchen because she lives in an Airstream trailer."

Lisa let out a delighted laugh. "Of course she does."

"Mom? Do you seriously disapprove of her just because of where she lives?"

Lisa looked at her son in bemusement. "When did I say anything about disapproving? I'm all in favor of minimalist living, for those who have the temperament for it. Besides, it's certainly better than that stifling suburban stucco box your father raised you in."

Brian took off his glasses and rubbed his forehead, feeling the beginnings of a headache coming on. "Dad raised me in that stifling stucco box because you left, and he was doing the best he could on his own, and that suburb you disdain so much had good schools and Little League and a low crime rate, and—"

"It had no culture. It had no heartbeat! I was dying there, Brian. You know that. I had to leave. I was running for my life."

"Really." He turned to face her. "What about my life? What about Dad's life?"

"Don't be dramatic, Brian. It doesn't suit you."

It suited her, though—down to her manicured toes. Brian went back inside and left her on the patio alone.

~

CASSIE NOTED the fact that when Brian came back inside, he went straight to his bedroom and closed the door without saying anything to her. She was certain he was upset, and she wasn't the one who'd upset him.

The cake, she reminded herself. *Focus on the cake.*

She took her baked layers out of the freezer, then unwrapped one of them and placed it on a cake board she'd already prepared. She brushed off a few loose crumbs, then began frosting the cake with the buttercream she'd made.

When Lisa came into the kitchen and began looking in the refrigerator, Cassie got the distinct feeling it was less about finding some food or beverage than it was about investigating Cassie.

"Mountain Dew, my God." Lisa shuddered and closed the refrigerator. "You'd think it's too much to ask for Brian to stock some Perrier."

"Um … I think he's got some herbal tea," Cassie offered.

"Does he? That's surprising." Lisa hunted around in the cupboards until she found it. "This will do. Would you like some?"

"Sure. I mean … yes, thank you. That would be nice."

Lisa went through the motions of making tea: she filled the kettle with water, put it on the stove, and took out two mugs and placed them on the counter, each with a tea bag string dangling from its side.

"So, Cassie. How did you and my son meet?"

Cassie realized that the true story—the one in which she'd been using the house without permission and he'd caught her wearing nothing but a towel—was not something she could tell Lisa.

She'd found that lies worked better if they closely resembled the truth, so she modified the facts as little as possible.

"Well, I was here at Otter Bluff when Brian arrived and surprised me. Elliot and I didn't know he was coming." All true, as far as it went.

"Ah. I suppose I should have called and informed you. Though, if I had, you and Brian might not have struck up a friendship."

Was there something arch in the way she'd said the word *friendship*? Or had Cassie imagined that?

"That's true," Cassie agreed. "Sometimes things work out for the best."

"How charmingly optimistic." Lisa took her mug to the kitchen island where Cassie was working and sat down on a barstool to watch.

At first, Cassie found it hard to focus under the scrutiny. But then, after a while, she got lost in the task. That was one of the things she loved about decorating cakes: it took her away from her own world and immersed her in one of sugary flowers, smooth frosting, and the challenge of making her vision into reality.

By the time Lisa spoke again, Cassie had almost forgotten she was there.

"My God, you've made that frosting look like silk. It's flawless. How in the world?"

Cassie, pleased by the praise, smiled as she worked. "A lot of it's in the making of the buttercream, but there are tricks to applying it, too. If you dip the spatula in cold water, you can get a really smooth finish." She demonstrated with her own spatula.

"Why, that's wonderful," Lisa said. "You know, I don't usually strive for that kind of gloss in my own work. It's all about chunky textures. I like to create a sense of the tactile."

At first Cassie wasn't sure what she was talking about, but then she remembered Elliot saying Lisa was an artist. Was it possible she was a rich and famous one? Cassie recalled something about that. She knew so little about the art world, it was certainly possible.

She was about to ask about it when Lisa propped her chin on her hand and said, "You know, this reminds me of the cake Brian's father and I had at our wedding."

"Was it beautiful?" Cassie asked.

"My God, no. It was a mess." But she smiled wistfully. "We had a bargain wedding—Garrett was a grocery clerk, you know, so we didn't have money to spare—and we used the cheapest baker we could find. And, my dear, it showed."

"Oh. That's a shame." Cassie finished the base layer of frosting and set to work making white orchids in buttercream.

"I suppose. On the other hand, the cake is supposed to serve as a symbol for the marriage, yes? For that, it was perfect. Cheap, shabby, and leaving a bad taste in one's mouth."

"That's ... I don't ..." Cassie didn't know what to say to that, and she found herself sputtering helplessly.

"Water under the bridge, darling. Now, what variety of orchid is that, exactly?"

CASSIE FINISHED THE CAKE, boxed it, cleaned up the kitchen, then got ready to take the cake home to refrigerate it until she could deliver it to the bride the following day.

By the time she was ready to leave, Brian still hadn't emerged from his room. Thor was in there with him, having scrabbled and whined at the door until Brian let him in.

"I wanted to say goodbye to Brian," Cassie said, standing at the door with her purse hanging from her shoulder and the cake box in her hands. "Do you think he's okay?"

"Of course he is. He's just hiding from me, dear. I imagine he'll come out when he becomes weak from hunger—or when I leave on Sunday evening. Whichever comes first."

"Oh." Cassie shifted her weight from one foot to the other. "There's obviously a ... a dynamic between you two that I ... that's none of my business. I'm sorry to have intruded."

"Nonsense, Cassie. Without you, I'd have had no one to talk to. Goodnight, dear. And when you text my son, please tell him that he's acting like a toddler and I'd like him to come out so we can chat. Would you?"

Cassie did text Brian, and she didn't wait until she got home to do it. She pulled out her phone and sent a message as she sat in her car at the curb outside his house.

I'm leaving now. Where did you go?

His response came a moment later. *My mother was right. I'm hiding from her.*

Cassie laughed. *You heard that?*

It's not as though she keeps her voice down.

He had a point. Lisa had projected her voice as though she were speaking to an auditorium.

What's the deal with you two?

Oh, you know. The usual. She abandoned me and my dad when I was six so she could pursue an art career in LA. Then, the only time I saw her was when she showed up for the occasional birthday to bring me a wildly inappropriate gift. Nothing you haven't seen a million times on The Brady Bunch.

Cassie stared at her phone, horrified. What could she say to that? How could she possibly respond?

Hold on. I'm coming out, he said.

As Cassie sat there, Brian emerged from a hedge at the side of the house. He came to her car and got in on the passenger side.

"You came out of a hedge," she said.

"I slipped out the sliding glass door in the bedroom and came around."

She'd intended to be subtle, but screw subtlety. "God. Did she really leave you when you were six?"

"She would specify that she left my father, not me. But damned if I could tell the difference at the time. I still can't."

"Wow. She's successful, right?"

"Very."

"She seems really …" *Big* was the word Cassie wanted. Not big in the physical sense, but in terms of her personality. Her presence.

"Yeah." He didn't wait for her to finish her sentence. "She is." He raised his eyebrows. "Any chance you want to help me escape? Maybe drive me across the border into Mexico and leave me by the side of the road?"

She smiled. "I don't think that's a good idea."

"Yeah, probably not." He sighed and looked at the house. "It's only a weekend, right?"

"That's the spirit."

"You know what would be good, though? If I could take you out to dinner tomorrow night, it would get me out of the house. Also, it would show her that I do have a life, contrary to what she seems to think."

Cassie didn't know whether to feel excited or offended. "So, what you're saying is, you don't actually want to go out with me for its own sake, you just want to do it to make things easier with your mother. Enticing offer."

"What I'm saying is"—he leaned closer and lowered his voice to a register that was intimate and sexy—"I've wanted to go out with you since we met. On a real date that isn't cake-related. So, will you? Please?"

"Oh." Just seconds ago he'd been cute man-child Brian, the goofy guy of the leftover pizza and Mountain Dew. But now, he'd transformed into the handsome, sexy Brian from the wedding. How did he do that? And could he make the change at will? "That's … that'd be good."

"Okay. I'll call you tomorrow. I'd better get back in there and face Medusa."

CHAPTER 14

"So, I met Brian's mother."

Cassie was sitting at her mother's kitchen table eating a plate of pancakes Nancy had made for her. Nancy was always moaning about how Cassie probably wasn't eating right in the trailer, so when she'd come in asking for her mother's pancakes, Nancy had been delighted.

At the stove, Nancy was working on a stack of pancakes for Cassie's father, Vince. Across the table from her, Lacy, who had already finished breakfast, was sitting with Trevor on her lap and a mug of coffee in front of her. Lacy had stopped by to eat pancakes and also to give Nancy her morning Trevor fix.

"Who's Brian?" Nancy wanted to know.

"Oh ... he's just a guy in one of the rental houses. His mother owns it. We maybe went out once."

"Honey, what does it mean that you *maybe* went out?" Nancy, a spatula in her hand, looked at her youngest daughter.

"We definitely went out, but it maybe wasn't a date," Cassie clarified. "But ... he asked me out again on what would definitely be a date."

"You met his mother after one maybe date?" Lacy wrinkled her nose. "That's kind of soon, isn't it?"

"No, no." Cassie shook her head and stabbed a forkful of pancake. "I met her, but it wasn't a thing. She just happened to be where I happened to be."

"And where was that?" Nancy had become so absorbed in Cassie's conversation that she hadn't noticed her pancakes were burning. She noticed now. She flipped them, then turned back toward Cassie.

"At Brian's house. Which isn't really his house, it's the vacation rental, and it belongs to his mom. Otter Bluff, the one on the water in Marine Terrace? She just happened to be there while I just happened to be there."

"Enough with the logistics." Lacy bounced her son on her knee. "Tell me about the mother. How was that?"

"It was interesting." Cassie ate another bite of pancake, savoring the butter and syrup and the soft texture on her tongue. "She was … odd. But kind of cool. She's an artist. I get the feeling she's kind of a big shot, but that's not something I'd know about."

"*Hmm.* Is she anyone I've heard of? What's her name?"

"Lisa Barlow."

Lacy thought, then shook her head. "No, but I'll ask Gen."

Genevieve Porter, one of Lacy's best friends, was an art dealer with a gallery on Main Street. If Lisa was, indeed, an art world big shot, Gen would know.

"The thing is," Cassie went on, "Brian says she left him and his father when Brian was six, and she's barely been in his life. She was all *darling* this and *sweetheart* that when she was talking to him, but he spent most of the time shut up in his room, avoiding her."

"Yikes," Lacy said.

Nancy shook her head and *tsk*ed. "I don't know how a mother could turn her back on her child. Especially one so young."

Cassie didn't know, either, and it was clear Brian had serious issues with it himself.

"You know, Cassie," Nancy began, then trailed off.

Cassie knew her mother well enough to know that Nancy was about to say something Cassie didn't want to hear.

"Yes, Mom?" Cassie prompted her.

"Here it comes," Lacy said.

"Oh, don't give me that, Lacy." Nancy scowled at her daughter. "All I was going to say is that it's a concern, this young man having such trouble with his mother. Cassie, if you and he were to end up together—"

"It's just one date, Mom. Or, two, depending on how you count them. Nobody said we're going to end up together."

"If you end up together," Nancy went on, undaunted, "you're going to have that woman for a mother-in-law. And ..."

"She already has us getting married," Cassie remarked to Lacy.

"*And,*" Nancy said, raising her voice over her daughters, "people who grow up with troubled family lives tend to replay those problems in their marriages."

"Mom. Brian and I aren't planning a wedding. I'm pretty sure he was just thinking dinner and a movie."

"I stand by what I said. Vince!" Nancy called to her husband, who hadn't come downstairs yet. "Your pancakes are ready!"

BRIAN CAME out of his bedroom at Otter Bluff the next morning to find his mother sitting on the sofa with her bare feet propped on the coffee table and her laptop open on her thighs. She was wearing a pair of red-framed reading glasses and a silk kimono.

"Good morning, Mom." Brian let Thor outside to pee, then went to the kitchen to pour some coffee, his hair standing up at odd angles from sleep.

"Brian, dear." She looked at him over the tops of the glasses, her fingers paused over the keyboard. "I should probably mention that Lorenzo will be here around midmorning."

Brian blinked at her. "Who's Lorenzo?"

She scowled. "I'm sure I've mentioned him to you several times. He's my personal assistant."

It escaped Brian why his mother needed a personal assistant. Yes, she was fairly sought-after these days in certain circles, and yes, she always seemed to be juggling one engagement or another. But was she so busy that she needed an assistant to follow her on her weekend getaway?

"Okay, but why's he coming here?"

"To assist me, obviously." She went back to typing something into the computer.

"Well … is he staying overnight? Where's he going to sleep?" Otter Bluff only had two bedrooms, and Brian wasn't about to give up his.

Lisa stopped typing again and gave Brian a slow, lopsided smile. "Oh … I don't think that will be a problem."

WEEKENDS WERE busy days at Central Coast Escapes, with various renters arriving and leaving. That meant Cassie had a busy day ahead of her on Saturday.

She had to clean two houses in the morning and cover Elliot in the office for a couple of hours in the afternoon. She had to deliver the sample cake to the bride-to-be and sell her on a plan for the full-sized cake. Then she had to plan her wardrobe—and her overall approach— for her date with Brian.

She couldn't plan what she'd wear until she'd thought out her philosophy for the date. Should she aim for devastating sex appeal, with the intention of making him want her desperately? Or should she go for cute and casual, just in case he had something closer to friendship in mind?

The wedding they'd attended together had been mostly friendly. But the way his voice had sounded when he'd asked her out—the way he'd looked at her? That suggested that the devastatingly sexy approach was called for.

She thought about it as she cleaned a house on Park Hill. Then she called Lacy on her way to her next assignment.

"So, sexy, right? Not cute and friendly?"

Since Lacy already knew about the date, there was no need to get her caught up on the background of the question.

"Well … what are the chances that you're going to friend-zone him?"

Cassie considered that. "I don't know. I mean … I guess that could happen. It's too soon to tell."

"Okay. Then, on a scale of one to ten, how much do you *want* the two of you to get friend-zoned?"

"Zero." The answer popped out of Cassie's mouth before she could think about it. Still, it felt true. She'd like for this to go somewhere, though she had no idea whether it would.

"Zero?"

"Yes. I'm sticking with that. Zero."

"Okay. Then irresistible sex kitten it is."

WHILE CASSIE WAS THINKING about sexiness, Brian was actively trying not to think about it.

Lorenzo arrived at around one o'clock, and the guy hadn't been in the door five minutes before he tongue-kissed Lisa and grabbed her ass. Thor, an excellent judge of people, growled at him.

Brian had assumed that was what his mother had meant when she'd said not to worry about sleeping arrangements, but assuming it and seeing it played out in front of him were two entirely different things.

Especially because Lorenzo appeared to be about the same age as Brian.

"Oh. God." Brian hadn't intended to express his disgust—at least, not out loud—at the sight of Lorenzo and his mother making out, but the words had leaped from his mouth.

"Problem, dear?" Lisa delivered the words with a smug grin on her face even as she leaned in and pressed her breasts against Lorenzo's chest.

"No, no. Nothing years of intensive therapy won't fix." He hadn't even been formally introduced to Lorenzo yet—a situation Lisa promptly addressed.

"Lorenzo, this is my son. Brian, this is my—"

"If you say 'fuck buddy,' I swear to God—"

"My *assistant*, Brian. And yes, we're seeing one another socially as well. My God, you're an adult, and the mention of sex still makes you respond like an adolescent boy."

"Please don't say *sex*."

Lorenzo let go of Lisa's left butt cheek and reached out to shake Brian's hand.

"Brian, it's lovely to meet you. Lisa's told me so much about you."

Brian shook the hand despite where it had been. "She's told me absolutely nothing about you."

"Ah. Well. We'll get to know each other this weekend, no?"

It was the *no* as much as anything that set Brian off. The sheer, affected pretentiousness of it, as though Lorenzo had only recently arrived from Milan and was still struggling with the nuances of the language. In fact, he had no accent, and Brian would have bet he'd been born in Des Moines or maybe Gary, Indiana. The *no* set Brian off more than the man bun, more than the leather sandals, more than the single hoop earring. More, even, than the bulging biceps, one of which was adorned with a yin-yang tattoo.

"Lorenzo, you and Brian are going to get along wonderfully, I just know it," Lisa declared.

"I'll just get the rest of my things out of the car." Lorenzo shot a finger gun at Brian—with the corresponding click of his tongue—and went out the front door.

"How old is he?" Brian asked as soon as Lorenzo was out of earshot.

"Why does that matter?"

"He's younger than me, isn't he?" Brian accused. "He's, what, twenty-eight?"

"He's thirty-two."

"Well, it's okay, then!" Brian declared, throwing his hands into the air. "Thirty-two! That's totally fine!"

"Brian." Lisa lowered her voice, tipping her chin downward and looking at her son in a way that was somehow both scolding and confidential. "Just because you don't currently have a satisfying sex life doesn't mean that I—"

"Oh, God." Brian slapped his hands over his ears. "I can't hear you. I can't hear a thing you're saying."

"Very mature, dear."

Brian wondered if maybe he'd be better off at his own house with the mold and the termites. At least if those things were breeding, they were too small for him to have to witness it.

CASSIE FINISHED work at Central Coast Escapes at two p.m. Then she went home, retrieved the sample cake from her mother's refrigerator, and drove across town to the home of her new client.

The woman, one of Deandra's cousins, lived in the Top of the World neighborhood in a house surrounded by towering pine trees and looking out over the distant ocean.

She received Cassie into the house with such bubbling enthusiasm that Cassie couldn't help but share in it.

"Come sit down!" Rachel, a perky redhead, waved Cassie in toward the living room. "My mother's here, I hope you don't mind. She wanted to see the sample. She was at Deandra's wedding, too, and we both thought the cake was so amazing. Mom! Cassie's here!"

Cassie remembered Rachel's mother from the wedding, and they shook hands and exchanged pleasantries.

"I wish Blake could be here, but he's working a double shift at the hospital," Rachel went on. "He's not really into the details, anyway. 'Just tell me where to stand and what to say.'" She imitated her fiancé's voice. "Which is fine, because I'm a control freak about this stuff."

"She is," her mother confirmed.

Cassie laughed, caught up in Rachel's giddy joy. "Well, after you told me what you had in mind for the ceremony and reception, I came up with a concept for your cake that's different from Deandra's. Here. Let me show you my sketches...."

FORTY-FIVE MINUTES LATER, Cassie left Rachel's house with a signed contract for a three-tiered wedding cake. Rachel had loved the concept and the sample cake, which Rachel, Cassie, and Rachel's mother, Joyce, had eaten with mugs of hot coffee.

Out of a sense of moral obligation, Cassie had disclosed her somewhat informal status.

"You should know that I'm not exactly legal," she'd said with a nervous laugh. "When I get a commercial kitchen to work from, I'll get a license and health department inspections and all of that. Until then ..." She'd left the rest of her thought dangling.

"Well, I guess you'll charge a lot more once that happens," Joyce pointed out.

"I suppose that's true," Cassie admitted.

"Cassie, when you do get all of that—the kitchen and the license and all—you're going to take off, I just know it. And we'll be able to say we knew you when." Rachel gave Cassie an impulsive hug.

Cassie left their house feeling excited and optimistic about her business—or maybe that was just the sugar high.

She couldn't wait to tell Brian about her triumph.

But first, she had to go home and get ready for their date.

BRIAN ARRIVED at Cassie's place to pick her up at around seven. She'd been reluctant to have him do that, fearing that her mother—or, even worse, her father—might harass him if they saw him approaching the trailer through the backyard.

But the way Brian saw it, Cassie had already had enough exposure to his mother. Lisa alone was bad enough. Lisa plus Lorenzo seemed like too big a risk for his budding relationship with Cassie to withstand.

Dinner at Indigo Moon was more casual than Deandra's wedding had been, but he still wanted to look nice, so he showed up in pressed khakis and a button-down shirt open at the collar. He wore leather loafers, and he was freshly shaved, with his dark, thick hair neatly combed.

"And where are you headed, all dressed up?" Lisa had wanted to know.

"Nowhere. Just … out." Brian stood near the front door, his hands shoved awkwardly into his pants pockets.

"You have a date, no?" Lorenzo grinned from where he was draped obscenely across the living room sofa, with Brian's mother draped obscenely across him.

"I have a date, yes," Brian said, unconsciously mirroring Lorenzo's sentence structure.

"With whom?" Lisa asked. "Is it that darling Cassie?"

There it was again—that word. *Darling*. Lisa's passive-aggressive attempt to be pleasant while suggesting that the woman in question was no more than a mindless Barbie doll, an attractive but useless plaything.

"It's Cassie, yes."

"Interesting," Lisa said.

Brian didn't care for how she said it. He didn't care for it at all.

CHAPTER 15

*C*assie opened the door to her trailer to find Brian standing there looking casually handsome. When his eyes widened at the sight of her, she knew her calculation to go with heart-stopping sexiness had been the right one.

She was wearing a little black dress from Whitney's closet—tight, form-fitting, low-cut, and short.

She was also wearing a pair of Whitney's heels, which were so tall they gave her an extra three inches of height, besides making her calves look sinewy and muscular.

She'd considered putting her hair up, but Whitney had urged her to leave it down, arguing that men loved long, loose hair. Cassie's hair wasn't long—it barely brushed her shoulders—but she'd given it the artfully mussed treatment, as though she'd just gotten out of bed looking this way.

He'd seen her looking elegant. He'd seen her in jeans, with flour dusted on her clothes. He'd even seen her wearing nothing but a towel. It was time for him to see her in an outfit that said, *I haven't been laid for a while and you're just the man for the job.*

"You look ..." He didn't finish the sentence, but he didn't have to. The way he was taking in the sight of her finished it for him.

"Shall we go?" She grabbed her purse from where it was hanging near the door.

"Sure. But … you mind if I take a look at your trailer first? I've always wanted to see inside one of these things."

AT THE RESTAURANT, they got a table in a secluded corner. Cassie ordered a glass of chardonnay, and Brian, explaining that he was more of a beer guy, ordered a local craft brew.

The conversation between them was awkward at first—Cassie could tell that something was bothering him.

"Whatever it is, you might as well come out with it," she told him. "Otherwise, I'm going to think it's me, and I'll go home tonight wondering what I did wrong and obsessing over my various inadequacies."

"I can't see any inadequacies from where I'm sitting." He took a sip of his beer, then carefully replaced the glass on the table.

"Then what's going on?"

Brian sighed, looked at the table, then fussed a little with his cloth napkin. "Okay, here goes. My mother is dating some hipster guy with a man bun who's only one year older than I am. And he's staying with us at Otter Bluff."

Whatever Cassie had expected to hear, it hadn't been that. She let out a guffaw that was probably less than ladylike. "You're joking."

"I wish. His name is Lorenzo." Brian said the name *Lorenzo* with a kind of flourish that told Cassie more about the guy than the man-bun hipster description had.

"You must be mortified," Cassie said.

"You have no idea. You know what's worse? Her bedroom shares a wall with mine. If I have to lie awake tonight listening to rhythmically squeaking bedsprings and moans of passion …"

Cassie laughed again—she couldn't help it. At the sight of Brian's scowl, she said, "I'm sorry. I know it's not funny. Not to you. But at the same time, it's … you know. It's kind of funny."

"It's like one of those recurring nightmares where you try to run but your feet are stuck to the floor." Brian rubbed his face with his hands. "You know? Mothers aren't supposed to ... They're supposed to become impregnated in a lab somewhere by a white-coated doctor with test tubes and surgical instruments."

"Oh, Brian," Cassie laughed. "If that's how you think sex works, then I shouldn't have bothered to wear this dress."

Cassie didn't fully realize what she'd said until she saw Brian's reaction to it. He was blushing and stammering, and he didn't seem to know what to do with his hands.

That was when she understood that she'd pretty much told him she wanted to lure him into bed.

Okay, that wasn't entirely true. She hadn't fully decided yet whether she wanted to lure him into bed. But when she'd chosen her wardrobe, she'd considered it a distinct possibility, and she'd just inadvertently admitted as much to Brian over the appetizer.

"That's ... wow. I didn't ... You're not ..." Brian seemed like he might actually swallow his tongue.

"What exactly is it you're trying to say?" Cassie prompted him.

He made eye contact and said, "I'm trying to say it's a hell of a nice dress."

CASSIE COULD HAVE WALKED BACK the thing about the dress and the sex, but she didn't. As their entrees came, she decided she didn't mind leaving the thought out there. At the very least, it would, as Lacy had suggested, prevent her from being friend-zoned.

They ate rack of lamb (him) and salmon (her), and they talked a little more about his mother and her boyfriend, Cassie's business, and Brian's plans for his career.

"I posted a video earlier this week," he told her. "Video game stuff —me giving commentary as I play, that sort of thing. Those do really well. This one did okay with views, but the comments were way down." He drank from his water glass, then put it back on the table.

"I've seen a drop in revenue without Ike, which is okay since I'm not splitting it in half anymore. Still, I haven't settled on a clear direction for the show now that it's a solo deal. I need an angle. I just don't know what it is."

"Okay. What are you considering?"

They talked about that—about Brian's ideas and the pros and cons of each. Cassie, who was a regular YouTube viewer, threw in some ideas of her own based on what she enjoyed.

"I always love watching Pinterest fails," Cassie said. "Those are hilarious."

That sent Brian into a discussion of some videos he and Ike had done of the two of them attempting something they were comically unqualified to do. Once, they'd tried to follow along with a Bob Ross painting tutorial, and another time, for a Halloween show, they'd tried to duplicate an elaborate pumpkin carving they'd found on the Internet.

"That stuff does work," Brian acknowledged. "But it's best if you have two people on the show. With just one, there's no reaction footage, and that's where the humor is."

Cassie thought about that as she took a bite of salmon. "I could teach you to decorate a cake."

He paused with a forkful of lamb halfway to his mouth. "What, you mean on camera?"

"Sure." She shrugged. "I could teach you something complicated that you're sure to mess up. Compare my cake to yours—that kind of thing."

"That could be good." Brian's far-away look told her he was envisioning it, pondering how such a thing might go. "We're coming up on Easter," he said. "We could time it to the holiday. Do a bunny cake or something."

"Except …" Cassie said.

"Except?"

"Except, that would involve me … you know. Being on camera."

"Well, that was part of the concept."

She'd suggested it because she hadn't expected him to like the idea.

She was just talking, just throwing things out there. Now that he was picking up on it, she realized she was terrified of having her face on video for thousands—or, considering Brian's audience, maybe hundreds of thousands—of viewers.

"I know. I know it was. But ..."

"Don't worry, you'll be great." Brian grinned at her, and she felt the genuine warmth of it, the sincerity. He believed what he was saying. He believed she could do this.

"Are you sure?"

"It won't hurt that you're gorgeous."

She suddenly felt too warm, and it had nothing to do with the temperature in the restaurant.

SHE KNEW a little about his family, so they talked about hers. Her three sisters, her brother, Nick. She told him she'd grown up in Cambria in a house full of kids and pets and a constant, cheerful mess.

"My mother was a stay-at-home mom. My dad's an architect. Moving out into the trailer was the first time I've been alone in thirty years."

"Did you always live with your parents until then?"

"No. No, no. There was college and the dorms, then there was an apartment with two roommates. Then I was a live-in nanny for a family with three kids. But this is the first time I've lived in a space that's just my own. Though, I spend more time in my parents' house than I do in the trailer, so ..."

"Sounds a lot like Ike's family," he said. "Lots of kids, lots of activity. A devoted mom."

The way he said it, she could feel the longing coming out of his pores. Especially with that last part—*a devoted mom.*

"That must have been hard for you, not having your mom around." Cassie reached out and put her hand over his on the tabletop. He turned his hand palm-up so he could hold her hand.

"I spent most of my childhood at Ike's house. I was an honorary Fitzgerald."

"I'm glad you had him."

"Me too." He shrugged. "My dad did his best, but he worked a lot. And he's not exactly a touchy-feely kind of guy. His approach to feelings was that if you don't talk about them, they'll get bored and go away."

"How has that worked out for him?"

Brian took a bite of his lamb, chewed, then shrugged again. "Well, he's got a drinking problem, so probably not very well."

WHEN DINNER WAS OVER, they drove to San Luis Obispo to see a movie. Thankfully, they both wanted to see the same thing—the newest release from the Marvel Cinematic Universe. Brian had worried that Cassie might be the art movie type—that maybe she liked things with heavy symbolism and subtitles—and he'd wondered whether they could make a relationship work with that kind of obstacle between them.

So when she'd suggested a superhero flick, he'd been nearly giddy with his good fortune.

They got a couple of soft drinks and a large popcorn to share, and about halfway through the movie, Brian was bold enough to reach out and take her hand. He held it atop the armrest that separated them, and after that, he barely noticed what was happening on the screen.

BY THE TIME Brian took her home, Cassie's mind and body were buzzing with the possibilities of what might happen once they got there. She didn't usually sleep with someone on the second date (because she did consider this their second date), but a little harmless making out wouldn't be unwelcome.

He held her hand as he walked her across the yard, their shoes crunching on the gravel path that led to the front door of the trailer.

If she decided to invite him in, the chances were high that her resolve would collapse and she'd tear her clothes off and throw herself into his arms. For now, she stood at the Airstream's front step and tipped her face up to him for a kiss. The moon was at three-quarters and the sky was clear, and they both were bathed in a gentle, silvery light.

He brushed his fingers over her cheek, then leaned in and let his lips gently caress hers.

Cassie's body felt warm and fluid as she leaned into him, deepening the kiss.

And that was when her father turned on the back porch light and opened the door.

"Cassie? Is that you?"

The magic, of course, was broken, as it always was and always would be in the presence of one's father.

Cassie jumped back, creating a foot of space between her body and Brian's.

"Yes, Dad. It's me. Hi. I'm just coming in." She gave her father a little wave.

"And who's that with you?" Vince squinted theatrically from his place on the stoop, backlit by the kitchen's ceiling lamp.

"I'm sorry," Cassie mouthed to Brian. Then she took his hand and led him over to the Jordan house.

The introductions were courteous but awkward. "Brian, this is my dad, Vince Jordan. Dad, this is Brian Cavanaugh."

Vince's big, meaty hand virtually swallowed Brian's as they shook. "Nice to meet you, son."

Cassie noticed that her father's voice had lowered somewhat, probably in an attempt to intimidate Brian. She was also certain that his use of the word *son* was calculated: the man vs. the child.

"You too, sir."

"Cassie, your mother's waiting up because she wants to talk to you about something. Why don't you go in there? I'll walk Brian to his car."

Cassie pouted like a teenager. "What could she possibly need to talk to me about at this time of night?"

"Who knows the thoughts of women?" Vince said.

"Dad—"

"Brian." Vince gave Brian a smack on the back that was supposed to appear friendly, but which caused Brian to pitch forward from its force. "What say we take a little walk to your car?"

WHEN BRIAN WAS GONE, Cassie stood in the Jordan kitchen with her hands on her hips, confronting her father.

"Mom did not want to talk to me. Mom is asleep."

"My mistake." Vince's eyebrows rose in a display of innocence.

"Mistake, my ass."

"Cassie …"

"I'm a grown woman," she went on. "I do have sex. Not with Brian —yet—but it does happen on occasion. With people. And you have no right to—"

"Of course I have a right. I'm your father." His tone had softened, and the way he was looking at her made her feel five years old again. "I'm always going to worry about you and what you do. With people." He said the last bit archly, tossing her own words back at her.

"Damn it." She plopped down into a kitchen chair. "He was kissing me. We were kissing."

"I noticed."

"It was a good kiss, too."

"Cassie." Vince winced painfully. "I really don't need to hear that."

"All this means is that next time I'll go to his place," Cassie said, her arms crossed over her chest.

"Another country would be even better." He kissed her on top of her head and walked toward the stairs, a glass of water in his hand. "Good night, sweetie."

"Good night, Dad."

She was still feeling distinctly sulky when he turned back toward her on his way to bed. "That guy treat you right?"

"He's been a complete gentleman. A fact I was hoping to correct tonight, until you—"

"Ah, jeez." Vince scrunched his face up as though in pain. "I'm gonna pretend I didn't hear that last part."

CHAPTER 16

*C*assie took it up with her mother the next morning over coffee. Vince had gone to his office early, and Cassie didn't have to be at Central Coast Escapes until ten.

"Could you please tell Dad to stop scaring away my dates?" Cassie was dressed in faded jeans and an old T-shirt, her hair up in a messy bun. Nancy had her Bunco group in a half hour, so she was dressed up in slacks and a bedazzled tunic, her hair freshly done.

"I'm not sure there's anything I can do about it, Cassie. He's your father, and you're his youngest. You're always going to be his baby."

"But I'm not a baby. I'm a grown woman. What does he think he's doing, guarding my virginity? I haven't been a virgin since twelfth grade."

"Oh, Cassie. I really don't need to hear—"

"Mark Pullman. Prom night. His parents had a van, so ..."

"Cassie!"

Cassie gave her mother a mischievous grin.

"You're punishing me," Nancy said.

"Sort of."

Nancy sat down in a chair across from Cassie at the kitchen table. "Honey, he loves you, and he worries about you. That's all."

"He doesn't stalk Whitney's boyfriends. At least, I don't think he does."

"Well, Cassie, Whitney doesn't live in our backyard."

And that was the heart of the problem, wasn't it? Cassie was an adult, but she didn't fully live like one. If she did, she wouldn't be close enough that her parents could monitor her activities by looking out their kitchen window.

When she got her bakery up and running, she was going to remedy that situation.

"Ugh." Cassie rubbed at her face with her hands. "I have to go to work."

No matter how many shifts she worked at Central Coast Escapes, no matter how many toilets she cleaned and bed linens she changed, she was never going to be able to afford her own place that way.

She needed to figure out the bakery thing if she ever wanted to live like the mature adult she was.

Not to mention if she ever wanted to get laid again.

Which she really, really did, and sooner rather than later.

"So. What are your plans?" Brian asked his mother as she stood in the kitchen at Otter Bluff making a hemp milk and kale smoothie for herself and Lorenzo. Thor was standing by in case she dropped something—though Brian doubted he would want it if she did.

"Well, darling, I've got a spa treatment booked this afternoon. I've also got a meeting with a gallery owner on Main Street, though it's not likely I'll want to place my work there. This isn't exactly an art world hub, and I—"

"I meant ... you know ... past that. Past today."

She blinked at him. "Well, tomorrow I thought I'd—"

"When are you leaving?" He hadn't meant to blurt it out, but she didn't seem to be taking the hint.

She turned toward him, looked at him as though she were in awe of his gall, and placed a fist carefully on her hip. "Why, Brian. Are you in a hurry to get rid of me?"

He thought about softening it—thought about coming up with some kind of spin to suggest he was only concerned about her and her needs—then decided that blurting had worked fine so far.

"Yes. I am in a hurry to get rid of you, Mom."

For just a moment, he thought he saw real hurt on her face, and he regretted having said what he'd said—even if it was true.

"What have I done to displease you now?" Her subdued tone told him he'd been right—she was hurt.

"Nothing. You haven't done anything." He sank down onto a barstool at the kitchen island. "It's just ... if you must know, you're interfering with my sex life."

"This is about Cassie."

"Yes, it's about Cassie. We had our date, and it went well—very well—and then I couldn't bring her back here, obviously, because you're here, and you can't exactly bring your date back to your place when your mom is in the next room. So we went to her place, but her trailer is in her parents' backyard, and her dad saw us kissing and ... well. Let's just say I left shortly after that."

Lisa laughed in a theatrical, tinkling way that left Brian wondering if she'd practiced it in a mirror. "Oh, sweetheart. You could have brought her here. I'm not a prude. It's not as though you and she would be having sex on the sofa. You do have your own room."

"Yeah, but you and Lorenzo are right next door, and there might be ... you know. Noises."

The way he'd said it suggested that it was his and Cassie's noises he was worried about. In fact, his concern was that if Lisa and Lorenzo made noises—which they'd done last night, to his horror—Brian might not be able to perform. And he really didn't need that kind of humiliation on top of everything else.

"Dear, I assure you, I won't be emotionally scarred by your noises."

But I'm emotionally scarred by yours.

"Well, still ..."

"So." Lisa folded her arms on the island countertop and looked closely at her son. "You really like this girl."

"Yes. I really do."

"*Hmm.*"

He didn't like the *hmm*, didn't like what it implied about whatever it was she was thinking.

"So, when are you leaving? And, more to the point, when is Lorenzo leaving?"

She rested her chin on the back of one hand. "I'm not sure yet, Brian. I'll have to see how things ... develop."

CASSIE HAD another week to make Rachel's wedding cake, which was plenty of time, but she still didn't have a kitchen of her own to work in. That meant she had to ask Brian if she could use Otter Bluff.

That was awkward with Brian's mother there, and it was also awkward that she'd be asking him for a favor when they were dating. Seeing someone was complicated enough without adding the power dynamic of one person needing something from the other.

Except, Brian needed something, too. He needed a YouTube video that would bring in a lot of views and please his subscribers. Maybe he could get what he wanted at the same time Cassie got her own needs met.

Maybe we can do the video we talked about at the same time as I do the wedding cake, she suggested to him in a text message that afternoon. *I know we talked about an Easter theme, but a wedding cake's harder, so the fail will be better.*

She watched as three bouncing dots on her screen told her he was formulating a reply.

Sounds good. When do you want to do it?

Cassie thought about her schedule. She had a day off on Thursday, which would work well for her to get the cake done for the weekend.

Thursday afternoon?

See you then. BTW, my mother will probably still be here. She was supposed to be visiting for the weekend. One weekend. Two days, three if there's a holiday, four if you add Friday and Monday. No definition of weekend stretches to Thursday, yet here she'll be, hovering and calling you darling.

Cassie couldn't help giggling at Brian's mini tirade about his mother.

That's fine, she responded. *If she doesn't mind me being there.*

BRIAN THOUGHT about telling Cassie that his mother had specifically stated she didn't mind Cassie's presence—even if Cassie stayed overnight while naked. But there didn't seem to be a way to say such a thing that wasn't mortifying. Instead, he confirmed their plan and ended the text exchange with a jaunty *See you Thursday!*

Then he began planning the video.

He called Shayla, his part-time assistant, and asked her if she was available to film the video for him. She was, so that was good.

Then he opened his laptop and started working on a script for the video. Of course, most of it would be unscripted—the informal nature of it would be the best part—but there'd be an intro, and that had to be planned in advance.

How would he introduce Cassie? As a friend? More than a friend? Would he simply call her a local baker?

It occurred to him that this wouldn't just be an entertaining video; it could also give her baking career a significant bump if the thing took off and people decided to hire her because of the show.

The whole thing was going to be a win-win.

He wrote the script for the intro, sent Cassie an e-mail asking her what supplies he should have on hand for his version of the cake, then watched an array of similar videos to see what had already been done, what worked, and what didn't.

After that, he spent some time on social media, leaving amusing quips on Twitter and Facebook.

He took Thor to the dog park and let him run until he was

exhausted and panting. Then he brought him home and gave him a new chew toy and a bowl of water.

Finally, Brian had to do the thing he'd been avoiding—he had to tell his mother about his plans for the video, since she was, after all, staying in the house, too. He needed to make sure she'd be out of the way on Thursday.

"Hey, Mom?"

Lisa was sitting on the back deck in an Adirondack chair, sipping sparkling water and reading something on her laptop. Brian had stuck his head out the sliding glass door to talk to her, and she looked up and set her reading glasses on top of her head so she could see him better.

"What is it, dear? And please, don't make me twist my neck like this to see you." She patted the chair beside her. "Come. Sit."

Reluctantly, he came outside and sat down.

"Where's Lorenzo?"

"He went to San Luis Obispo to try to find me some decent art supplies. I have an idea for a new painting."

"Oh. That's great."

Brian didn't often ask about Lisa's art career, but he had the impression it was going well. A couple of years before, one of her paintings had sold for more than two hundred thousand dollars at auction, and the sale had made her an art world celebrity. Her picture had been in all of the art magazines, she'd had a prestigious solo show at a hot New York gallery, and she'd found herself being invited to the same parties as Madonna and Leonardo DiCaprio.

He didn't know if she was still riding that high, but she had a full-time personal assistant, so he assumed she was.

The idea of her launching into a new painting gave him a moment of hope.

"So, does that mean you're going back to LA so you can use your studio?"

Her eyes narrowed, and he knew he hadn't been nearly as subtle as he'd thought. "It does not. If I were going home to do the painting, I wouldn't need Lorenzo to buy supplies here, now would I?"

Brian's shoulders fell. "I guess not."

They sat for a moment watching the waves crash against the rocks below the house.

"So … Cassie's coming over on Thursday." It had been on the tip of Brian's tongue to ask for his mother's permission, but that was stupid —he wasn't sixteen, asking his mom if he could bring a girl home. In fact, when he *was* sixteen, he'd never asked his mom if he could bring a girl home, because his mother hadn't been there. Why should he start asking her permission for such things now?

"Is that so?" She raised her eyebrows in question.

"Yeah. We're going to work on a video for the show. So … you might want to, you know, have a spa day or something."

"Hmm. What is the nature of the video?"

"I don't think that's—"

"For God's sake, Brian, I'm asking about your work. I'm not inquiring about state secrets."

He wasn't sure he'd ever heard his mother refer to his YouTube videos as "his work" before—as though they were a legitimate career. She'd never given any indication that she was interested in what he did or that she had any respect for it.

"Cassie's going to teach me to decorate a cake."

Lisa allowed him a half smile. "And you think that's something you'll be able to do?"

"No. That's the point. I'm going to fail. Entertainingly."

"I see." She put her glasses back in place and looked at her laptop screen, her interest in the topic apparently exhausted.

"So, can you give us the kitchen on Thursday?"

"Of course." She shrugged to indicate the insignificance of it all.

"And you'll … you know. Leave?"

She looked at him over the tops of her glasses. "I don't believe I will, actually."

"Mom …"

"Brian, I want to watch. I want to see what you do. Is that so wrong?"

He supposed it wasn't. He'd always wanted her to take more of an interest in him, and that's what she was planning to do. So, why did he feel so uneasy about it?

"You and Lorenzo will have to stay out of the way while we're recording. And be quiet. And ... you know. Not be the center of attention."

Her lips curved slightly. "It'll be a strain, dear, but I'm sure we'll manage it."

CHAPTER 17

*B*rian had everything ready by Thursday. He had the extra supplies Cassie had asked for, and he'd used a cake mix to bake a simple two-layer round cake he'd be decorating.

The cake was lopsided, but that was okay. The point of the whole thing was for him to fail, after all.

When Cassie showed up that afternoon, he met her at the door. She was holding a kind of tackle box that she used for her cake decorating stuff, and she had an additional bag of supplies slung over one shoulder.

"Ah … there's just one thing," he said.

"Uh-oh. What?"

"My mom's here. And so is Lorenzo."

"Oh. That's okay." She leaned in and whispered, "I kind of want to get a look at him anyway."

"Right. Well, that's fine, then." He put his hands into his jeans pockets and rocked back and forth on his feet while Thor sniffed Cassie's legs.

Cassie's eyebrows drew together as she studied him. "Is everything all right?"

"Yeah. Of course. Sure." He rubbed the back of his neck. He knew he was doing a crappy job of convincing her that he was a man in top form.

"Well, maybe let me in, then. This stuff is getting heavy."

"Oh. Jeez. Here, let me take that." He took one of the bags from her and stepped back to let her in.

"Cassie, is that you?" Lisa came out of the bedroom to greet her. She was wearing some kind of loose, flowing silk top with an artsy print on it, skinny jeans that hugged her long legs, and a full complement of jewelry—bracelets, necklaces, and dangling earrings.

Lisa grasped Cassie on both shoulders, leaned in, and did a two-cheek air kiss that never failed to make Brian roll his eyes.

"Come in, darling, come in," she told Cassie. "Brian has told me what you're doing today with your video. I can't wait."

"Oh. Well, that's …"

"You haven't met Lorenzo, have you?" She raised her voice and called down the hallway, "Enzo, darling, come meet Cassie."

CASSIE WAS SO preoccupied with whatever was bothering Brian that she didn't fully see Lorenzo when he first came into the room. Her brain simply didn't register him. She glanced at him, then looked at Brian.

That was when it clicked that Lisa's boyfriend was some kind of faux-Italian god with a man bun and six-pack abs. The abs were visible because he was wearing nothing but loose linen pants slung so low on his hips that they appeared to be in danger of falling off.

The fact that she didn't really see him and then suddenly did caused her to do a visible—and probably comic—double-take. She was aware that Brian had noticed it, but now that it was out there, she had no way of taking it back.

"Cassie. Lovely to meet you." Lorenzo took both of her hands in both of his, then did the same air-kiss thing Lisa had done.

"Oh. I … you too." Cassie tried to keep her eyes on his face and not on his naked chest.

"Did you forget to pack shirts, Lorenzo?" Brian asked. "Would you like me to loan you one?"

"Oh! Ha, ha." Lorenzo chuckled and said to Cassie, "He's very funny, no?"

Thor, who'd come to investigate, licked Cassie's hand, and she rubbed him behind his ears.

"Can we just get this done?" Brian said.

THEY WERE STILL WAITING for Shayla. Brian had told her not to come until a little later, to give him and Cassie time to set things up and go over the plan.

That's what they were doing now in Otter Bluff's big kitchen as Lisa sat at the island, observing them.

"Here's my cake." Brian brought his cake out of a plastic container he'd put it in and set the layers in front of Cassie. "I didn't freeze it because it seemed to me a lot of visible crumbs will increase the fail."

Cassie nodded. "Yeah, it should."

"So your intention is to do a poor job?" Lisa asked, a mug of herbal tea on the island in front of her.

"Yes," Brian deadpanned. "It's humor."

"I suppose that's a matter of individual interpretation," Lisa said.

Cassie had her own layers made and frozen, and she removed them from the plastic Ziploc bags she'd brought them in.

The two of them laid out the tools of Cassie's trade: frosting, piping bags, metal tips for the bags, spatulas for spreading frosting, a couple of round cardboard cake boards, some food coloring, and various other things with purposes that were unknown to Brian.

By the time they were done with all of that, the doorbell rang and Shayla was there with a video camera, a tripod, and an armload of lighting equipment.

"Oh, jeez," Cassie said when she saw all of Shayla's equipment.

"What?" Brian asked.

"It's just … I guess I thought it would be you and me and an iPhone. But this is real. It's like a real show."

"Well, yeah. You've seen the show. You know what it is."

"Yes, but it always looked so … informal. I didn't think it would be this professional."

"I'll take that as a compliment," Brian said. "It was supposed to look informal, like a couple of guys goofing around. If that's what you saw, then I guess it worked."

Brian introduced Shayla around—she got a pair of air kisses from Lisa and another from Lorenzo, while Cassie simply offered a handshake.

"Is this one going to be on camera?" Shayla motioned toward Lorenzo.

"No, just me and Cassie," Brian said.

Shayla gave Lorenzo what could only be described as a leer. "What a shame."

WHAT FOLLOWED WAS, to Cassie's mind, an odd combination of chaos and professionalism.

The cake decorating part—or, at least, Brian's part of it—was the chaos. Icing went everywhere, what should have been roses ended up looking like pink poop emojis, an entire corner of Brian's cake fell off and onto the floor, and the end result looked like it had been mauled by rabid weasels.

Cassie's cake, on the other hand, looked utterly lovely.

Of course, Cassie had expected all of that—the chaos. It was the professionalism of Brian and Shayla's video production skills that came as a surprise.

It wasn't that she'd thought he wasn't good at what he did. Of course he was, or he'd never have made a living at it for so many years. But watching him switch back and forth between his goofy numbskull persona and the guy behind the scenes, blocking out shots and troubleshooting the lighting, issuing orders to Shayla regarding camera angles and lenses, had Cassie seeing him with new eyes.

"You really know this stuff," she said with some wonder while they were taking a break between shots.

"Well ... I've been doing it for a while." He rubbed a hand over the back of his neck, inadvertently smearing pink frosting onto his skin.

"Yeah, but ..."

"I mean, you watch the show," he said.

"I do. But it always looked so ... unplanned. So casual."

"It wasn't."

She was beginning to see that.

While they worked, Lorenzo was somewhere else—he'd left a while ago to do some errand or another—but Lisa lingered nearby, politely staying quiet while the camera was on but adding comments here and there in between takes.

"Why, Brian, I had no idea you were a real director!" she'd said at one point. Then, at another: "Cassie, you're an artist. A real artist!"

When it was over, Cassie had the bottom tier of Rachel's wedding cake covered in fondant and decorated, ready for the top two tiers to be added later. It looked perfect, just the way she'd imagined it.

The kitchen at Otter Bluff, on the other hand, looked as though it had been hit by some sort of explosive device made of cake and shrapnel.

"Holy shit." Shayla was packing up her video camera, and she gave a long, low whistle as she looked at the mess. "You oughta think about bringing in a power washer and hosing the whole thing down."

Thor was busy licking up a splotch of frosting from the floor, and Brian took him by the collar and began to lead him into a bedroom. "C'mon, big guy. All I need is to have you puking frosting in the middle of the night."

The dog whined in protest as Brian removed him from what looked like a sugary crime scene.

When Brian came back, he looked around in awe at what they'd done to the place. Then he went into the bathroom, came out with a wet washcloth, and wiped frosting off his face and hands and out of his hair.

"I guess I'd better get on this," he said, indicating the mess.

"I'll help," Cassie said.

Brian winced. "I hate to do that to you. You were doing me a favor, after all."

"And you were doing me one," she reminded him. "It won't be so bad if we work together."

They both looked at Shayla, whose eyes widened in innocence. "Oh. Gee. You know, I'd love to help out, but I have an appointment, right around"—she checked the time on her phone—"now! Right around now." She reached out, picked up a bite-sized chunk of Brian's cake from where it had plunked onto the countertop, and put it in her mouth. "Tastes good, at least."

She gathered up her equipment and headed out the door before anyone could protest.

Brian looked at Lisa. "Mom, I don't suppose you'd—"

Lisa let out a scoff. "Dear, you know I don't clean. That's what I hire people for."

She went to the refrigerator—stepping around fallen chunks of cake and frosting—pulled out a Perrier, and took it out onto the back deck. Brian and Cassie watched through the sliding glass door while she lowered herself into an Adirondack chair, twisted the cap off the bottle, took a sip, then raised her face toward the sun.

"I guess it's just us, then," Brian said.

"I guess so."

He'd missed a bit of frosting at the corner of his mouth, and Cassie had the nearly irresistible urge to lick it off. She grinned at him, thinking about it.

"You look like you're up to something," he observed.

"I might be," she admitted.

They were standing very close together, and they'd both lowered their voices to something soft and intimate.

"If that something involves me ..."

"It might."

"Then, I'm just saying, I hope you'll feel free to … you know … follow through on whatever it is."

"Really."

"Well … I wouldn't want to be the one to hold you back or—"

She leaned forward and, with the tip of her tongue, licked the little bit of pink sugar from the edge of his bottom lip.

THEY'D BEEN DOING the show, having fun, and then all of a sudden, Cassie was licking him. And now it wasn't fun anymore. It was … well. It was electrifying.

Yes, she'd been giving him that look. And yes, he'd encouraged her to go with whatever it was she'd been thinking.

But the feel of her tongue on him …

It was a lightning bolt that went straight from the point of contact, down through his body, and to his nether regions. He shifted a little to ease the pressure in his pants.

He looked at her, holding himself in check for just a beat, then he shoved his hands into her hair and took her mouth with his.

She tasted like frosting and warm woman and something else … something that might have been happiness.

He deepened the kiss, touching his tongue to hers as her body melted against him.

When they parted, her eyes still closed, she let out a little hum. Then she opened her eyes and blinked once, twice.

"Oh, boy," he said.

He said it not because he regretted what he'd done or even to express the immeasurable pleasure of it. He'd said it because he knew this wasn't just a kiss. This was going to lead … somewhere.

Somewhere big.

Whether it was big good or big bad, he'd just have to find out when he got there.

CHAPTER 18

*C*assie couldn't go out with Brian that weekend because she had a packed schedule. She had to finish Rachel's cake, deliver it, work eight-hour shifts at Central Coast Escapes, and attend her mother's birthday dinner.

Things with the cake went fine. She finished it at Otter Bluff while Brian gamely kept his distance to avoid distracting her. She delivered it on Saturday, took pictures for her portfolio, and left a plastic holder of business cards on the cake table—with the bride's permission—in the hope that she would attract more clients.

She cleaned houses the rest of Saturday and all day Sunday, worked the reception desk at Central Coast Escapes, squeezed in some time during her lunch hour to buy her mother a gift, and was near exhaustion on Sunday night as she gathered with her family at the Jordan house to celebrate the birthday.

"God. Is that wine? Give it to me." Cassie had barely come in the back door to the kitchen before she snatched a bottle of chardonnay out of Whitney's hand.

"Glass?" Whitney raised a perfectly sculpted eyebrow and offered Cassie a wineglass.

"Oh, I thought I'd just chug it out of the bottle if that works for everyone." But she took the glass from Whitney, pulled the cork, and poured herself a sensible serving.

The kitchen was humming with activity. Of course, Nancy wasn't cooking since it was her birthday. So Cassie's siblings were bustling around stirring pots, checking on things in the oven, and chopping things at the center island.

"Is everything all right?" Lacy asked. She looked up from where she was poking a meat thermometer into a pot roast.

"Oh, sure. Things are good, actually." Cassie took a sip of the wine, savoring its crisp, fruity flavor. "The wedding cake I did for Deandra's cousin came out great. She was thrilled with it. I'm just exhausted, that's all."

"Ooh. Did you bring pictures?" Jessica, who'd been chopping vegetables for a salad, put down her knife and reached out for Cassie's phone.

Cassie brought up the photos on her iPhone and handed it to Jess.

"Oh, my God. This is gorgeous." Jess swiped through the photos, then handed the phone to Whitney, who swiped and handed it to Lacy, who swiped and tried to hand it to their brother, Nick.

"If I can't eat it, what do I care?" he said, a stack of plates in his hands.

"Very supportive," Cassie said, taking back her phone.

"It really is stunning," Whitney said. That was quite a compliment coming from Whit, who'd always been the family's arbiter of taste. "You're a genius. You've got to get your own bakery soon."

"With what?" Cassie leaned her butt against the counter and sipped more wine. "Central Coast Escapes barely pays me enough to buy groceries and make my car payment."

"Speaking of that," Jess said. "You need a better job."

"Gee. You think?" Cassie quipped. "And anyway, I don't want a job. I want my own business."

"Have you checked with the local restaurants to see if you can sell baked goods? That could really bring in some money," Lacy suggested.

"Yes, and two of them said they'd be interested once I get a commercial kitchen and a health department inspection. Which leaves me back where I started."

"And what about the guy?" Jess wanted to know. She waggled her eyebrows at Cassie.

Of course everyone knew about Brian. Lacy had known from the start, and Cassie had to tell Whitney when she'd borrowed the dress for her date. One or both of them had to have told Jess and Nick—it was what they did. There were few secrets in the Jordan family.

"He's good." Cassie tried not to display a goofy smile, but she couldn't seem to help it.

"Oh ho!" Jess said.

"You're blushing," Whitney pointed out.

"Does that mean you did the deed?" Lacy asked.

"Oh, crap. I don't need to hear this." Nick grabbed a handful of flatware and went out to finish setting the table.

"No, we haven't done the deed." Cassie rolled her eyes. "We might have last weekend if Dad hadn't scared him away."

"Wasn't that only your second date?" Jess wrinkled her nose in barely suppressed judgment.

"Yes. We kissed, and that was it, so you can stop looking at me that way," Cassie told her.

"I'm not looking at you any particular way," Jess protested. "I just think—"

"She thinks you should be saving yourself for marriage," Whitney said, smirking.

"I hate to tell you, Jess, but that ship sailed a long time ago," Cassie said.

"I'm aware." Jess scowled. "I found your birth control pills when you were in your senior year in high school, remember?"

"In any event," Cassie said, trying to get the conversation back on track. "He asked me out this weekend, but I was swamped, and now I'm here, so it didn't happen. But we did a video a few days ago."

She told everyone about the YouTube video and Brian's plans for it.

"That sounds like fun. When's he going to post it?" Lacy asked.

"I don't know. He's got to edit it. He's going to let me know. Jeez, I hope I look okay on camera. I did my hair and everything, but there was powdered sugar everywhere, so …"

"Are you kidding? I'm sure you looked flawless." Whitney perched one fist on her hip. "With your peaches and cream complexion and that wholesome farm girl thing you've got going on?"

"Wholesome farm girl? Now, wait a minute." Cassie didn't know whether to be flattered or offended.

"What's taking so long? I'm starving." Cassie's father poked his head into the kitchen.

"Almost done," Jess told him. "Five more minutes."

"You've been saying five more minutes for twenty minutes," he grumbled before retreating back into the dining room.

BRIAN WATCHED the edited video of himself and Cassie, and he felt that tingly feeling he got when he knew he'd done something good.

It wasn't that the idea was all that original or compelling. Cake decorating fails had been popular long before Brian and Cassie had added their contribution to the genre. It was something less definable —something you couldn't force.

They had chemistry.

Brian sat back in his chair at the dining room table at Otter Bluff and watched the video again. His mother and Lorenzo were out, so he had the kind of precious solitude he experienced so rarely these days.

What he was seeing was chemistry, pure and simple. He'd had it with Ike, and that's why their show had done so well.

That magic, that undefinable something that drew viewers in—he was seeing it again for the first time since he and Ike had done their last show together.

It was possible he was imagining it, that he was seeing what he wanted to see.

Brian grabbed his cell phone and called Ike.

"You got a minute?" he asked when Ike picked up the phone.

"God, yes. Benny wants us to go shopping together. *Shopping.* Dude, the longer you stay on the phone, the less time I'll have to spend sitting in the guy chair outside a dressing room answering questions like, 'Does this make me look fat?'"

"I heard that!" Benny hollered in the background.

"The answer to 'Does this make me look fat' is always no," Brian said.

"Like I don't know that. Like I'd have survived to this age not knowing that."

"Right. Well, anyway ... I wanted you to watch something."

Brian e-mailed a link for the video to Ike, then he waited while his friend watched it. He heard Ike's fiancée, Benedetta, talking about the video, too—they were both watching with Ike's phone on speaker.

They laughed in all the right spots, so that was good. The laughter sounded natural, too—not like they were being polite.

When they'd finished, Brian asked both of them, "So? What do you think?"

"Oh, my God. That was a scream," Benny said. "I've seen that girl around Cambria. How did you find her?"

"Oh, she does the maintenance at my mom's vacation house, and I'm staying here, so ..." He decided not to share the story about Cassie getting caught using his kitchen without permission. Or the story about him seeing her nearly naked. They were good stories, and he'd told them to Ike, who was, after all, his best friend. But it wouldn't be gentlemanly for him to tell those stories to Benny.

"She's good on camera," Ike said. "Really good. Has she done this before?"

"Not that I know of."

"Well ... she's kind of a natural."

Brian thought so, too, but he'd wanted to get Ike's reaction without influencing it by offering his own opinion.

"You think so?" he said.

"I do. You said you just met her?"

"Yeah."

"Huh."

"What does that mean?" Brian asked.

"It's just … I wouldn't have thought that. The two of you seem like you've been together a while. The chemistry …"

And there was the magic word. This was going to work—he just knew it. The question was whether Cassie had any interest in being a regular on YouTube. Another question was whether it was smart to mix his professional life with his personal life.

That kind of thing was fraught with peril. And yet.

"You thinking of taking her on as your new partner?" Ike asked. "Or, wait. She's the girl you're dating, right? That could be complicated."

Ike and Brian had been friends so long that he'd just voiced Brian's own thoughts, as though he were somehow in Brian's head.

"Yeah, I'm thinking it. And yeah, it could be."

"Okay, you watched the video and answered the questions," Benny told Ike over the speaker. "Let's go shopping."

CHAPTER 19

*C*assie was behind the reception desk at Central Coast Escapes on Monday when Brian sent her a text message to tell her that their YouTube video was up.

Oh, God.

It had been one thing to make the video. It was entirely another to know it was out there, available for the world to see.

Okay, thanks, she texted back. Then, after some hesitation: *How did it come out?*

Just watch it and see.

Well, that was no help. Why couldn't he just tell her? Why couldn't he just be straight with her? Was it because the video was bad? Was that why? Had he avoided the question because he knew what a train wreck it was?

Oh, no. This was terrible. Cassie would never be able to show her face in public again. Especially not in Cambria. Everyone knew her here. The comments would be brutal. The looks people would give her—pity, she imagined. On the other hand, Cambria tended toward an older demographic. Maybe no one would see the video. Maybe no one would know….

Oh, God.

She avoided watching it at first, reasoning that she was at work—it would be unprofessional to watch YouTube at work. Never mind the fact that nobody had been into the office for more than an hour, and she really had nothing to do. Still. She was on the clock. This was Central Coast Escapes' time, not her own.

She made busywork for herself as a means of avoiding the video. She cleaned the office bathroom. She vacuumed the carpet, even though she'd already done it once today and it looked fine. She emptied the wastebaskets, even though there wasn't much trash to dump out.

With all of that done, she went back to her desk and sat down, looking for paperwork to do. She couldn't find any—she'd done it all.

Finally, with no other way to occupy her time, she followed the link Brian sent her and clicked on the video.

One of her fears had been that she would look terrible. People always said the camera added ten pounds, and everybody knew that you never looked the same on camera as you did in your own head.

So, as the video began, Cassie was relieved to see that she looked … like herself. The Cassie in the video was the one she'd always known. So that was okay.

At first, she was thrown off by the odd sound of her own voice. Was that how she sounded? But as the video progressed, something else happened.

She stopped worrying about it and started enjoying it.

The experience was almost like she was watching someone else— someone she didn't know but whom she liked just fine. She and Brian laughed, joked, decorated cake, and through it all, Cassie felt herself wishing she were a part of that camaraderie, that jovial friendship.

Then she remembered that she was.

When it was over, she felt a kind of inner glow—a sense of having done something well and being satisfied by it.

She texted Brian: *It's good, isn't it?*

He responded in under a minute. *It's already picking up steam. Ten thousand views, and it's only been up an hour.*

And that was when she started freaking out again.

Is that good? she asked.

In an hour? Yes, it's good.

Okay. So, the video wasn't going to pass by unnoticed the way she'd halfway hoped it would. People were watching it. A lot of people.

Cassie took a deep breath, closed her eyes, and tried to calm her nerves.

WHEN CASSIE READ the comments that had been posted on the video's YouTube page, she began to think maybe this whole thing would turn out to be good for her.

—*Oh my gosh. That cake is beautiful! Cassie's, not Brian's, LOL. How can I buy one of her cakes?*

—*We need a link to Cassie's website.*

—*My mom and dad are going to have their twenty-fifth anniversary and they live on the Central Coast. I want Cassie to make their cake. How can I get in touch with her?!!*

Of course, there were also comments about Brian being funny, questions about when Ike was coming back, inquiries about what Brian had planned for the future, and comments about people being glad they didn't have to clean up the mess.

But there was enough positive feedback about Cassie's work—enough comments about Central Coast people wanting to buy her cakes—that it buoyed her hopes for the business she wanted to build.

And then there were the commenters who thought Cassie should be a regular part of Brian's show.

That was something to think about another time.

For now, she needed to figure out how to get a commercial kitchen and health department approval so she could start advertising her business in earnest.

She spent the rest of her free time at Central Coast Escapes online researching the legal requirements for bakeries; commercial property available in Cambria; and how to get a small business loan. She made notes on a yellow legal pad and became so absorbed in her work that she barely noticed when five o'clock came and it was time to go home.

～

ONCE HE'D GOTTEN out a video he felt good about, Brian had some time to relax.

Relaxing meant letting his mind wander, and of course, when his mind wandered, he began thinking about Cassie.

She'd been busy lately, but her day off from Central Coast Escapes was coming up, and the wedding cake she'd been working on was completed and in the past. He hoped that meant she might go out with him on another date—potentially with more kissing at the end of it.

Or maybe more than kissing, if all of the stars aligned and their various parents left them alone.

He wanted to call her or text her, but he knew she'd been slammed with everything she had going on, and he didn't want to be that guy who demanded all of her attention, giving no respect to her many obligations.

He wanted to be the guy she looked forward to seeing as sweet relief from all of the pressures of life.

So he hung out at Otter Bluff on Tuesday, biding his time, playing with his dog, and trying not to think too hard about his mother and Lorenzo.

Which was hard, since his mother and Lorenzo seemed to be everywhere.

"Oh, darling, there you are. Lorenzo and I were wondering if you wanted to join us for brunch."

Brian and Thor were out on the back patio, Brian in an Adirondack chair and Thor lounging on the ground beside him, when Lisa poked her head out the sliding glass door.

"Isn't brunch a Sunday thing?"

"Well, it doesn't have to be. Why should I be constrained by a concept that was pure invention in the first place? If I want to eat scrambled eggs at eleven a.m. on a Tuesday, I don't see why—"

"Okay, I get it." He'd stepped right into that one. "Thanks for offering, but I'm good."

She narrowed her eyes. "Brian, if you'd give Lorenzo a chance …"

"That's not why I don't want to go," he lied. "I just don't feel like it. You two have fun, though."

She seemed to consider that, then came out onto the patio and sat down beside him. "Are you all right, Brian?"

"Yeah. I'm good. Why?"

"It's just that you haven't been talking much lately. I know Lorenzo was a shock to you, but—"

"It's really not that." This time, he was telling the truth.

"What, then?"

Should he tell her? For the past thirty years, since he'd learned to talk, he'd made it a firm policy not to tell his mother anything significant about his life. It had always worked for him. But she was here, and he was here, and she seemed genuinely interested, and he wondered, what could it hurt? Where was the harm in letting her in, just a little?

"I just have a lot on my mind. I'm wondering when I can go back to my house and how much the work is going to cost me. I miss Ike. I need to figure out what I'm going to do with my show now that he's gone so I won't lose momentum. The video with Cassie and the cakes is doing well, so that's good. But I need a plan going forward. And then …"

"Then what?"

"And then there's Cassie."

Her eyebrows rose delicately. "Is there a problem between you and Cassie?"

"No. No problem. Not at all. That's just it. Things are good. I think … I think this might be something."

"Really." She said it not as a question, but as a kind of statement of surprise.

"I think so. I really like her."

"And she likes you as well." That wasn't a question, either.

"You think so?"

"I know it, dear. I watched her while you were making that video. She positively glows when she looks at you."

Brian felt a rush of sensation at that. Was she right? Did Cassie glow? It seemed to him that she always glowed—that it was just a natural part of her.

A second shoe was going to drop here—he just knew it. "You don't approve," he guessed.

"What?" Her eyebrows shot upward again. "Did I say that, Brian? Did I utter even one word to suggest that?"

"No, you didn't. But I know you. I know that a woman who lives in her parents' backyard and works for minimum wage and wants to bake cakes for a living would never meet your standard of sophistication."

Left unspoken was the fact that Brian, with his YouTube show and his affection for video games and blockbuster movies, didn't meet that standard, either.

"I'm not nearly as big a snob as you seem to think I am," she protested.

"Yes, you are."

He'd expected her to argue the point, but she didn't. She simply sat back in her chair, looked out at the ocean, and sighed.

"I don't disapprove. It's just ..."

Wait for it.

"It's just that I imagined you'd move to Los Angeles one day, and you won't do that, I assume, if you're involved with a woman who lives here."

This came as a surprise to Brian. "You thought I'd move to LA?"

"Well ... yes. I live there, after all. And now Ike does, too. And you're in the entertainment industry. There's a lot for you down there. I'd thought ... I'd thought that you and I could repair our relationship."

She thought that? How in the world might that happen, given how she'd virtually abandoned him when he was barely out of toddlerhood?

"Mom ..."

"Is that so far-fetched an idea?" she asked, interrupting him. "Is it so impossible?"

And, God help him, for a moment he considered it. He considered what his life might be like if he could let his seething resentment for his mother go—if he could have that weight off of him.

"It's not completely beyond the limits of possibility, no."

And yet.

Brian didn't consider for a moment that Lisa really was okay with Cassie. After all, Lisa's art centered mostly on disdain for domesticity. The piece that had sold for two hundred thousand dollars had been a collage of women in bondage made out of the packaging of consumer products: mac and cheese boxes, cleaning products, frozen food containers. She loathed anything that might suggest housewifery— and he couldn't imagine she'd make an exception for baking.

"She's going to open a bakery here," he said. "And I want to see where this thing with us might go. So ... I'm not planning a move any time soon."

"I see."

Brian could virtually smell his mother's thought processes, starting with the fact that he was choosing Cassie over her, progressing through her evaluation of Cassie as an inadequate partner for him, and ending on her idea of Cambria and the entire Central Coast as a fine place to visit but an inferior place to build any kind of reputable career.

"Weren't you headed out to eat?" Brian asked.

As if on cue, Lorenzo opened the sliding glass door and called to Lisa. "You're ready for brunch, no?"

Brian was glad he'd declined. Could he sit through a meal with that man-bunned asshole?

No.

CHAPTER 20

The next day, just when Cassie was wondering when Brian might call, he did. They made plans to see each other that evening, and that was a development she'd fully expected.

Barely an hour later, his mother called.

She hadn't expected that.

Cassie was at Jitters on Main Street, in line to order a vanilla latte, when the call came in on her cell phone.

"Cassie, is that you? Darling, it's Lisa."

Cassie was so surprised that she didn't say anything for a moment. Then, the thought popped into her head that this had to be about the house, because why else would Lisa be calling her?

"Oh. Lisa. Hello." She regained her composure as she moved forward a little in line. "Is there a problem with Otter Bluff? Is it the power socket in the bathroom? I told Elliot—"

"No, no. The house is fine. Well … the interior design is terribly dated, of course, but I have no one to blame but myself."

"Oh. Is Brian okay? I just talked to him earlier today, and—"

"Yes, yes. My son is fine."

Clearly, Cassie wasn't going to be able to guess what this was about. There was nothing to do but wait for Lisa to get to the point.

"Lisa, can you hang on a second?" Cassie muted the phone and ordered her latte. She paid for it, then stepped aside to wait for her drink. She unmuted the phone. "Okay, I'm back. What can I do for you?"

"Dear, I just wanted to tell you how impressed I was with your cake decorating skills. You're an artist with frosting."

Coming from an actual artist—one who was, by all accounts, enjoying a hugely successful career—that meant something. Cassie picked up her drink at the counter, found a table by the window, and sat down.

"Thank you so much. I really appreciate that."

"Well, it's simply the truth."

As flattering as it was, there was no way Lisa had called just to tell her that. Something more was coming, and Cassie already felt uneasy about it.

"That's very kind," she said.

"Listen, dear, I'm sure you're busy, so I'll get to the point. Brian told me you're interested in opening a bakery, but you don't have the capital."

"That's ... that's true. I'm looking into getting a small business loan, but—"

"Well," she went on as though Cassie hadn't spoken, "my financial adviser has urged me to find a business to invest in, and I thought perhaps you and I might enter into a mutually beneficial partnership."

Cassie blinked a few times, wondering if Lisa could possibly mean what she seemed to be saying.

"You and I? A ... partnership?"

"I'd like to bankroll your business, Cassie. For a percentage of the profits, of course. Do you have an attorney? If not, I'd suggest that you get one, as the legal details of these things can be utterly excruciating. I can offer you some names."

Cassie still was having trouble processing what Lisa was saying. "You want to ... to help me open my bakery? But I can't ask you to give me that kind of money. It wouldn't be ..."

"I wouldn't be 'giving' you anything," Lisa corrected her. "It's an investment, as I mentioned. But that will be worked out by the lawyers, God bless them. If I had to deal with paperwork loaded with legalese all day, I'd lose whatever sanity I have left."

Cassie took a sip of her latte, needing the caffeine to help her get her brain working properly, then rubbed her forehead with her hand. "But how can you be certain the business will run a profit? I'm sure the first year, at least, will be tight, and after that …"

"I'm aware of the realities. The question is, are you interested?"

"Does Brian know you're making this offer? Did you tell him about this?"

The beat of silence that followed told her the answer, and that caused a growing sense of unease in Cassie's belly.

"Lisa …"

"I'll tell him, darling. I just haven't yet because there was no sense in it if you weren't interested in the first place. So, are you?"

Wasn't this everything she'd been wanting? Hadn't she daydreamed about just such a windfall, just such a serendipitous development that would make her dreams come true?

"Of course I'm interested."

"Wonderful, Cassie." Lisa's voice brimmed with enthusiasm. "Let's set up a meeting, shall we? We'll need to discuss the details."

BRIAN WAS EXCITED about his date with Cassie. Part of the excitement was the promise of getting away from his mother and Lorenzo, and part of it was the hope of possible sex.

Most of it, though, was about the pure pleasure of being with Cassie.

Brian hadn't dated as much as most people seemed to think, despite the fact that, at the height of his YouTube fame, he'd had plenty of interest from female viewers.

The truth was, despite his on-screen persona, he was an introvert who liked to have a few serious relationships—like the friendship he shared with Ike—instead of numerous superficial ones. That meant that he usually found dating to be uncomfortable at best and painful at worst until he really got to know the woman.

This thing with Cassie had been different. He'd felt like he knew her from the beginning, which allowed him to bypass the awkwardness and discomfort and go straight to the part where he was just happy to be with her.

He showed up at her trailer at six p.m. feeling nearly giddy with anticipation, though he made a valiant attempt to suppress the giddiness on the grounds that it was unmanly.

They'd both dressed up for their last date, but this one was more casual—a walk on the beach in Cayucos followed by fish and chips at Duckie's—so he'd opted for jeans, sneakers, and a long-sleeved rugby shirt to protect him from the evening chill. She opened the door dressed in jeans artfully ripped at the knees and a loose, V-neck sweater over a tank top that gave him a peek of her cleavage. Her blond hair was loose over her shoulders, making him want to bury his face in it.

"Hi." She grinned at him, and the flirtation in the grin made him feel a little weak-kneed.

"You ready?" He shoved his hands in his pockets because he didn't know what else to do with them.

"Almost. I just have to do one thing first."

"What's that?"

She came down the steps, put her hands on his shoulders, and kissed him. Whatever thoughts he'd had in his brain promptly fled at the feel of her lips on his.

"Now I'm ready," she said.

THEY DROVE south to Cayucos under a bright and clear sky, the sun just beginning to edge toward the horizon. A light breeze created a hint of chop on the ocean.

They ate fish and chips and drank mugs of beer at Duckie's, a funky, surf-themed place just steps from the pier. Then Cassie held Brian's hand as they walked on the beach, the surf lapping onto the sand near their feet.

During dinner, she'd waited for an opening to tell him about her conversation with his mother. The opening had come when he'd asked her how her plans for the bakery were progressing, but she'd let the opportunity pass.

She was nervous about it. She wanted Lisa's help—wanted it so much she could barely think of anything else—but what if he had an issue with it? She knew he had a shaky relationship with his mother. What if he objected so strongly that it threatened to disrupt this new and fragile thing they had together?

One thing was certain: She couldn't simply fail to tell him. Secrets got bigger and more dangerous the longer you kept them, and this one had to come out before it became obvious that she was intentionally keeping him in the dark.

"Hey. Brian?" They were walking hand in hand, going around a pair of kids building a sandcastle.

"*Mmm?*"

He seemed happy. She didn't want to step on his happiness, and yet it had to be done. She supposed there was always the chance he'd be supportive of the idea.

Cassie stopped walking and turned to face him, her hand still in his, the breeze ruffling her hair.

"Did your mom tell you about our phone call?" She kept her tone light, as though she was certain he already knew and that it wasn't an issue at all.

His eyebrows drew together. "What phone call?"

"Oh, I thought for sure ..."

"Cassie? What phone call?"

Okay, the casual act wasn't working. She sat down on a log of driftwood and motioned for him to join her.

"Your mom offered to put up the capital for me to open my bakery.

She wants to have a meeting, with lawyers and everything. She said she was impressed with my skills and she thinks it would be a good investment."

Her heart pounded as she waited to see how he would respond.

At first, he didn't say anything. He looked out at the ocean, then rubbed his eyes with his hand, pushing his glasses out of the way. Then he straightened the glasses and looked at her.

"She did what?"

"Brian ..."

"When did this happen? When did you talk to her?"

"Today. This afternoon."

She'd held out hope that maybe he would even like the idea—maybe he'd be excited for her. Clearly, that wasn't how it was going to go.

"You didn't say anything. At dinner, I asked you how your plans were coming, and you didn't say anything."

"Well, I'm telling you now."

He pulled his hand away from hers, and that wasn't a good sign. No, that didn't bode well at all.

"Well ... wow." Brian rested his forearms on his knees and didn't look at her.

"I thought ... I thought I wouldn't be able to do it. It all seemed so out of reach, you know? Finding a commercial kitchen space, coming up with the money I would need to do that ... and now, it's going to be possible. My dream is going to be possible."

What she really meant was, *Please let me have this. Please don't take this away from me.*

"She's manipulating you. Or me," he said. "She's manipulating someone, though I'm not really sure how yet. When she starts pulling the puppet strings—"

"That's not fair." But, was it? Brian certainly knew Lisa better than Cassie did. Maybe he saw something that Cassie didn't. Still, it didn't seem right for him to immediately jump to the judgment that Lisa was using her and Cassie was naïve enough to allow it.

Brian stood up, walked a few feet away, and turned back to Cassie. "What did she say? What did she say exactly?"

Cassie stood up, too, to avoid a severe height disadvantage. "I told you what she said. She wants to invest in my business."

"In exchange for what?"

Cassie blinked a few times, gathering herself. "In exchange for a percentage of the profits. That's how investments work."

"But … she doesn't need that." He shook his head. "She's loaded. She doesn't need …" Brian pressed his mouth into a tight line and jammed his hands onto his hips. "Oh, God. I know what this is. I know what this is. She's going to wait until it's almost a done deal, wait until you've picked out the place and are all excited about it, then she's going to …"

"What?"

"She's going to tell you to break up with me or she's pulling the money."

BRIAN KNEW what he was saying was true. He knew it as well as he knew the shape of his own hands or the taste of his own tongue. And yet it wasn't until the words were out of his mouth that it occurred to him that his take on things might hurt Cassie's feelings.

"But … why would she want that?" Cassie asked, the injury already in her eyes and on her face. "Has she said something? Did she tell you she doesn't like me?"

"No." Now he could either pull back what he'd said or double down on it. He chose to double down. "She doesn't work that way. She doesn't tell you things straight out. At least, not at first."

"So, what does she do, then?"

"She …" He hesitated, thinking about it. "She hatches a plan, like Lucy Ricardo and Ethel Mertz, but with money."

"But I'm asking you why." Cassie's voice lowered, and the open, happy expression on her face had changed to one of guardedness. "Why would she want you to break up with me? What does she think is wrong with me? Why wouldn't I be good enough for you?"

That was when he knew for sure that he'd stepped in it.

"Cassie ..."

"I'm asking. I really want to know."

Shit. What could he say now that wouldn't make this situation worse? What could he tell her that wouldn't make her stomp down the beach away from him?

He tried to form his words carefully. "She might think ... It's possible she wants to see me with someone more ..."

"What are you trying to say, Brian? For God's sake, spit it out."

"Okay. Fine. She wants me with someone high-powered who's going to drag me kicking and screaming into what she thinks is a respectable career. And aspiring bakery owner doesn't qualify."

CASSIE TRIED to process what Brian had just said to her: his mother didn't think she was good enough for him. But his mother had never said that. Which meant Brian was the one assuming she wasn't good enough for him.

Part of her brain acknowledged that Brian's criticism was of his mother, not of Cassie. After all, his assessment was that his own career wasn't good enough, either. But another part of her—something primal—told her he wouldn't have come to that conclusion if he hadn't believed it himself.

"Why don't we just walk back?" Cassie avoided eye contact with him, focusing instead on brushing sand off her jeans.

"You're mad. You're mad, aren't you? Listen, I get it. She's impossible. She's—"

"Right now, she's not the one I have an issue with." Cassie said it deliberately, carefully, meeting his eyes with her own. If she didn't stand up for herself now and this became a relationship, then it could stretch out into months, years, potentially a lifetime of not standing up for herself. She didn't want to set that kind of precedent.

"What do you mean?"

She started walking away from him toward the pier.

"Cassie? What do you mean?" he called after her.

She spun around to face him. "What I mean is, she never said I wasn't good enough for you. She didn't say it to me, and she didn't say it to you. Only one person said that. You. Just now."

"I didn't mean …" He rubbed his face with his hands. "Cassie, wait. That's not what I meant."

"It's certainly how it sounded." She'd said what she needed to say. Now, she turned and walked back toward the car without stopping.

THEY DIDN'T SAY much on the way home. They'd intended to have a longer evening—drinks at Ted's, maybe, or a movie at his place or hers—but from the tension in the car, it was clear that wasn't going to happen.

They'd just passed the town of Harmony on their way back to Cambria when Brian finally said something.

"I don't think you aren't good enough. Wait. With the double negative, that's confusing. I *do* think you're good enough, Cassie. In fact …"

"In fact, what?"

"In fact, I think you're a little out of my league. I think I'm playing above my division here. Or at least, I was until I stuck my foot in my mouth and ruined everything. It's just … my mother makes me crazy. I know she's going to try to ruin things between us somehow, and I just … I don't want that to happen."

She'd been trying to keep her eyes forward, but now she sneaked a look at him. "You think I'm out of your league?"

"God, yes. Just look at you."

A smile tugged at Cassie's lips, but she suppressed it. Yes, it was nice to know he was attracted to her, but that wasn't good enough. If all she had was her looks, then what was the point?

"That's all?" she said. "You like how I look. That's it?"

"No. Of course not." Brian's knuckles went white for a beat as he squeezed the steering wheel. "You being out of my league has to do with the whole package. Your looks, yes, but also your talent, your personality, the way you just have your shit together. It's everything."

"You think I have my shit together?" The idea was surprising, especially because Cassie's sisters always seemed to believe otherwise.

"Yes. I do. Well ... despite the fact that you were stealing the use of my kitchen and wearing only a towel when I met you."

Now she did grin—she couldn't seem to help it. "Despite that."

"Actually, I think the towel thing has to go in the plus column rather than the minus. Because obviously." He shot her a quick grin that was sexy as hell.

Was this how it was going to be? Was it always going to be impossible to stay mad at him? Because that might make things difficult for her in any number of ways.

"You've really got the charm-your-way-out-of-trouble thing down," she said.

"Well, in fairness, I've been working on it for a number of years."

"PARK HERE. RIGHT HERE." Cassie indicated a spot at the curb several houses down from her parents' place.

"But—"

"Just do it." He did. They got out into the dark night, and Cassie used the flashlight app on her phone to light their way as they walked toward the Jordan house.

"What are we—"

"*Shhh!*" She quieted him and motioned for him to follow her.

They walked to the Jordan house quietly, by the light of Cassie's phone, and sneaked around the side of the house and into the backyard, their feet swishing through the overgrown grass.

"Cassie, do we really have to—"

She turned to him and hissed, "Do you want to come into my trailer, or do you want my father to roust you off the property again?"

There seemed to be only one correct answer to that question. "I want to come in."

"Then follow me and don't make any noise!"

They got to the trailer without triggering the dreaded back porch light at the Jordan house—which would have been a sure signal that they'd been caught.

Cassie unlocked the trailer, went inside, and soundlessly waved him in.

"Do you always have to do this when you bring a guy home?" he asked as she went through the tiny space turning on lights.

"I've never brought a guy here before."

"Really." This came as a surprise, though he wasn't sure what he'd thought. Of course he hadn't expected to learn that Cassie brought home a new guy every weekend—she didn't seem the type. But it had never occurred to him that he might be the first man in her trailer—a phrase that sounded to him like some kind of off-color metaphor.

"Yes, really. It's not that I haven't dated, it's just ... well. The sneaking is awkward and makes me feel like I'm fifteen, and that's not usually the image I want to project to the men in my life."

"And I imagine you can usually go to their place without having to deal with their mothers. Or their mother's pretentious boyfriend."

"Yes, that. It's weird. I mean, here I am, a full-fledged adult, and I still have to sneak around so my parents won't know I plan to have sex with my boyfriend."

More than one element of that sentence struck him right in the central nervous system, making parts of him tingle and other parts of him come to attention. "So ... you think of me as your boyfriend? And you're planning to have sex with me?"

"Oh." Her voice softened. She was standing very close to him. "The boyfriend thing ... I didn't mean ... What I'm trying to say is, yes, I do think of you that way, but if you're not there, it's not a big deal, we can—"

"Stop backtracking. I liked it."

"Oh." She inched closer.

"And the sex thing?"

She tipped her face up to him. "Why don't you kiss me, and we'll see what happens?"

He did. He touched his lips to hers tentatively at first, then deepened the kiss, thrilling at the taste and feel of her.

"So … I noticed you've got a full-sized bed in this thing," he murmured. Her hands were on his back, and he gently rubbed her cheek with his thumb.

"I do. You want to try it out?"

CHAPTER 21

The thing about Brian was, if you watched him on YouTube goofing around with his friend, you'd imagine that he couldn't find a clitoris with a flashlight and a diagram.

In real life, though, he had no trouble finding it—and he knew what to do with it once he did.

Being skilled was one thing. Cassie was delighted to find that he was also sensitive, caring, and generous as a sexual partner. He took direction when she gave it, he put her pleasure before his own, and he checked with her throughout to make sure she was still okay with whatever it was he was doing.

Which pretty much meant that, as far as men were concerned, he was as rare as a magical unicorn that shot gold dust out its ass.

"I mean, you wouldn't think it, right?" Cassie asked Lacy on the phone the next morning. Brian hadn't spent the night, as he'd wanted to get off the Jordan property before Lacy's dad knew he was there. "You'd think he'd be this … I don't know. This frat boy or something. Eager, but no nuance. But, oh my God. There was nuance. So much nuance."

"Is *nuance* a code word for orgasms?" Lacy wanted to know.

"Yes. Yes, it is."

"That's so great." In the background, Cassie heard Trevor fussing and one of the older kids—it sounded like Caleb—asking when she was going to make his breakfast. Lacy shooed him away, telling him she'd be right there. "Daniel and I used to have … *nuance* … every day. You know, before the k-i-d-s." She spelled the word out so her son wouldn't be offended. "Now, we're lucky if it's once a week."

Cassie winced in sympathy. "Really? God."

"Don't get me wrong," Lacy went on. "I love my life. I want this. I want all of it. Still, I wouldn't mind a little more nuance, if you know what I mean."

Cassie sat with that thought for a bit while Lacy changed the TV channel for Caleb and went into the kitchen to pour his cereal.

"You know," Cassie said when Lacy returned her attention to the conversation, "I could babysit sometime if you and Daniel want some alone time."

Lacy laughed.

"What's so funny?"

"They'd destroy you in ten minutes. No offense, Cass, I know you love the kids, but on your own? You'd be ready to throw yourself in front of a bus before Daniel and I were out of the driveway."

Cassie pouted a little. "That's not fair."

"And yet it's true."

It probably was, she could admit to herself.

"But I need practice," Cassie said. It popped out before she knew she was going to say it.

Lacy was silent for a moment. Then she said, "Really."

"I didn't mean—"

"You didn't mean that you're already thinking about having Brian's babies? Okay. Let's go with that."

Damn it, she *had* been thinking that. Was she insane? Had she entirely taken leave of her senses? It seemed that she had.

Some good nuance could do that to you.

～

BRIAN WAS SO pleased with the direction his life had taken that he almost forgot to be pissed at his mother.

Fortunately, the morning after his date with Cassie, Lisa reminded him.

"If you came home last night for the sake of appearances, you needn't have." She smirked at him as she loaded up the blender with hemp milk, kale, and God knew what else. "I'm thrilled that you're getting serviced. Maybe it'll relax you."

Her characterization of what had happened between himself and Cassie as him being serviced—as though Cassie were a mechanic who'd tinkered around under his hood—took some of the glow off his good mood, and that reminded him that his mother was tampering with his personal life.

"First of all, what makes you think anything happened between me and Cassie?"

"Oh, please. You're happy, relaxed. I think I actually heard you humming."

Had he been doing that? Okay, fine. He wouldn't argue the point.

"Second," he went on, "I didn't get *serviced*. I'm not a broken washing machine. We had an evening of ..." What could he call it? Lovemaking? Mutual intimacy? Either of those would make him sound like a wuss. "Well. Just don't call it that."

"Whatever you say, dear. My point is, I'm glad you had a good night, and you didn't need to cut it short for my sake."

"None of this is any of your business." He walked over to the kitchen island, where she was assembling her smoothie, and waited as the blender whirred. When it was done and she was pouring a green mixture into a glass, he went on. "Speaking of which, why did you offer to finance Cassie's bakery?"

Lisa leaned her kimono-clad butt against the edge of the counter-top, sipped some of her smoothie, and assessed her son with a look Brian thought was damned smug.

"She told you."

"Of course she told me. What are you doing? What are you up to?"

Lisa cocked her head slightly, appraising him. "I think she's talented, and I believe her bakery will be a good investment."

"Bullshit."

"You don't think she's talented?"

"Of course I do. But that's not why you're doing it. There's an ulterior motive, I just don't know what it is yet."

Lorenzo, wearing only a pair of sweatpants that hung perilously low on his hips, came into the kitchen, kissed Lisa extravagantly, then poured himself a smoothie from the contents of the blender. Then he smacked Lisa on the ass and went back into their room.

"Is he leaving sometime soon?" Brian wanted to know.

"Why must you be such a prude?"

"Why must you parade your sex life in front of me?" They glared at each other for a moment, then Brian realized they'd gotten off track. "But, forget that. Forget him. What's going on with you and Cassie?"

"There's nothing 'going on.' I made her a business offer, and she's considering it. Did she tell you whether she's going to accept?"

"No. She didn't say."

"Well … she will. Of course she will. And then, assuming all goes well with your relationship, the three of us will be a happy little family, won't we?" She blew him a kiss, then went into the bedroom with Lorenzo.

BRIAN HAD ASSUMED that Lisa was scheming to get Cassie out of his life. But her "happy little family" comment suggested otherwise. Okay, so if Lisa didn't want to end the relationship, she must want to use it in some way.

If Cassie was financially dependent on Lisa, it stood to reason that Lisa could use that as leverage to manipulate Brian in any number of ways. If she wanted something from him and he failed to deliver it, she could simply remind him that Cassie's future was in her hands.

What could he do? He'd be at his mother's mercy.

The whole thing nagged at him all day as he went to San Luis Obispo to check on his house; stopped in Morro Bay to pick up a prescription for his mother; worked on marketing for his YouTube show; and brainstormed ideas for new videos.

He texted Cassie a few times—flirty messages about how much he'd enjoyed the previous night and how he couldn't wait to see her again—but he avoided the topic of what she was going to do about his mother's offer.

"I don't know what to say to her, man," he told Ike over the Bluetooth in his car as he drove on Highway 1. "I can't tell Cassie not to take the money. That bakery is her dream. Am I supposed to tell her to give up her dream?"

"You can't do that," Ike agreed. "But maybe there's some other way for Cassie to get what she wants."

Was there? That was the question.

"The video we did together is doing well," Brian said. "Maybe that's something. If we do some more, and they pick up a viewership, maybe that would help her get startup money."

"Sure," Ike agreed. "But that'll take a while. This thing with your mom is right now."

"God. Literally everything about this is waving more red flags than …" He trailed off.

"Than what? I'm waiting."

Brian scrambled for a comparison. "… Than the Albanian Olympic team."

"Dude. You must be upset. Your joke delivery is way off."

"I know," Brian said miserably.

"There's one obvious option," Ike said.

"Which is?"

"You could stop seeing Cassie. Then she gets her bakery, and your mother has no hold over you."

"That's not an option." Brian said it immediately, definitively.

"So you really like her, then."

"Yeah. I really do."

"Well, then you'll just have to hope that whatever the two of you have together is strong enough to withstand your mother's meddling."

It was strong enough on his end. But what about Cassie's?

CHAPTER 22

*C*assie and Brian avoided talking about the Lisa issue, as it seemed fraught with so many potential problems. They fell into a happy pattern of spending time together at his place or hers, then sneaking into her trailer for sex that was sometimes energetic, sometimes slow and leisurely. Brian sneaked out in the morning before sunrise to avoid being spotted by the Jordans.

The YouTube video had led to more cake orders, so Cassie worked in the kitchen at Otter Bluff as though it were a perfectly normal thing to do. She made polite conversation with Lisa and Lorenzo but would not commit when Lisa approached her about the offer to finance her bakery.

Cassie didn't want to let the opportunity pass her by, but she didn't want to upset Brian, either. She put off making a decision, telling Lisa that she was thinking about it.

In truth, she wasn't thinking about much else.

She wasn't going to be able to delay forever. New renters had reserved Otter Bluff for the month of May, and once they moved in, Cassie wasn't going to have anywhere to bake—unless she took Lisa up on her offer.

Cassie was still waffling about it toward the end of April, when

Otter Bluff erupted in activity after Lisa got word from her agent that she'd been offered a solo show at Art Basel, an annual art fair in Switzerland—a huge opportunity that virtually guaranteed Lisa's art would be acquired, at astonishing prices, by some of the top collectors in the world.

"I have to get back." Lisa was bustling around Otter Bluff, shoving things into various pieces of luggage as Lorenzo stood by taking notes on things Lisa wanted him to do for her. "I have work I can show, of course, but it won't be satisfactory. I need new pieces—something that will create buzz. Lorenzo, I'll need an order of supplies as soon as possible. You know what to do. Oh, God. I've wasted nearly a month here, when I should have been working. It's intolerable."

Cassie was in the kitchen working on a cake, and Brian stood nearby with his hands shoved into his pockets, looking unsettled.

"The show's not until the fall, though, right?" Brian offered. He rubbed the back of his neck with one hand.

"Yes, but if I'm going to create enough new work for the show, I'm still going to be pressed for time. I'll be practically living in the studio for the next few months."

Cassie listened while trying not to be obvious about it. What did this mean for Lisa's offer? On the one hand, if she was going to be that busy, surely she'd be too preoccupied to worry about Cassie's bakery. On the other hand, it sounded like this show was going to bring Lisa a lot of sales—and a lot of money. Which might make her more likely to send some of that money Cassie's way.

In any event, Cassie figured the time to dither about her decision was over.

When Lisa and Lorenzo had packed their things, Cassie and Brian helped them carry their luggage to the car.

"Congratulations, Mom." Brian hugged her awkwardly, giving her shoulder a little pat to punctuate the conclusion of the hug.

"Yes, congratulations, Lisa. This is wonderful news," Cassie said. "Brian? Uh … why don't you check the house one last time to make sure they didn't forget anything?"

"Sure." He went back inside, looking relieved to be doing something other than standing there.

When he was gone, Cassie turned to Lisa, thinking, *It's now or never.*

"Lisa? I know you have so much more to think about now, and I know this isn't your first priority, but ... does your offer still stand?"

Lisa's eyebrows shot up, and she raised her oversized sunglasses and placed them on top of her head so she could see Cassie better. "Why, of course it does. Have you decided to accept?"

"I'd like to have the meeting. The one you suggested, with ... with the lawyers." It all seemed so odd to Cassie to be talking about meetings and lawyers. "If you have time."

Lisa made a tutting sound with her tongue. "I won't need time, dear, that's what I hire people for. I'll have my lawyer call you. You should find representation in the meantime." Lisa appraised Cassie with a hint of a smile. "I'm glad you've decided to see sense, Cassie."

Brian came out, announced that they hadn't forgotten anything, and opened the passenger side door for his mother. Thor stood by, wagging his tail and looking hopeful that someone might pet him.

"This is exciting, no?" Lorenzo asked.

"Ah ... yes." Brian gave him a perfunctory wave, and moments later, Lisa's Mercedes was heading down the road toward Highway 1.

As Cassie and Brian watched the car turn and move out of sight, Cassie felt a wave of guilt over the fact that she hadn't told Brian about her plans to accept Lisa's offer.

But why did she have to tell him now? There was a chance the meeting wouldn't come to anything. Maybe she would hear the terms and discover that the whole thing wasn't viable. Maybe her own lawyer—once she found one—would tell her to run like hell. If that happened, telling Brian would cause undue turmoil for no purpose, wouldn't it?

That's what she told herself, anyway.

BRIAN'S HOUSE wasn't ready yet—it seemed like it would never be ready—and living in Cassie's trailer with Thor clearly wasn't an option. So he and the dog moved out of Otter Bluff at the end of the month and booked a different two-week rental house with Central Coast Escapes.

His contractor had assured him that two more weeks would be enough, and Brian hoped he was right. He couldn't throw his money around willy-nilly, even though things were looking up with his YouTube ad revenue since the video with Cassie.

The video had been a hit that exceeded Brian's expectations. It continued to perform well weeks later, and the comments about her were very positive—from people who wanted her cakes to people who simply wanted to see more of her, including guys who thought she was hot.

That last part bothered him a little, though he certainly couldn't argue with their opinions.

One morning, from his new temporary home on Happy Hill—a neighborhood overlooking Moonstone Beach that was home to Cambria's prostitutes back in the town's mining days—Brian called Cassie and told her his idea.

"We could make it a regular thing. The cake fails, I mean. Each video, you could try to teach me a new technique. The cool thing about it is the product placements. Do you have any idea how many cake decorating products there are on the market? Well, of course you do. That's a lot of potential revenue."

He explained to her how that worked—they would use a particular product in a video in exchange for payment from the manufacturer. He and Ike had done it all the time with products ranging from Flamethrower Crunchie Snacks to breakfast cereals to Slip 'N Slides.

"I had no idea," Cassie said. "I thought you just made your money through ads."

"Most of it, yeah. But there's more than one kind of ad. Some of them are more covert than others. And you need multiple revenue streams." He said some things about marketing that would have bored him to tears if he'd been listening to someone else say it. Which meant he was probably boring Cassie to tears.

"So, it would just be more like the last one?" she asked.

"Well, we'd mix it up here and there. You don't want them to be too similar. But the same concept, yeah."

"And I could make money doing that?"

"As a matter of fact …" He told her about what he'd made from the first video, and how, after subtracting Shayla's cut, he was planning to split the rest of the revenue between the two of them.

"You're going to pay me?" Cassie sounded shocked.

"Well, yes. Of course I am. Did you think I was just going to keep the revenue for myself?"

"I don't know what I thought. I guess I thought it was just fun," Cassie said.

"It is fun. Getting paid makes it even more fun."

"So … how much?" She sounded as though she were a little afraid to ask.

He told her the figure.

She didn't say anything at first, and he wondered if that was good or bad.

"Holy shit," she said after a while. "Are you kidding? Oh, God. I have to sit down."

Okay, so it was good, then.

Brian had thought of the revenue from the cake video as solid but not spectacular. But viewing it through Cassie's eyes, he could see that the number might be surprising. After all, she got paid minimum wage for her work at Central Coast Escapes, and when you broke it down by the number of hours worked, her cake income wasn't much better.

Why shouldn't she bake and get more highly paid for it?

"So, are you in?" he asked.

She laughed. "Are you kidding? Of course I'm in."

WHEN BRIAN HAD CALLED, Cassie had been scrubbing the bathroom floor at Seaside Cottage, one of the rental houses in her care. Now that they'd hung up, she slid her phone into her back pocket, grabbed the mop, and got back to work.

At first, she felt giddy at the idea of being paid—and paid well—for doing the video, which she'd thought of as pure play. If she could have more of that, why not? There was no downside.

The more she thought about it, though, the more she realized that being in the public eye could be its own downside.

What if the viewers didn't like her and were cruel? What if they did like her and were creepy? Either one seemed like a distinct possibility. Never, in the entire time that Cassie had been pondering what she might do with her life, had she considered a career in entertainment. Now that she was considering it, the concept was freaking her out.

"He wants me to be on YouTube. Regularly," she told Lacy on the phone as she was driving back to the office from Seaside Cottage.

"What did you say?"

"I said I'd do it. But now …"

"Is there any money in it?" Lacy asked.

Cassie told her what Brian had said about her share of the video they'd already done.

"Holy shit," Lacy said.

"That was exactly my response," Cassie told her.

"Who needs to open a bakery if you can get this kind of money for making videos?"

"I do. I need to open a bakery. I can't get distracted, Lacy. I've got to stay focused on my goal."

Lacy was quiet for a moment, considering it. Then she said, "Well, okay. But maybe doing this for a while could help you reach that goal."

CHAPTER 23

*T*hat night, Cassie celebrated her YouTube windfall by taking Brian out to dinner at Neptune—a restaurant she usually couldn't afford. He'd objected at first, arguing that he couldn't let her pay, but she'd been so happy and excited that he'd ultimately let her do it.

After a good meal and even better wine, they'd gone back to Brian's new rental, which was blissfully free of parents—either his or hers.

They let Thor outside to pee, and when they called him in, Cassie was unbuttoning Brian's shirt before they even got the door closed.

"I'll bet you're glad to be rid of Lorenzo," she said as she untucked his shirt and slid it off his shoulders.

"Don't say that name."

"I just meant—"

"No, seriously, don't say that name if you want me to be able to … you know. Perform."

As it turned out, performance wasn't an issue. He even took a couple of curtain calls.

They both took full advantage of the fact that they could be as noisy as they wanted without alerting anybody's family to their activities. Back at the trailer, Cassie more than once had slapped a hand over Brian's mouth to keep him quiet in the throes of passion. Here, in a space that was only theirs, noise was not only tolerated but encouraged.

When they finished in the bedroom, they even took a shower together—something that would not have been possible in Cassie's trailer.

"I could get used to this," Brian said when they were back in bed, showered and sated. "All that sneaking around at your place made me feel like I was sixteen. Not that it wasn't fun. But this ... It's full-grown adult sex. It's a whole different animal."

"Right?" Cassie snuggled up closer to him. "I've got to get out of that trailer. I mean, it's been nice not to have to pay rent. Better than nice—it's been essential, given how expensive rent is here and how Elliot pays me like he's Scrooge McDuck. But I'm too old to have my dad waiting up for me and chasing men away."

"Men?" Brian's eyebrows rose. "Plural?"

She rolled onto her stomach and grinned at him. "I was speaking generally."

"Well, speaking more specifically, now that we're together ... in both the dating sense and the physical sense ... I wonder if maybe it makes sense to make the plural ... you know. Singular."

Her smile widened. "Brian, are you asking me to go steady?"

He blushed a little, and that was cute as hell. "I'm just saying, I won't be seeing anyone else. Not while this thing with us is still going on. And I hoped ..."

"Yes, I'll go steady with you. And I won't bring anybody else to my trailer." She stretched toward him and kissed him, covered only in a sheet.

"Great. That's great. And about your money situation ... have you given any more thought to my mother's offer?"

Cassie had been avoiding the subject, hoping she could have the meeting with Lisa's attorney under the radar. What point was there in upsetting Brian if the thing with the bakery didn't work out anyway? But now that he was asking her a direct question—while they were both naked—she couldn't lie to him.

"I … ah … I have a video conference with her attorney on Monday."

"Cassie—"

"It's just a meeting. I don't even know what she's going to offer me, specifically. I don't know the terms. It might not even work out. It's just … It makes sense to at least *listen*, doesn't it?"

He kissed her forehead and rubbed a hand over her shoulder. "Yes. It does."

"I know you don't like this, and I can see why. I really can. But the bakery means a lot to me, Brian. And without something like this—without the kind of money your mother can give me—I don't think I'll ever be able to make it happen."

"Well, I disagree with that. I think we can come up with other options. Still. I get that you need to have the meeting. You need to see what she's offering."

She hadn't realized how worried she was about his reaction until that reaction came. Now, she was so relieved that he hadn't blown up at her that tears sprang to her eyes.

"Thank you."

"You don't have to thank me. I still don't think it's a good idea. But I don't want to be the guy who steps on your dreams."

"Then, thank you for not being the guy who steps on my dreams."

She settled in beside him with his arm tucked around her and wondered if he was right. Maybe this was a bad idea. Maybe she was being manipulated.

And maybe there were other ways to get what she needed—maybe even the YouTube idea.

Still, it wouldn't hurt to listen.

～

ON MONDAY, Cassie went to the office of Clayton Drummond, a local attorney whose name she'd been given through the Cambria grapevine. Cassie had asked Lacy, and Lacy had asked her friend Genevieve Porter, who'd asked her husband, Ryan Delaney, who'd asked his brother, Colin Delaney, a Harvard-educated lawyer who did all of the real estate and investment work for his wealthy family.

Colin himself was too busy—and lived too far away—to handle the matter himself, but he'd said Clayton Drummond was reliable and solid and, more importantly, wouldn't rip Cassie off.

On Colin's urging, Drummond had agreed to forego a retainer and simply charge his hourly rate for the consultation, reasoning that they could renegotiate if the meeting turned into anything more complicated.

That was fine, but his hourly rate—at three hundred dollars—still was a lot for her to hand over without knowing whether Lisa's offer would come to anything.

Still, she needed to approach this like an adult, and an adult knew when to be frugal and when it made sense to spend the money. In this case, she knew spending the money was the right thing to do.

She went to Drummond's office at the appointed time, trying to ignore the nerves that roiled in her stomach like birds flapping their wings.

"Cassie. Sit down." He ushered her into his office and got her settled in his visitor's chair.

Drummond, a grandfatherly man with a stout frame and a balding head, folded his hands on top of his desk—a bargain model that looked like it came from Ikea—and smiled.

"Why don't you tell me about your goals, first of all, so I'll know what we're looking for going in?"

CASSIE LEFT DRUMMOND'S office with an offer from Lisa that spelled out the details: what expenses Lisa would cover, what percentage of the profits she would receive, what roles she would and would not play in daily business decisions, and how either one of them could go about severing the agreement, should they decide it was no longer beneficial.

Drummond negotiated a few things, managing to secure a few more percentage points of the profits for Cassie to keep for herself. Overall, though, he thought it was a solid offer, and he told Cassie she should strongly consider it.

Lisa had only been adamant on one point: she wanted veto power over Cassie's choice of location for her business. Cassie could look wherever she wanted, but Lisa had to agree before the rental papers were signed.

Cassie hesitated on that, unsure whether she wanted to give up that power, but on the other hand, it was reasonable, wasn't it? If Lisa was going to be paying the rent, why shouldn't she have a say in where the bakery would be located?

She didn't sign the contract that day, because Drummond advised her to take a couple of days to think about it.

"How did the meeting go?" Brian asked on the phone later that afternoon. He'd caught her while she was scrubbing a toilet at a rental house in Leimert, and she put him on speaker as she continued to work.

"It was good. My lawyer said it was a good offer. He didn't flat-out tell me to take it, but I could tell he wanted to."

He was silent for a moment while she attended to the underside of the bowl.

"So, what do you think? Are you going to do it?" he asked finally.

She straightened up and wiped a bead of sweat from her forehead with the back of one hand. "Honestly? I think I might. I know you're unsure about it, but do you know how long it would take me to pull together the money without her help? I'll be baking cakes on the moon, because people will be living there by then."

"I could help you. I have some savings. Maybe I could—"

"No."

"But Cassie—"

"I said no." It had come out more forcefully than she'd intended it, and she softened her tone. "Thank you for offering. Really. It's sweet of you. But this thing we have is too new for us to get into a money thing together. There's a good chance it would ruin everything, Brian, and I don't want that."

Of course, they were already getting into a money thing with the YouTube videos, but she thought it best not to bring that up.

"There's a chance that you going into business with my mother could ruin everything, too," he said.

"Well." She flushed the cleaning solution down the toilet and closed the lid, replacing the brush in its holder. "I'm just going to hope that doesn't happen."

BRIAN WALKED out onto his patio, looked out at the ocean view—this one distant, unlike the close-up view at Otter Bluff—and worried that the best relationship he'd had in a long time was about to go swirling down into some fiery hell-pit.

With his mother involved, how could it do anything else?

He tried calling his mother, thinking he'd warn her not to mess with either his love life or his girlfriend, but Lorenzo wouldn't let him talk to her. The bastard wouldn't let him talk to his own mother.

"She's painting," he said. "For Art Basel. She told me she would cut certain parts of my body off with a kitchen knife if I interrupted her. I'm fond of those parts, Brian."

So here he was, feeling helpless to stop the train wreck he was sure was coming.

But then again, maybe it wasn't. Maybe Lisa really did think the bakery would be a good investment. Maybe she wanted to help Cassie because Brian cared about her—and maybe it was Lisa's way of making amends for being a crappy mother all of his life.

Maybe this was even a turning point for them, the place after which they would have a better, closer relationship. Maybe he would one day look back on this time, this event, and say to himself, *That was when I realized she'd changed. That was when I knew she really loved me.*

Or maybe monkeys would fly out his ass.

The two possibilities seemed equally probable.

CHAPTER 24

*C*assie signed the contract two days later using a notary who
worked at Clayton Drummond's office.

She had a lot going on right now: three new cake orders had come
in as a result of Brian's YouTube video, she was still maintaining a
full-time schedule at Central Coast Escapes, and now she had a
bakery to set up.

She was so excited she could barely think about anything else
besides the bakery.

"What about Blue Iris?" Nancy asked over dinner that night as
Cassie sat at the kitchen table with her parents. A plate of meatloaf,
mashed potatoes, and green beans sat in front of Cassie, largely
untouched because she'd been too excited to eat.

"What about it?"

"The building. The restaurant went out of business six months
ago, and it's still vacant. Maybe you could try there."

Cassie summoned up the restaurant in her memory—she'd eaten
there a few times, and she tried to recall the space.

"It's too big," she decided. "There's a dining room, a bar—I don't
need all that. All I need is a kitchen, a display case, and a sales
counter."

"Maybe you're thinking too small," her dad suggested. "Why not have tables where people could sit and eat pastries? And you could use the bar for espresso and fancy coffee drinks."

"Oh, but—"

"Oooh. I like that," Nancy said. "And you could have lunch items. Quiches and whatnot."

"Mom. Dad. I can't afford all that," Cassie said.

"Maybe not," Vince said. "But Lisa Barlow can."

AT FIRST, the idea of Blue Iris seemed completely impossible. But if her parents thought it could be done, then maybe it could. Nancy and Vince Jordan were among the most sensible people Cassie knew, and they wouldn't urge her to hope for the unattainable.

She found a sign in the window of the shuttered restaurant, took down the name of the leasing agent, and, with her hands shaking slightly with nerves, she made the call.

The rent was shocking, but Cassie wasn't the one who'd be paying it. All Lisa could do was say no.

She thought of taking Brian with her to look at the property, but then she changed her mind and asked Lacy instead. Brian was too ambivalent about the whole thing—he might dislike anything she considered just because his mother was involved. And she didn't want to hear negativity right now. She wanted to be excited.

From the moment Cassie walked into the place, it was clear that this wasn't right for her. The dining room was too big, the kitchen was more than she needed, and the price was so high it was unlikely she'd be able to turn a profit.

But walking through the place, with its hardwood floors, its gleaming bar stretched across one end of the room, its kitchen with acres of stainless steel work space, she had ideas—one after another.

Of course she could have a small seating area where customers could enjoy pastries and coffee and maybe work on their laptops. Of course she could have espresso drinks. Of course her bakery could be a gathering place —not just a commercial kitchen to satisfy the health department.

"God, Lacy. This could be so great." Cassie whispered it to Lacy out of earshot of the agent.

Lacy looked thoughtful. "It's a little big. I mean, yes, you might have some breakfast and lunch foods, but—"

"Not this place. It's huge. It would never work. I meant the bakery in general."

"Oh." Lacy perked up. "Yes! It's going to be awesome. I can't wait."

When Cassie gave her decision to the agent, a middle-aged brunette in dark slacks and a powder blue polo shirt, the woman said she had another property across town that might work better. Did Cassie want to see it?

"What is it?" Cassie asked.

"Do you remember Moonstone Mocha? It was a coffeehouse that was open for about five minutes last year?"

Cassie turned to Lacy. "I don't. Do you?"

Lacy had been a barista at Jitters on Main Street until she'd left work to become a stay-at-home mom, so she tended to keep up on the coffee-related developments in town. "Yeah, I do. Great location, but they had really limited hours and a tiny menu. I remember thinking at the time that they wouldn't stay in business long, and they didn't."

"That's the one." The agent nodded. "It's adorable. Shall we take a look?"

CASSIE FELL in love with it the moment she stepped inside. The former Moonstone Mocha was a converted cottage on Main Street at the end of East Village. It had a covered porch, front and back yards landscaped in drought-tolerant plantings, two small rooms that would accommodate cafe tables, and a kitchen with new appliances that looked like it had been updated by the previous owners.

"When was this place built?" Cassie asked.

"Around 1890. The Moonstone Mocha people redid the kitchen, as you can see—it's a shame the business didn't last. The place is darling, don't you think? You can put cafe tables with umbrellas in the front and back yards. It'll be lovely in the summer."

"What's the rent?" Cassie braced herself—she was already in love with the place, and she didn't want to find out the entire venture was impossible.

The agent told her.

The number was high, but not as high as Blue Iris had been. Earning enough to turn a profit might be hard, but it didn't seem impossible.

"I need to take some pictures and measurements and talk to my investor," Cassie said. She pulled a tape measure out of her purse. "Grab the other end of this, Lacy, would you?"

Cassie was buzzing with excitement when she got off work that evening. She'd told herself she would keep most of the bakery stuff away from Brian, since he was so hesitant about his mother's involvement, but she couldn't keep quiet about it. She wanted nothing more than to tell him, and it couldn't wait.

Instead of going home, she went straight to his place on Happy Hill. When he opened the door with Thor beside him, Cassie hurried inside, already talking.

"You won't believe the place I found for the bakery. You remember Moonstone Mocha? Maybe not, since you live in SLO. They went out of business, and the place is still vacant. It's a historic cottage on Main Street. God, it's cute as hell. Do you think your mother will say yes? I hope she says yes. It's the perfect size for what I need, and the kitchen's been redone, and there's an adorable outdoor area, and ... I have pictures. Here. Let me show you."

Thor, apparently bent out of shape at having been ignored, sat down at Cassie's feet and whined. "Oh, hey, big guy. How are you?" She went down on one knee and rubbed his sides.

"Hi, Cassie. Come on in. How was your day?" Brian said wryly.

She laughed and stood up straight again, giving Thor one last pat. "My day was great. How did you guess?"

He pulled her into his arms and kissed her. "Mine's starting to get better," he said.

YES, Brian was worried about this business arrangement between Cassie and his mother. Yes, he thought it portended doom, pain, and heartache. But Cassie was so happy, he didn't want to do anything to ruin that. He loved seeing her happy.

He loved seeing her, period.

So when she showed up bubbling over with enthusiasm about the place she'd found, he smiled, hugged her, asked her questions about it, and agreed that it really did sound perfect.

He was uneasy as hell, but he tried not to show it, because he didn't want to be that guy who pissed all over his girlfriend's happiness.

Eventually, he had to ask the question.

"So, what did Lisa say about it?"

"I haven't told her yet, but I'm sending her all of the information tonight. I took a ton of pictures, and I've got the rental agreement I can send her. And if she has any more questions, I can get her in touch with the leasing agent. It's perfect, Brian. I love it so much. This is all like a dream that's coming true. I just can't believe it."

Brian couldn't believe it either—that was the problem.

His mother was up to something, and when they both found out what it was, Cassie's dream was going to be crushed—and their relationship along with it, most likely.

CASSIE STAYED OVER THAT NIGHT, and Brian called Ike the next day to get his perspective on the situation.

"Lisa's gonna drop the hammer any time, man, I just know it. And then what? You think Cassie's going to want to be with me after she sees what a shit show my mother is?"

"Or," Ike said.

Brian waited, wondering what positive spin his friend could possibly put on all of this.

"Your mom could be trying to do something nice to make amends for all she's put you through over the years," Ike said.

Brian supposed it was conceivable. He wanted to believe it.

"You think so?"

"I wouldn't go that far. I'm just saying it's possible."

"Okay. But it's also possible that she's trying to get me to do something, or not do something, and this is her way of forcing the issue instead of just ... you know. Asking nicely, like most people would do."

"Yeah. Knowing Lisa, that's probably more likely than the first thing I said," Ike admitted.

"I warned her," Brian said. "I warned Cassie, and she got offended, so I can't warn her again."

"Well ... you could help her find a way to do it without Lisa. Or ..."

"Or?"

"Or, you could just sit around with your butt clenched, waiting for the bomb to go off."

THE IDEA of going around with his butt clenched didn't appeal to Brian, so he called his mother later that morning. At first, Lorenzo hadn't wanted to let the call through, but Brian threatened to drive down there, grab the nearest easel, and use it as a club to beat Lorenzo senseless. Brian privately doubted whether he could do it—Lorenzo worked out, and he didn't—but the threat worked. The asshole put the call through.

"Mom. Cassie found a place for her bakery."

"I'm aware. She sent me a voluminous e-mail. I haven't had a chance to look at it yet, as I'm up to my neck in work."

"Well ... look at it. And don't screw with her. If you're doing all of this to mess with me in some way ..."

"Brian, I've told you. I'm simply trying to help her while at the same time making a good investment."

He ran a hand through his hair, making it stick up at odd angles. "But it's not a good investment. Most new businesses fail in the first year. You know that. I know that. And Cassie knows it, too. It's not a good investment—it's a risky one. So you have some other reason for doing it, and I'm telling you, you'd better not hurt her."

"Why, Brian. It seems you really care for this girl." He could hear the smug smile in his mother's voice.

"Yeah. I do. And that's why I didn't want you anywhere near her. But since that's not going to work out, you'd better not screw with her. If you do ..." He trailed off, uncertain what kind of threat he wanted to make.

"Yes?"

"I know you don't really care whether I'm in your life. You never have. But if you care at all, you won't do whatever you're plotting to do. Because I'll be gone."

Brian's heart was pounding. He'd finally said what he'd been thinking since childhood but had never before voiced—that his mother didn't care about him. He'd wanted to say it so many times, but he'd feared that it was true and that putting it out there would confirm his worst suspicions. It had taken Cassie to make him bold enough to say it out loud.

"That's not fair." Her voice was quieter now, and she'd lost her usual swagger. "It's not."

But she didn't say she loved him.

He hung up on her before that omission could become even more glaring.

CHAPTER 25

*C*assie and Brian made another cake fail video, this one with a product placement—they shot it to prominently display a cake storage container that Cassie had to admit was pretty innovative and useful.

She made and delivered another wedding cake, using the kitchen at Brian's rental. The kitchen wasn't nearly as good as the one at Otter Bluff, but it was better than the one in the Airstream, so she made do.

The whole time she was working on the video, then planning, decorating, and transporting the wedding cake, she waited for a response from Lisa about the property on Main Street.

That answer came via e-mail on a Saturday while Cassie was behind the reception desk at Central Coast Escapes.

Lisa thinks you can do better. She's asked me to research properties in Los Angeles. Much better—you can get more high-end clientele, get into the food magazines, etc. When can you come down to view some options????

—Lorenzo

Cassie stared at the message, her jaw slack. Los Angeles? Nobody had ever said anything about Los Angeles when she and Lisa were discussing the contract. Cassie didn't want to move to Los Angeles. She lived here.

For some reason, the sight of the four question marks pissed her off. Lorenzo was supposed to be this sophisticated urbanite—he'd clearly looked down on her, had considered her so much lesser than he was. Well, she might be a small-town girl, but at least she knew that a sentence only needed one goddamned question mark.

She took a deep breath, coached herself to stay calm, rational, and professional, and composed her response.

Please thank Lisa for her comments. However, it was always my intention to locate the bakery in Cambria. I'm sorry if I failed to communicate that in our negotiations.

—Cassie

The response came fifteen minutes later:

Lisa says it'll be more profitable in LA. I must agree. Please send me a list of dates when you can come down to view properties, and I'll set up meetings accordingly. —L.

Cassie stewed about it for the rest of her shift.

When Brian came to pick her up after work so they could grab dinner together, and he asked about it immediately.

"So, did you hear from my mom yet?"

Cassie's shoulders fell. "Yes. Or, from Lorenzo, anyway."

"So, what did she say?"

They were walking on the sidewalk on Main Street, and Cassie stopped and turned to him. "She said no. She said I could do better. She said … she said she wants me to open the bakery in Los Angeles, not Cambria." She'd told herself to keep her tone calm and steady, but her voice wobbled, and a tear slipped out of one eye.

"LA?" Brian sounded mystified. "Is that something you two had talked about?"

"No! No, it isn't! And that's why I'm so … so stumped! Why is she throwing this at me out of nowhere?"

Brian sighed and rubbed the back of his neck. "Well … she's always thought LA was the center of the universe. I mean, that's one of the reasons she left me and my dad—because she just had to be in the city where she thought everything was happening."

"But if that's so important to her, why didn't she mention it? Why is she just springing it on me like this?"

"I don't know, Cass."

BUT HE DID KNOW. He knew as soon as she'd said it. There was nothing in it for him to tell her, though—the last time he'd spoken up about his mother's motivations, Cassie had gotten mad at him, and he didn't want that to happen again.

He should have seen this coming, and he was surprised he hadn't.

His mother didn't want to force a breakup between him and Cassie. She wanted to push Cassie into moving to LA so Brian would follow her. She wanted Brian nearby so she could stick her fingers into his life on a daily basis instead of just now and then.

How many times had she suggested to him that he needed to move to Southern California? She'd started pushing the issue when Ike moved down there, pretending that she was only thinking of Brian and his longtime friendship.

The ironic thing was that she'd never cared where Brian lived when he was a kid—as long as he didn't live with her. She'd never cared what he was doing when he was in college, or when he'd been establishing his YouTube career.

Hell, she'd barely found the time to take his calls.

It had only been over the last couple of years that she'd become interested in him and his life, but as far as he was concerned, it was too late. She'd had her chance. Why should he uproot his life for someone who was so self-centered, who'd been so quick to throw him away like he was an item of clothing she'd bought and then grown tired of?

"Brian?" He'd been quiet, and now Cassie was looking at him with concern. "What are you thinking?"

"Just … I'm thinking it sucks that she didn't okay the property you found. That's all."

"Do you think I can change her mind?"

He smiled slightly, not because he felt even vaguely optimistic, but because he was forcing himself not to be too negative in front of her.

"I don't know. You could try."

BECAUSE CASSIE WANTED to show that she was flexible and open to new ideas, she agreed to make the trip to LA to look at the properties Lorenzo had told her about.

Her hope was that if she at least looked, if she at least considered Lisa's idea, then maybe that show of good faith would help her convince Lisa to approve the Moonstone Mocha property in Cambria.

Plus, it would give Cassie a chance to talk to Lisa about it in person instead of going through Lorenzo.

"Will you come with me?" she asked Brian over the phone a couple of days before her trip.

"Oh. Well. My time's almost up in the rental, and the house in SLO isn't ready yet, and—"

"Please?"

He hesitated, and she could almost see the look on his face, that expression he got when he wanted to say no to her but couldn't bring himself to do it.

"You can see Ike," she said. "It'll be fun."

He agreed, but she could tell by his voice that he didn't think it would be fun at all.

BRIAN SPED up his work schedule to get a new video out before the trip. Cassie told Elliot she'd be out of town on her days off—Monday and Tuesday—and he therefore couldn't call her in for emergency maintenance or cleaning tasks. He seemed put out about it, but then again, Elliot was always put out about something.

Brian had checked out of his rental on Sunday afternoon and he and Thor had spent the night at Cassie's trailer. That made it convenient for them to leave early on Monday morning, before Cassie's parents realized he was there.

Brian had a regular petsitter he used for Thor, and they dropped him off on their way through San Luis Obispo. Then they stopped at a donut shop, bought a sack of donuts and two cups of coffee, and headed south on Highway 101 toward Los Angeles.

The spring day was cool and clear, and the sky was a crisp blue as they drove south through Pismo Beach with the ocean at their right. Because it was such a glorious day, and because spending time with Cassie was always a good thing, he tried not to focus on the reason for the trip—his mother's meddling—and attempted instead to think about the positives. He was on a road trip with his girl, and he had some truly excellent donuts.

There was a lot to appreciate about that.

As Brian drove, they talked about their all-time favorite road trips; their experiences in Los Angeles; places they wanted to visit while they were down there; and their favorite music for driving. Both of them were keeping it light, figuring the big issue of whether Cassie might or might not decide to move could be dealt with later.

The driver's side window was open, and Brian felt the ocean wind on his face as he drove. He glanced over at Cassie, whose lips were sprinkled with powdered sugar from her donut. It made him want to kiss her.

Of course, just about everything made him want to kiss her.

THEY STOPPED at an In-N-Out Burger in Sherman Oaks for lunch, and by the time they were throwing away their trash and heading out the door toward Brian's car, Cassie was starting to feel nervous.

"I'm not going to move down here," she said, more to herself than to him. "I'm just doing this to show her that I'm flexible. To show her that I'm considering her suggestions. That I'm not rejecting every-thing she has to say out of hand."

"No, I get it," Brian said.

"I'll look, but that's it. I'm staying in Cambria. Everything I want is there."

He could only hope that one of the things she wanted was him.

~

THE FIRST PLACE Cassie looked at was on Sunset Avenue in Venice. It was a huge space with what looked like acres of glass display cases. The seating areas—both indoors and outdoors—could accommodate one hundred.

"I think Lisa might have misunderstood the ... the scope of what I have in mind," Cassie told Lorenzo as they walked through the cavernous front room, their shoes echoing in the open spaces.

"Oh?" He raised his eyebrows, and Cassie wondered for a moment whether he had them waxed.

"It's just ... I was thinking me and maybe two employees. This place would need a staff. Dozens of people. Breakfast and lunch menus. And the location ... I mean, it's got to be expensive."

He told her how much, and Cassie nearly swooned.

"I can't believe she's even considering paying that," Cassie said.

"She is," Lorenzo assured her.

~

BRIAN STAYED silent during the visit to the place in Venice. The property was so outsized, so ostentatious, that it had to be Lisa's way of making a statement.

What that statement was, he couldn't say.

Probably, there were a couple of things going on here. One was that, if he was right about Lisa's motives, she was trying to woo Cassie down here with a bakery site beyond her wildest dreams. The other was that Lisa probably saw Cambria as unbearably provincial and believed that any business she had a part in should be more upscale. More chic.

If Cassie had asked him his opinion of the place, it would have been the same as hers—it was completely out of proportion for the business Cassie had in mind for herself.

But since she didn't ask, he simply smiled, kept his mouth shut, and waited to see how things would develop.

LORENZO HAD two more property viewings lined up for that day—one in Santa Monica and another in Beverly Hills—and at each one, Cassie could feel her dreams dying.

These gleaming, upscale spaces weren't her. The neighborhoods, the people—none of it had anything to do with the business Cassie had built for herself in her imagination.

"Please tell me the places we're seeing tomorrow aren't like this," Cassie said to Lorenzo as they toured the final property of the day.

He raised his eyebrows and tilted his head, making his man bun bob slightly. "Well, no."

"Good."

"Tomorrow's properties are a little bigger, a little more grand." He flicked a hand as though to dismiss that as a concern. "But Lisa wouldn't have me show them to you if she weren't willing to pay that kind of rent. So, just enjoy."

Clearly, the man wasn't reading the room.

"I need to talk to Lisa," she said.

"Oh, I'm afraid she's not available. She's painting twenty-four seven to get ready for Art Basel. That's why she asked me to take care of it."

"But—"

"I'm sure she can spare a minute," Brian put in. "For her son."

Lorenzo's expression might have indicated that he'd smelled something unpleasant. "I'll see what I can do."

CHAPTER 26

They checked into their hotel near Lisa's place in Silver Lake just before dinnertime. Cassie let her bag drop to the floor then collapsed onto the bed, her arms and legs outstretched as though she were preparing to make snow angels.

"This isn't going to work." She blew a lock of hair out of her face. "It's just … it's not going to work. I don't know how I managed to miscommunicate with her this badly. I don't know what either one of us was thinking."

The way she was lying on the bed, she hadn't left much room for him. He squeezed into the space between her outstretched body and the headboard anyway.

"I don't think you miscommunicated," he said. "I think she's got her own agenda."

"Which is?"

The last time they'd talked about it, Cassie had ended up yelling at him, and he didn't want to have that happen again. "I don't know. I'll talk to her."

"If Lorenzo will let you in. What's up with that guy? He guards access to her like he's trying to protect state secrets."

Brian wanted to know what was going on there, too. It was true that Lisa often had hangers-on doing her bidding. But this thing where Brian wasn't allowed to see her or talk to her was new. Was that happening at Lisa's direction, or was Lorenzo trying to control her for his own purposes?

It made him concerned not just for Cassie's sake, but for his mother's.

"I'll find out more tomorrow," he told her. "For now, let's just go meet Ike and Benny, have a nice dinner, and forget about it. It'll be fun. We'll have beer and dessert."

"Not both at the same time, I hope."

"Not both at the same time."

He reached over and ran his hand gently over her forehead and into her hair. She rolled onto her side, scooted into his arms, and kissed him.

"Could we maybe have dessert first?" She grinned at him, looking mischievous, and tugged his shirt out from where it was tucked into his jeans.

If she meant what he thought she meant, he was all for it.

LATER, after they'd showered—which took longer than it should have because they did it together—they got dressed and arranged to meet Ike and Benny at a Thai place in Hollywood.

It was Cassie's first time meeting Brian's best friend, and she was nervous as they went inside the restaurant and Brian waved to Ike and Benny, who were already seated.

Ike was enormously tall, with a sculpted beard and a friendly smile. Benny was an attractive brunette in her mid-thirties wearing a Star Trek T-shirt, skinny jeans, and black Doc Martens.

Cassie liked them both immediately, which was a relief because she already knew Ike held a lot of influence with Brian, and Benny held a lot of influence with Ike.

They talked and laughed over beer and Pad Thai. Ike and Benny told them about their wedding plans for the following spring, and Brian and Cassie filled everyone in on life in Cambria. Ike told them how he was getting along at the UCLA law school, and Benny talked about her job as a college marine biology instructor.

Brian and Ike laughed a little over a video Brian was planning, then Ike brought up the ones Brian and Cassie had made together.

"They're really good." Ike leaned his long body back in his chair, a bottle of beer in one hand. "You know, Cassie, you have great comic timing. Not to mention the fact that you can decorate the hell out of a cake. The ones you made for the show were amazing."

"I'm really hoping you'll do ours," Benny said.

Cassie blinked at her a few times. "Really?"

"Oh, hell yes. The one you made on that first video was stunning. And I saw the ones you posted on your Instagram. And"—she pointed one finger at Cassie—"I'm telling you now, we're paying full price. I don't want you giving us some ridiculous discount just because we're Brian's friends and you'll be coming to the wedding."

Cassie absorbed the fact that they assumed she would be coming to their wedding as Brian's date a year from now. They'd just met her, and yet they were taking it for granted that she was here to stay. That had to mean Brian had told Ike he was serious about her.

She felt warm all over in a way that was distinctly pleasant.

"Hopefully, I'll have my bakery up and running before then," she said, avoiding the question of what Brian had said to them and what it all meant.

"How's the search going? You find a place you like here in LA?" Benny asked.

Cassie's shoulders fell, and she took a hefty slug of her beer. "No. No, I didn't. Let me tell you what happened...."

THE VISIT with Ike and Benny was just what they'd both needed to release some of the tension of the day. Later, when they were alone, they released some more tension in a way that would have been decidedly inappropriate at a restaurant.

They couldn't put off dealing with it forever, though, so Cassie brought it up when they were lying in bed together in the dark.

"I think we should just go home. If I can see Lisa in person and talk to her about the Cambria property, then yes, I want to do that. But if she won't even talk to us …" She shrugged. "Lorenzo isn't going to show me anything I want to see."

Brian rolled onto his side to face her in the silvery moonlight streaming through the hotel window. He rubbed her shoulder gently. "We'll go over there in the morning. To her place. And I'm not asking Lorenzo's permission. Then, if we don't get anywhere with her … yeah, we'll go home."

"You warned me this wasn't going to work out." Cassie tried to keep the tears out of her voice. "You warned me, and I didn't listen."

"Maybe it'll still be okay," he said. "Let's try tomorrow, and we'll see."

BRIAN DIDN'T THINK it was going to be okay. He didn't think Lisa was going to listen, and he had his doubts about whether she'd even pry herself away from her studio long enough to hear their arguments.

But he couldn't say that to Cassie—not when she was feeling so vulnerable. He had to keep up a show of optimism for her sake.

The fact was, he was furious with his mother. But, hell, that wasn't a new feeling for him. He'd been furious with her before, and he would be again. But usually, that anger was roused by something she'd done to him. Now she was playing games with Cassie, and that was an entirely different thing.

He wasn't going to let his mother screw around with the woman he loved.

It wasn't until he'd thought about it just that way, lying in bed with Cassie nestled against him, that he realized he loved her.

He loved her.

He wouldn't tell her—not now. He wasn't sure she was there yet, and he didn't want to freak her out. But for him, the matter was settled.

Now that he knew he loved her, he wasn't going to let anyone—even his mother—hurt her.

CHAPTER 27

The next morning, Brian and Cassie had breakfast at the hotel, packed their things, checked out, and drove to Lisa's place in Silver Lake.

She lived in a converted warehouse loft space that was right out of *Flashdance*, if the woman in *Flashdance* had been rich. Exposed brick and ductwork gave the place urban ambiance, along with a huge, steel front door that rolled instead of swinging open. Half of the interior was arranged as a living area, and the rest was designated as Lisa's studio.

Not that Cassie saw much of it until after a good deal of arguing and confrontation.

Initially, Lorenzo met them at the door and refused to let them in.

"Lisa is working. You understand that, no?" Cassie tried to ignore the fact that the man was wearing nothing but a pair of running shorts. He worked out, obviously, but she didn't think this was the time to admire his abs.

"I understand that she's my mother and I don't need your permission to speak with her," Brian said.

"Ah, but I'm afraid you do." Lorenzo smiled and shrugged. "She's asked me to keep her environment free of distractions, so ..."

"Maybe put on a goddamned shirt if you don't want her to be distracted," Brian said. Then he leaned into the doorway past Lorenzo and shouted, "Mom? Lisa! I need to talk to you right now. Tell this asshole to let us in."

Moments later, Lisa came to the doorway, and Cassie was surprised by her appearance. She looked older and more tired than she had when Cassie had seen her last. She was wearing a pair of loose sweatpants and a cardigan sweater, which she was hugging around herself. She had no makeup, no jewelry, and she looked like a different version of herself—as though she had a twin sister who'd become a librarian, maybe, or a grocery store clerk instead of a high-profile artist.

"What is it, Brian?"

Clearly, he, too, was surprised by her appearance—and maybe also by the lack of fight in her voice. Because for a moment, he didn't say anything. He just looked at her, his jaw slack.

"Well?" she prompted him.

"I … ah … Can we come in? Cassie and I want to talk to you."

She looked at them for a moment as though she weren't going to admit them. Then she nodded and stepped back so they could enter.

The first thing Cassie noticed was the art. Huge canvases, some so tall that Lisa needed a ladder to reach the tops of them. The art was a combination of oil paint and collage, and the subjects were all the same: domesticity and the subjugation of women.

Cassie gaped at them, hugging herself, as she saw what appeared to be a series in progress, all focused on women in frilly aprons. They were all baking wedding cakes.

In one, a woman in a Donna Reed–era dress and high heels decorated a pink and blue cake while wearing shackles around her ankles and wrists. Surrounding the image were blown-up news articles, book pages, and photographs related to bondage, slavery, imprisonment, and mind control.

Cassie walked from one canvas to another. All of them played on the same themes.

"What is this?" She looked at Lisa helplessly. "What is all this?"

"It's the work for Art Basel," Lisa said crisply, walking past them and toward the kitchen. "Can I get you two some tea?"

"I don't understand." Brian sounded as shocked as Cassie felt. "You seemed so interested in Cassie's baking at Otter Bluff. Is this what that was about?"

Lisa shrugged, her face tight. "I might have gotten some inspiration from her. It's possible. I get inspiration from any number of places."

Lorenzo occupied himself doing minor tasks in the studio, sweeping up in an area where Lisa had scattered the news clippings and other random items she used for her work. He looked over his shoulder and smirked at them as he swept.

"Is this what you think of me?" Cassie swept an arm toward the paintings. "Is this really how you see me?"

Lisa let out a scoff. "Dear, don't be dramatic. I'm making an important social statement. It isn't about you."

"But it is, though. Isn't it?" Cassie felt gut-punched by what she was seeing, at the knowledge that she was being simultaneously ridiculed and used. "Why did you offer me the money, then? It certainly isn't about you believing in what I do. Not with ..." She gestured toward the paintings with disgust. "With *this*."

Lisa didn't say anything. She just pulled her cardigan more tightly around her body as though it were armor.

"Tell her, Mom." Brian's face was grim. "Tell her why."

"Brian, what are you talking about?" Lisa turned her ire on her son. "What exactly is it you think you know?"

"Just that the whole bakery partnership has something to do with me. Doesn't it?"

"Well, of course it does!"

Lisa threw her hands into the air and whirled toward her son. "What did you think, that I wanted to throw tens of thousands of dollars into a brand new business run by a woman who, at her age, still earns minimum wage and lives with her parents? Is that what you thought I wanted? I was doing this for you, Brian. For *you*. Because you have feelings for her, and I thought ..."

"Go on." Brian's voice was deadly calm.

"I thought that if I could convince her to start her business here, in Los Angeles, then you might follow her. And then I might see you more than a couple of times a year, at Christmas or my birthday. You might not be able to forget I exist. We might … We might have an actual relationship, the way mothers and sons do. And if you want to hold that against me, then my God, Brian, you go right ahead. I plead guilty of loving you and wanting you in my life."

BRIAN HAD KNOWN THAT, of course. Lisa had made no secret of the fact that she'd wanted him to move closer to her. But having confirmation that she'd used Cassie to achieve her goals infuriated him.

"You had no right to bring Cassie into something that should be between the two of us." He pointed one threatening finger toward his mother. "This is her life you're playing with."

"I'm right here," Cassie said. "You're both talking about me like I'm not here, but I'm standing two feet away from you and I can hear every word."

Lisa gave Cassie a dismissive wave and rolled her eyes.

Brian looked at Cassie, tightened his jaw, then looked back at his mother. "You can't control this," he said, "and you can't control me or my feelings."

Lisa reached out to her son, putting her hand on his arm. "If you could only see how I—"

He shook her hand off. "For what it's worth, Lisa"—he pointedly used her first name—"the reason we don't have a better relationship has nothing to do with where I live. You think this is about geography? About travel time? It's about the fact that you're so epically narcissistic that you couldn't be bothered to raise me, you look down on everything I do, and you've never shown even the slightest hint of interest in me or the things I value. But, sure, get me to move to LA and I'm sure all of that will go away."

Lisa reared back as though she'd been slapped.

"Come on, Cassie. Let's go." He walked toward the door, expecting her to follow him.

CASSIE WATCHED Brian walk to the door, but she didn't go with him. Not at first. She was too stunned by everything that had happened, everything that had been said, to move.

Somehow, she'd gotten wrapped up in something that had nothing to do with her. She didn't want to be in the middle of this, and yet here she was. Feelings roiled inside her. She was seeing her best shot at her dream go up in a cloud of foul-smelling vapor. She'd been insulted, and it had turned out Brian was right that his mother disapproved of her. All of that left her feeling crushed. Devastated.

But she was also watching two people—one whom she cared about deeply and the other whom, regardless of what she'd done, was still a human being with feelings—hurt each other in ways that might never be repaired.

"Cassie? Are you coming?" Brian, usually such a relaxed and happy guy, looked grim and gutted.

"I … yes. Yes, I'm coming." She followed him out without another word. As she went, she saw Lorenzo smirking at her.

THEY DIDN'T TALK in the car as Brian maneuvered through the traffic of the city and toward the freeway that would take them north out of town. At first, they didn't talk because the tension of the shit show they'd just experienced was too thick to let anything through.

After a while, though, the fact that they weren't talking to each other became its own thing, its own source of discomfort and angst.

They didn't talk as they got onto Highway 101, they didn't talk as they moved through Hollywood, then Studio City, then Sherman Oaks.

Finally, Cassie couldn't take the silence anymore.

"Are we going to talk about this?" She was slumped down in her seat, her arms crossed over her chest.

He stretched his neck and didn't look at her. "Not yet."

"Are you mad at me?" Cassie asked, thinking as she said it that she sounded like a toddler who'd gotten caught writing on the walls. "Is that what's going on? Are you mad at *me*? Because, Brian, that's really—"

"No. I'm not. I just don't want to talk about any of this yet. So if you could just … just not talk about it yet, that would be great."

Tears in her eyes, Cassie slumped down even farther in the passenger seat, thinking that it was a long way to Cambria. It was going to seem even longer.

CHAPTER 28

*C*assie had imagined that Brian would crack at some point during the drive; he would become uncomfortable with the silence and talk about what had happened—certainly before they arrived in Cambria.

He didn't.

They stopped for lunch at a McDonald's in Ventura, and their total conversation amounted to what Cassie wanted and whether she preferred the medium combo or the large.

The longer it went, the more angry she became. Surely he couldn't think any of this had been her fault. Surely he understood that she'd been wronged here, not only by his mother's refusal to accept the Cambria location for the bakery but, more importantly, by her judgment of Cassie. *At her age, still living at home. Still making minimum wage. Still nobody,* in other words. Shouldn't he be reassuring her that she was, in fact, somebody? Shouldn't he be affirming that he didn't share his mother's view of her?

Instead of doing any of those things, he stared forward at the road, occasionally messing with the radio or bobbing his head along with whatever song was playing.

When he dropped her off at home, she didn't invite him in, and he didn't ask. He did help her carry her bag—at least he was still that much of a gentleman—but he dropped it inside and said an awkward goodbye, his hands stuffed into his pants pockets. Then he headed back to his car and drove away.

I will not cry, Cassie told herself. *I will not fall apart.*

IN HER TRAILER, she looked in her refrigerator, but she wasn't hungry. She tried to take a nap, thinking it might calm her down, but she couldn't so much as doze. She unpacked her bag, but that took only a minute, since she'd been gone barely a day.

She paced around her tiny space, thinking about everything that had happened. Then she did what she always did when she was having a problem.

She called Lacy.

LACY AND DANIEL'S house was located south of town off a winding road that led into the rolling, grass-covered hills. The house itself had been recently remodeled, with an addition to accommodate their quickly growing family. In back was Daniel's glass-blowing studio, down a gravel path from the house.

When Cassie got there, it was late afternoon. Lacy was in the kitchen arranging slices of cheese, crackers, and chunks of fruit on plates for the children's afternoon snack.

"Come and get it," Lacy called to Danny and Caleb, and the two boys ran into the kitchen, scrambled into their chairs, and began eating as though they'd just emerged from a week in the wilderness.

Trevor got a handful of Cheerios at his high chair.

With that done, Lacy turned to Cassie.

"Okay, that should occupy them for a few minutes. What's up? You sounded upset on the phone."

Cassie slid onto a barstool at the kitchen island where Lacy was putting away cheese and discarding strawberry tops and apple cores.

"I don't even know where to start," she said.

"I take it the trip to LA didn't go well."

Tears sprang to Cassie's eyes, and she wiped them away, taking in a shuddering breath.

"Oh, boy," Lacy said. "That bad, huh?"

"Yeah. That bad."

"Okay. After the boys finish their snack, I'll put on a movie for them. Then you should be able to tell me about it without things getting too crazy."

~

FIFTEEN MINUTES LATER, the older boys were watching a Pixar movie, Trevor had been put down for a nap, and Lacy and Cassie were sitting at the kitchen table, cups of tea in front of them.

"All right," Lacy said. "I'm ready. Let me have it."

Cassie told her everything: the grand, breathtakingly expensive properties that were completely unsuitable for Cassie's business; the paintings depicting women in slavery baking wedding cakes; Lisa's admission that she'd only offered to finance Cassie's bakery so she could manipulate Brian; the way Brian and Lisa had fought, talking about Cassie as though she weren't there; the tense, silent drive back to Cambria; and the way he'd dropped her off and left as though they'd been strangers carpooling to save gas.

"And now ..." Cassie threw her hands into the air. "Now, the deal with Lisa is over, obviously. And Brian's not speaking to me, even though I didn't do anything wrong. And Lisa said things about me."

"What things?"

"Oh ..." Cassie slumped down in her chair. "That if it weren't for Brian, she would never get into a financial deal with someone who was still living with her parents and making minimum wage *at my age*. She thinks I'm nothing. She thinks I'm a failure. And maybe Brian thinks so, too. Why else was he so quiet on the drive home? Why else did he just bring my bag into the trailer and walk away? Oh, God." She scrubbed at her face with her hands. "I never imagined I'd fall for a guy whose mother disapproved of me. What's to disapprove of? I'm a good person! I'm nice! I'm not a … a drug dealer or a hooker! What more does she want?"

Lacy gave her a wry smile. "That is a high standard, all right."

"You know what I mean."

Lacy put a hand on her sister's arm. "Yes. I do. And no, it's not reasonable for her to disapprove of you, but it seems like she does. So, what are you going to do about it? Are you going to walk away to avoid the potential headache? I mean, she might be your mother-in-law someday if this thing with Brian keeps going. Do you want to deal with that?"

"No. I really don't."

"On the other hand, Brian isn't his mother. And it wouldn't be fair to judge him based on her actions."

"I know that. Lacy, I know that! But … God. It's all such a mess. You should have seen how he was on the drive home. He could barely look at me, and he certainly didn't talk to me. Maybe that was because he thinks she's right. Maybe he does think he can do better than me. I do make minimum wage! I do live in my parents' backyard!"

"So did I until a few years ago," Lacy reminded her. "Does that make me someone who's not worthy of love?"

"Of course not."

Lacy rubbed Cassie's arm, then wrapped her hands around her tea mug and took a sip. "Maybe he's just embarrassed by how his mother acted. Maybe he feels bad about what happened, and he doesn't know how to talk about it yet."

"Maybe," Cassie agreed. "But either way, I don't have my bakery, I don't have any hope of getting it, and Brian's not speaking to me. I went into this weekend so excited about everything. It seemed like everything I wanted was about to happen for me. And now … I'm back to square one."

"Maybe not." Lacy shrugged. "I think Brian will come around. And as for the bakery … I think this might be a blessing in disguise."

"Really."

"Well … now you can get your business started on your own, or with the help of people who really believe in you instead of someone who was using you. And that's going to be better all around, isn't it?"

BRIAN FELT LIKE WARMED-OVER SHIT. Everything involving Cassie had been fucked up, and the pure scope of the fuckery made him certain that she would never want to see him again.

Not all of it had been his fault, true. But it was *his* mother, after all, who'd ruined things with Cassie's business. It was also Lisa who'd said ugly things about Cassie and had hurt her feelings. And Cassie would never have met Lisa if it hadn't been for Brian.

So, in a way, it really was his fault.

Also, he knew he'd been an ass on the drive home. He knew she'd been hurt by his complete inability to talk about everything that had happened. He just hadn't known what to say, and he'd been sure that if he had tried to say something, it would be the exact wrong thing, making the smoldering pile of ashes that was his life burst into lively flame.

God, he'd bungled things. And now, he didn't know how to get anything—even one thing—back on track.

He thought about all of it as he picked up Thor from the petsitter, took him for a long walk in the neighborhood, then brought the dog into the house and let him off his leash.

Brian's house was habitable again, so that was something. There was still some painting to be done where the mold and termite repairs had happened, but he could live with that until the contractor came back and fixed it.

The fact that he could live in his house again was the one positive thing that had happened to him in the past forty-eight hours. Thor seemed glad to be back; he ran around the place sniffing everything, then went to his favorite dog bed and curled up with his hedgehog squeaky toy.

Brian picked up the stack of mail on his kitchen counter that the contractor had collected from the mailbox and put there for him. He sorted through a couple of things, then tossed them back into the pile. He couldn't deal with things like mail when Cassie was angry with him. Right now, it felt as though nothing else mattered.

He needed to talk this out with someone, so he fished his cell phone out of his pocket and tried Ike. He didn't get an answer. Who the hell else was he supposed to talk to about this?

Well, you could talk to Cassie, dumbass.

He dialed her number, then thought about what he was going to say, rehearsing his strategy as he waited for her to pick up.

She didn't—probably because she was screening her calls.

Not that he blamed her.

IKE CALLED BACK LATER in the day while Brian was drinking a Dr Pepper and watching TV, trying to forget about all of the problems that were plaguing him.

"What's up?" Ike asked. "I saw that you called."

"I did."

"Is everything okay?"

"Oh, hell no. Everything is not okay." Brian rubbed his forehead with his hand.

"Shit. All right. Tell me."

Brian went through it, keeping it as short as possible. He hit the highlights, emphasizing his own dumbassery and the awkward way he and Cassie had left things.

"And you haven't talked to her about it yet?" Ike sounded surprised, which Brian supposed was fair enough.

"I tried calling her, but I think she's blocking my calls. I probably would if I were her."

"Then keep trying. Or go over there. Do something. Don't just leave it as you giving her the silent treatment for two hundred miles."

"It sounds bad when you say it like that."

"Well ... food for thought."

"Okay. All right. I'll go over there. But..." He ran a hand through his hair, making it stand up at odd angles. "I'm not really sure what I'm going to say."

"Tell her the truth, man. It's always worked for me when Benny's pissed."

"Yeah. Okay. Okay."

"And, Brian?"

"Yeah?"

"You need to make this right. Cassie's great. I mean it. I've met a lot of your girlfriends over the years...."

"You've met all of them."

"Right. I've met all of them, and this one is special. I'm telling you."

"I know that. I do."

"Yeah, well. I'm just saying. Don't screw this up."

CHAPTER 29

*B*rian called two more times, then texted, then went to Cassie's place, knocking on the trailer door and calling her name. When she didn't answer any of his attempts, he went home, dejected.

He went to Central Coast Escapes the next day, reasoning that she'd be a captive audience if she was working the reception desk, and she'd be unable to walk out on him.

Of course, if she was off doing maintenance at one of the houses, he'd be out of luck. Still, it seemed worth a try.

He lucked out, because Cassie was alone in the office when he got there at around ten a.m. She was sitting behind a computer at an artificial wood grain desk, a potted plant on the floor beside her.

"Hey. I'm thinking of vacationing in Cambria, and I wondered if you had a twelve-bedroom with an ocean view and a hot tub." He gave her a little wave from the doorway, hoping his lighthearted opening line wouldn't get him thrown out on his ass.

"What do you want?" No smile, no hint of pleasure at seeing him there. Okay. This was going to be a challenge.

"I want to talk."

"I'm working right now."

"Yeah. I see that. But … you didn't answer my calls or my texts. I went over to your place, but you weren't there."

"That's because I'm here."

"Well, it was yesterday. But still."

She stood up, put her hands on her hips, and glared at him from behind her desk. "I don't have time for this. I work here. This is my job. I need to do it."

"Elliot's not here. What are you working on right now?"

She didn't answer. Her lips pursed, then her eyes flicked down to her computer screen.

Taking a chance, he came over and looked at her screen.

"Solitaire." He pointed at the game with one finger. "You can put the red seven on the black eight."

"Shut up." But she couldn't quite suppress a grin.

"Look, Cassie. Can we talk? I get that you're at work, but I promise I'll take less time than an average hand of solitaire. Please?" He looked at her with his most endearing facial expression, eyebrows raised and face open and pleading. He knew this was his most endearing facial expression because it had been focus-group tested for the show. He hated to be so calculating, but on the other hand, this really mattered, and he had to get it right. Was it so wrong to use data to get the job done?

Cassie looked at something on her screen. "Fine. My last solitaire game lasted three minutes and twenty-five seconds. You've got that much time." She picked up her cell phone from her desk and set the timer. "Go."

"You're actually timing me?"

"You've just used four seconds."

He ran his hands through his hair, trying to focus so he could make his case in the allotted time. "I'm sorry for everything that happened with my mother. I'm sorry about the things she said to you. And I'm sorry about how I acted on the drive. I was just so … I felt like everything was my fault. Like you wouldn't have been involved with Lisa in the first place if it hadn't been for me, and you wouldn't have gotten hurt that way. I was worried that you wouldn't want to see me anymore, and every time I thought I might try to talk about it, I worried that the thing I was about to say would make it worse. So I just didn't say anything. And the more I didn't say anything, the worse it got."

He paused for a breath. "And finally, I want to say that she was just wrong about you. She was wrong to judge you. You know what you want, and you're taking steps to get it, and it's nobody's business how long that has or has not taken for you. I hope you didn't take what she said seriously. Because she doesn't know you. She doesn't know how special you are. She doesn't know how driven and talented and smart you are. But I do. I see all of that." He finished and cleared his throat.

She looked up from her phone. "You have a little time left."

"Ah. Okay. Well ... I just want to say ... that I hope you won't hold her actions against me. Because ... because I love you."

She blinked twice and put down the phone. "You do?"

"Yes. I do."

"Well ... you really know how to conclude a speech."

"So, can we get past this?" He allowed himself a slight, hopeful grin.

"Maybe."

"Maybe?"

"Yes, maybe. But right now, I have to work."

"Can I call you later?"

"Yes."

He turned and headed toward the door. He had his hand on the knob and was on his way out when she said, "Oh. By the way. I love you, too."

WHEN BRIAN WAS GONE, Cassie felt better and lighter than she had since this whole thing had started. He loved her. He'd said it. Now that it was out there, he couldn't take it back, even if he wanted to.

She hoped he wouldn't want to.

There would be time for them to talk it out, time for them to work out what it meant that his mother disapproved of her—if it meant anything at all. They could work out the problems that faced them, whatever those turned out to be, because they were in love.

She was in love.

And, by God, if she could have that—if she could have Brian's love and give her own love to him—then there was no reason she couldn't have her bakery, too.

She just needed to figure out another way to get it.

Elliot came in about a half hour later, relieving Cassie on the reception desk. Now that she was no longer needed in the office, she went off to tackle her list of houses that needed cleaning or small maintenance jobs.

She started at Dolphin Dreams. She dragged out the cleaning products, the mop, the broom and dustpan, and the vacuum from the utility closet and got to work. As she dusted and scrubbed, vacuumed and polished, she thought about her bakery and how she was going to finance it without Lisa's help.

The thing was, Lisa didn't actually care about Cassie or her dreams. But there were other people who did.

There were people who would help her who truly had her best interests at heart. But she had to find a way to show them that she was serious and that she knew what she was doing.

As she worked, she composed a mental to-do list in her head. it was a long one, but she felt increasingly hopeful that she could do it.

BY THE TIME Cassie got home that night, she had a workable plan in her head. She sat down on her bed in the trailer, opened her laptop, and created a spreadsheet of everything she had to do and in what order. There was a lot she was uncertain about, since she'd never done this kind of thing before, but she knew people who ran their own businesses—two of Lacy's best friends were proprietors of shops on Main Street—so she had resources if she needed help.

If all of this worked, it was going to be so much better than it would have been if Lisa had been involved.

And if she acted fast, she might even get the Moonstone Mocha property she so longed for.

She went to bed excited and optimistic, and she couldn't wait to show Brian her plan.

In fact, she couldn't wait to share everything with Brian, whatever it happened to be. Her ideas, her dreams, her fears and hopes—all of it seemed better with him involved.

"So, I researched the numbers on this, and here's the amount of business I would have to bring in to be able to pay the rent, utilities, and insurance on the property and cover the rest of my overhead— supplies, wages for two full-time employees, that sort of thing." Cassie had her laptop open in front of Brian the next morning at his house in San Luis Obispo. They were sitting at his dining room table with Thor stretched out on the floor at their feet.

"The thing is," she went on, "I think I can do it. Not just with wedding cakes, of course. I've already called some local restaurants to look into selling them desserts, bread, rolls, that kind of thing. A couple said no because they like their current suppliers, but two others said they'd be willing to try some samples and meet with me. And I've talked to a few local wedding planners about doing cakes for their clients. Nobody promised anything, obviously, just based on an initial phone call, but they're willing to try samples, have a conversation, look at my references." Cassie was practically glowing with enthusiasm—she could feel the excitement radiating out of her own skin.

Brian grinned at her as he looked over what she'd written. "Yeah, it seems like it could work."

"And I'd want to keep doing videos, if it's okay with you. Because I got some orders from the ones we did, and that seems like a really good way to make people aware of what I have to offer."

Brian nodded. "Yeah. You're right. It really could boost sales, and it's a hell of a lot cheaper than buying advertising."

"So, based on these numbers and this plan, I want to start looking for investors. People who aren't your mother."

Brian looked at her. "I have some money tucked away. I could—"

"No. No!" Cassie's tone held a little more horror than she'd intended, so she put a hand on his arm in consolation. "I mean, thank you. That's a very nice offer. But I don't want my business dealings to have anything to do with our relationship. We've already seen how that worked out with your mother. What if you invest in the business and then we break up?"

"Why would we break up?" He looked hurt and maybe a little offended.

"I don't know. People break up. Things happen. And if things do happen … whatever they might be … I don't want that to affect my bakery."

"Okay." He nodded. "I guess that makes sense. I get that."

"I wasn't showing you this because I wanted you to give me money. I showed you because I want to know what you think. You've got a good head for business. Will it work?"

His eyebrows rose as he considered it. "Well … at the moment, the plan is based on a lot of what-ifs. But they're reasonable what-ifs. They're what-ifs that seem possible."

She bounced up and down in her seat, grinning. "Really?"

He rubbed at the stubble on his chin. "Yeah. Really. So … who are you going to ask?"

CHAPTER 30

Cassie had given a lot of thought to whom she could ask to invest in her bakery. She'd also given thought to the question of loan versus investment. If she sought investors, she'd be giving a portion of her profits to that person, which could be good or bad for the investor depending on how the business did. If it was a straight loan, she'd be required to make payments with interest regardless of whether she was making a profit.

After lengthy consideration, she'd decided to look for investors. True, that would introduce the idea of other people having a say in how she ran her business. But that arrangement would allow her the time to build her bakery before she had to worry about paying anyone back—which she might not be able to do for a while.

Naturally, she started with her parents, not because they were drowning in a sea of money, but because they'd be offended if she didn't include them.

"So, that's my plan," she told them after dinner that night, after she'd laid out everything she'd shown Brian. "If you say yes, I'll work with a lawyer—I've already got one—to put together a contract and work out the terms. And if you say no, it's okay. It really is. I would never expect you to get involved if you can't afford it or if you don't believe in it. So don't worry about that." She waited, barely able to breathe, while her parents looked at each other.

Vince put down his mug of tea, folded his hands under his chin, and regarded his youngest daughter as the three of them sat around the kitchen table, Cassie's laptop open in front of them. "You've really thought this out."

"Yes. I have."

"Nancy? What do you think?"

Nancy's eyes were shimmering with tears, which alarmed Cassie.

"Mom? What's wrong? Oh, God. I didn't mean to upset you. I didn't—"

"You didn't upset me, Cassie. I'm just so proud. You're going to do this—you really are."

"Oh." Cassie felt her throat close and her eyes fill with tears. She leaned over and embraced her mother, hard. When she let go, she wiped her eyes and let out a shaky laugh. "You guys should take some time to think about it, though."

"I think we're together on this." Vince raised his eyebrows at Nancy, who nodded. "How much do you need, total?"

She told him.

"Well, that's a lot."

"It is," Cassie agreed.

"Nancy? How much do you think we could swing?"

She told him a figure—one that nearly made Cassie gasp.

"You don't have that much," Cassie protested.

"Like hell we don't," Vince said. "We've been saving. We've always been savers, you know that."

"Yes, but … what about your retirement?"

"Let us worry about our retirement," Nancy said.

"But … but most businesses fail in the first year," Cassie said. "I want you to be prepared for that. I don't want—"

"Are you trying to talk us into it or out of it?" Vince gave his daughter a stern look.

"I just want … I want to open the bakery, but I also don't want my parents living in a box on the side of the road if I fail."

Vince laughed. "Honey, I wouldn't offer you anything we can't afford. Now, are you going to let us invest, or not?"

~

"Did you know Mom and Dad have money?" Cassie asked Lacy on the phone later that day.

"Of course. You didn't?"

"No! How would I know that? They've lived in the same too-small house for thirty-five years. They hardly ever take a vacation, and when they do, they stay in budget motels. Why would I have thought they had money?"

"That's why they have money," Lacy said. "Because they never spend it on anything."

They talked a little about what Nancy and Vince had decided about Cassie's business; how Lacy's kids and Daniel were doing; the latest gossip from the Main Street coffeehouse where Lacy used to work and where she still hung out; and about Lacy's plans to get a job in the next year or so, once Trevor was old enough for her to feel okay about leaving him with a babysitter.

Then Cassie got around to the reason for her call.

"Do you think you could get me a meeting with Jackson Graham?"

Jackson was the head chef at Neptune, and he was also married to Kate Bennet, one of Lacy's best friends. If Cassie could secure a deal to provide baked goods to Neptune, that would go a long way toward convincing potential investors to take a risk on her bakery.

"I'm sure I could," Lacy said thoughtfully. "But Jackson would never work with you before the health department signs off."

"Oh, I know. I get that. But if he'll consider it—if he'll just say that he's seriously thinking about it—I think that would really help. And ... there's one more thing." Cassie didn't see the need to mention that the *one more thing* was the main reason she was calling.

"Sure. Shoot."

"Could you maybe ask Gen if she'd consider talking to me about this?"

Genevieve Porter was a local art dealer. She had a gallery on Main Street and, more significantly, she had married into the Delaney family. The Delaneys, who owned a large cattle ranch, weren't just rich. They were wealthy, which was an entirely different category. Gen was a close personal friend of Lacy's, and while Cassie didn't particularly relish taking advantage of that connection, she also wasn't too proud to at least try it.

"Oh, boy," Lacy said.

Cassie understood the reason for Lacy's reaction, but she pressed forward anyway. "I know it's a lot to ask. I know Gen and Ryan probably get all kinds of people approaching them for their money, and you've never been one of those, and it's weird for you to start being one now. For me. So, if you want to say no, I get it. I really do. But—"

"I'll ask her," Lacy said.

Cassie felt a burst of joy and enthusiasm well up in her chest. "You will?"

"I will. But, Cassie, if the answer is no, then it's no."

"Of course!"

"I mean it. She's one of my best friends. If she doesn't want to do it and you pressure her ..."

"I won't. I swear."

"Okay. Then I'll set it up."

THE NEXT FEW days were busy ones for Cassie. She consulted her attorney to nail down the specifics of what she would be presenting to Gen, she baked a variety of things to give to Jackson Graham, she wrote a formal business plan, and she still had to work at Central Coast Escapes, cleaning houses and working the reception desk.

She fell into bed exhausted each night—usually with Brian beside her.

The more work she did, the more she was sure she could make this happen.

By the time she met with Jackson on a Thursday afternoon, she had rehearsed every word she intended to say. She showed up wearing a skirt, a blazer, and sensible pumps, carrying a stack of bakery boxes full of samples and a file folder with the information she wanted to show him.

She was more than a little nervous, not just because of all that was at stake, but also because Jackson was notorious for his bad temper.

As it happened, the whole thing was shorter, more casual, and far less stressful than she'd thought it might be.

"Huh." Jackson peered into the box with his eyebrows raised, appraising the rolls, pastries, and miniature cakes she'd brought. The two of them were sitting in his office off of the kitchen at Neptune.

Cassie had already apprised him of the situation—how she was attempting to get her bakery up and running, and she needed to know that her products were viable so she could pursue investors. He'd already taken a brief look at her business plan.

"I don't expect any kind of commitment," she said nervously as he looked into one of the boxes, appraising her work. "And I'm sure you already have a provider for your baked goods. So this probably isn't—"

"Are you trying to talk me out of it?" he asked, echoing what her father had said.

"No. Of course not."

"Maybe less talking, then." He pulled a sourdough roll out of the box, broke off a piece, and popped it into his mouth.

If she'd expected him to rhapsodize over the flavor and texture, she was mistaken.

His expression didn't change as he chewed, then swallowed.

Next he poked into one of the boxes with a fork and tried a bite of her dark chocolate cake with chocolate ganache. Again, no response.

"Jackson?" she asked timidly.

He put up a finger to quiet her, then poked the fork in again and tasted a classic New York–style cheesecake.

By the time he'd tasted most of what she'd brought, she was certain the answer was no. After all, he'd shown no reaction to anything he'd tried.

Finally, he put down his fork, closed the boxes, and leaned back in his chair, putting one ankle atop the opposite knee. His chef's coat was still crisply white, as it was still early in the day.

"Well," he said finally, "I can't offer you any kind of deal until you get the permits and licensing worked out. But once you do, give me a call."

She blinked at him and sat up straighter in her seat. "Give you a call? What does that mean? Does it mean—"

"It means give me a call." He laced his fingers behind his head, leaning back so far in his office chair that it threatened to topple. "I do have a supplier, obviously, but they've lost their best baker—guy moved to San Francisco to get married—so the quality's been going downhill. You get the paperwork done, I'll give you a try. That cheesecake is really something, by the way."

"Oh. Oh, my gosh." Cassie jumped up, ran over to him on her uncomfortable pumps, and hugged him. She wouldn't have done that during a business meeting, usually, but she and Jackson knew each other through Lacy, so it wasn't like he was just any random chef she'd approached about her baked goods.

Her impulsive embrace threatened to make them both fall off of his steeply tilted chair, so he straightened, giving her back a friendly little pat-pat-pat.

"Ah, man. Okay." He laughed a little, and she finally let go of him.

"You don't know what this means to me, Jackson."

"I don't? I had to start somewhere, too." He straightened his coat, maybe blushing slightly from her hug. "But, listen. You screw up—you don't give me the quality I need, or you come in short on the quantity —and I won't give a shit whether you're my wife's friend's sister. I'll cut you loose even if it means I sleep in the guest room for a month."

"Understood."

Cassie left the restaurant smiling so hard she wondered if her face might break.

CHAPTER 31

 he road toward owning a business wasn't always smooth.

Cassie contacted a number of restaurants—and a handful of coffeehouses—and was told at each one that they already had a supplier they were happy with or that they were unwilling to take a chance on an unproven baker.

But Jackson Graham's favorable response would go a long way in giving her credibility while she tried to gather capital.

Which was exactly what she was doing when she met with Genevieve Porter and her husband, Ryan Delaney, at Gen and Ryan's house the following week.

Cassie knew Gen and Ryan through Lacy. She'd been to their house for barbecues, parties, informal gatherings. When she ran into either one of them around town, they stopped to ask after each other's families and enjoy some friendly conversation. They weren't strangers. They were friends.

And that was what made this awkward. If she hadn't known them at all, this would have been a simple business meeting. But because she did know them, it became so much more fraught with potential difficulty.

"First, I just want to tell you that it's okay to say no. In fact, I *want* you to say no if you don't think this is the right move for you. I don't want you to worry about your friendship with Lacy, or with me, or … or anything but business. After all, I'm new at this, and I'm going to make mistakes, and—"

"Why are you arguing against yourself before you even make your pitch?" Gen asked.

"That's pretty much what Jackson said," Cassie told her.

They were sitting in Gen and Ryan's kitchen in their house on the Delaney Ranch property, sipping coffee at the big farmhouse table. Cassie's laptop was open on the table, and she'd brought a folder of papers detailing her business plan. She told them what she intended to do, where she wanted to open the bakery, who her intended customers would be, what she predicted her revenue to be in the first year, and how she intended to market her business.

When she was done, she sat back and tried not to hold her breath.

Gen nodded appreciatively, looking over the printout of the business plan. "I can see this working. I really can. If you were just doing wedding cakes, I think that would be too narrow a focus to make it viable. But this? You're targeting the tourist trade as well as the local restaurants and the wedding business. This could be good."

Ryan rubbed at the stubble on his chin. "This location, it's the old Moonstone Mocha place?"

"Yes." Cassie nodded. "It's a great space, plus the kitchen was recently renovated. It's perfect for what I want to do."

His eyebrows rose as he considered it. "That's Joe Carter's place. The building's been empty for months, and Joe's been hurting without any rent coming in. Be nice to help turn it around for him."

Cassie felt a surge of hope at his words.

"And," Gen said, "it's not good for the town to have empty buildings on Main Street. It affects the property values for everyone."

"Does that mean you'll consider it?" Cassie tried not to jump up and down with glee, as that wouldn't be professional. It would also be downright embarrassing.

"What kind of figure were you thinking?" Ryan asked.

Cassie had already written out the terms she was hoping for. She took the sheet of paper out of her folder and slid it over to Ryan.

"That's a lot," Ryan commented.

Gen made a rude *ppfft* noise and smacked her husband on the shoulder. "Ryan, you earn that much interest in a week."

He grinned slightly, looking at the sheet of paper. "Well."

"Have your lawyer draw something up," Gen said.

THAT NIGHT, Cassie popped open a bottle of champagne at Brian's house as the two of them sat on his sofa, Thor lounging on the cushions between them.

"Here's to Cassie's Cakery," she said, pouring frothy champagne into his glass.

"So, you picked a name? I like it." Brian waited for her to fill her own glass, then clinked his against hers, and they drank.

"I thought about something more straightforward like Central Coast Cakes," she told him. "But in the end, I wanted the name to be fun. Central Coast Cakes tells you what you need to know, but Cassie's Cakery has personality."

"I agree."

She downed half of her glass in one triumphant gulp. "God. I can't believe this is actually going to happen. My dream. It's going to come true, for real. How many people can actually say that? I just hope …"

"What?"

"I hope I don't screw it up. People are investing their hard-earned money with me. I hope I don't let them down."

"You won't." He kissed her, and it made her head feel even more foggy than the champagne did.

"How do you know I won't?"

"Because I know you. I know how much thought you put into this and how much you want it. You won't let anybody down."

She leaned across Thor to kiss Brian, and Thor let out a whine of discomfort at the tight space. He wiggled around, stood up, and jumped down off the sofa, giving them what Cassie thought might be a scowl of disgust.

"More room for me," Brian said, scooting closer to Cassie.

"Do you really think I can do it?" she asked.

"I know you can. I just wish you'd let me invest."

"No. I don't want to do that." She snuggled up close to him to soften her words. "But there is something you can do for me."

"Well, okay, if I must." He reached for her T-shirt and began pulling it up over her head. "Let's get this off so I can get started."

"Not that." She giggled—she actually giggled—but let him take off the shirt.

"What then?" He kissed her neck, then trailed kisses down past her collarbone and toward her breasts.

"I …" She momentarily forgot what she was going to say. "I wanted to talk about… maybe some … some help with marketing."

He paused what he was doing and looked at her. "Sure. I can do that. Right now?"

"No, not right now." She gave his head a nudge to get him back to what he'd been doing. "We can do that later. Much later."

"Good plan," he said, and swept his tongue inside the lacy edge of her bra.

Now that Cassie had gotten the funding for her bakery worked out, Brian had the time and mental space to think about his mother.

Things had been left unfinished with her. Cassie had made it clear that she was not going to do business with Lisa. But so much else was left unresolved. Brian still had things to say to his mother about how she'd tried to manipulate both him and Cassie.

And he was worried, too. She hadn't looked right when he'd seen her before. She'd seemed tired. Defeated. That was unusual for her—she usually was so self-confident. And it made no sense considering the fact that she was scheduled for a career-making solo show.

So, what was going on?

Brian didn't like how she'd looked, and he didn't like the fact that Lorenzo seemed to be trying to keep people away from her.

Part of him said he should just mind his own business. His mother had decided early in his life that she didn't want to be closely involved with him. So why should be trouble himself to become involved with her now?

But another part of him knew that was crap. She was his mother. Regardless of what she had or had not done, she was still the woman who had given birth to him, and he still cared about her.

Something was going on, and he needed to know what it was.

"I'm going down there," he told Cassie one night while they were in bed together, relaxed and sated after a particularly athletic round of lovemaking.

"Where?"

"To see my mother." He was looking at the ceiling instead of at her, because he didn't want to be lured into staying here with her forever, until the polar ice caps melted and the sun burned itself out, until mankind's decline and the rise of something newer and possibly better. It was tempting to ride out eternity right here in this bed.

Cassie rolled onto her side to face him. "Okay."

"It's just … I didn't like the way she looked when I saw her last. She wasn't herself."

"Yeah. I don't know her very well, but it seemed that way to me, too. Something was going on."

"Something having to do with that Lorenzo asshole."

"Are you sure that's it?" Cassie laid her hand on his chest in a way he found immensely soothing.

"No, I'm not sure. But it seems likely, doesn't it?"

"Maybe it's got something to do with her work. Maybe her painting isn't going well."

"Yeah, maybe." But he doubted it was that simple. Lisa Barlow faced the world with a level of bluster and ego that might seem absurd to someone who didn't know her. It might seem, to an outsider, like an affectation. But Brian knew it was just her. It was how she was, how she lived. To see her looking older and somehow deflated had scared him.

"Do you think she's in some kind of trouble?" Cassie asked.

He shrugged. "I don't know. But I think I have to find out what's going on."

~

CASSIE HAD MIXED feelings about Brian's announcement that he was going to Los Angeles to see his mother.

On one hand, she did agree that something seemed off with Lisa. And she wholeheartedly supported a son doing what he needed to do to take care of his mother.

On the other, some selfish part of her worried about what would happen if he went down there and spent time alone with Lisa. Brian's mother had made it clear that she'd only approved of his relationship with Cassie if it meant Lisa could use Cassie to her advantage. Now that she couldn't do that, she had no reason to support the relationship at all.

What would she say to him about Cassie while he was there? What further manipulations might she try now that her first gambit had failed?

Privately, Cassie was terrified that Lisa might come up with some winning combination of argument, emotion, and scheming that would convince Brian to end the relationship.

All because Lisa thought Cassie wasn't good enough.

And she wasn't entirely wrong, was she? After all, Brian had built a successful business out of nothing, and what had Cassie done? She'd dreamed, that was all. Until now, all she'd done was hope and plan. Yes, she was taking action on it, finally, but it had taken her this long. She really was earning minimum wage and living in her parents' backyard, just as Lisa had said.

For God's sake, Brian was an entrepreneur who earned enough that he'd easily and casually offered to invest in Cassie's business. What made her think she was his equal?

Of course, she couldn't say anything to him about her worries. She didn't want to be that woman who was so insecure she thought she needed to compete with a man's mother for his love.

She had to keep her insecurities to herself. She'd air them to Lacy, no doubt, and she'd worry herself sick about it while he was gone. But she couldn't utter a word of it to Brian.

"When are you planning to go?" She kept her tone neutral, even supportive.

"Next week, probably. If Thor's sitter can take him."

"I can do it."

"Really?" He raised up a little to look at her.

"Sure. He and I already know each other. It'll be fine."

"That's great. Thank you. So, next week, then."

"Okay." She put her head on his chest and listened to his heartbeat, trying not to play out worst-case scenarios in her head.

CHAPTER 32

*B*rian headed out the following week after the last work on his house was finished and he'd wrapped up his latest YouTube video—this one a man-on-the-street taste test of breakfast cereal with various non-milk liquids, including orange juice, Mountain Dew, lemonade, sports drinks, and Red Bull.

He'd offered to have Cassie stay at his house with Thor while he was gone, reasoning that it would make things easier if Thor could have his own familiar space.

But Cassie opted to take the dog back to her place. Yes, it was cramped, but she had a lot to do in Cambria, so being there would make things easier.

She'd gotten the funding for the bakery—she'd gotten the funding! —and now she was ready to begin work in earnest.

The morning Brian left, she took Thor for a long walk and let him run around at the dog park. Then she put him in the trailer with his dog bed, a chew toy, some kibble, and a fresh bowl of water, and went to work at Central Coast Escapes.

Elliot didn't take it well when Cassie gave him her two-week notice.

"Well, Cassie, this really puts me in a bind," he fussed, his eyebrows drawn together in consternation.

"I'm sorry, Elliot, but this is good news for me. I'm ready to move on. Be happy for me."

"I suppose." He sat at his desk in the office. He picked up a pencil, fidgeted with it between his fingers, and put it down again. "But how am I supposed to find someone else on such short notice?"

"It's not short notice. It's the standard two weeks."

"Yes, but I don't just have to find someone in that time. I have to train them, and—"

"You'll manage, Elliot."

He never did congratulate her. Instead, he assigned her a crushing list of to-dos on an array of houses—so many things that she suspected he'd invented some of them just to punish her.

She didn't mind, though—at least, not much. As she changed light bulbs, applied caulking, cleaned under refrigerators—a task she'd never been asked to do before—and repainted things that didn't need repainting, she thought happily about her business.

On her lunch break, she called the leasing agent about the Moonstone Mocha property.

"Nobody else has asked about it, have they?" she asked the agent, fretting about whether she might be too late.

"A few people have inquired, but not seriously. I hear you've got the Delaneys backing you."

"You heard that?" Cassie puzzled over how that might be, though she knew Cambria was a small town with the corresponding small-town gossip.

"I did. So, are you ready to sign the lease?"

She signed late that afternoon after she got off work, exhausted and dirty from all Elliot had put her through.

She didn't even feel the fatigue, though, as she met in the Realtor's office to sign the paperwork.

"Oh, my God. I'm so excited. I love this property. I can't wait to get started." Cassie was barely able to contain her glee.

"We'd normally put you through a lengthy application process, a credit check, references and all that, but with the Delaneys on board …"

Clearly, going to Gen and Ryan had been the right thing.

AT HOME THAT NIGHT, after she'd walked Thor, Cassie called Brian on his cell phone to share the news with him.

"I signed. I have the Moonstone Mocha property. I guess I can stop thinking of it that way. It's Cassie's Cakery now. Can you believe it?"

"I can. I really can. Congratulations, Cass. That's awesome. I just wish I could be there to celebrate with you."

"I wish you could, too. How are things with your mom?"

He was silent for a long beat, and that told her more than anything he could have said.

BRIAN TOLD himself to keep things positive for Cassie, since he didn't want to ruin her triumphant moment.

"Things are okay." *Okay* was the best thing he could say at the moment without lying. And, by some standards, things were, in fact, okay. Nobody was bleeding. Nobody was on fire.

But Lisa was definitely not okay by most people's interpretation of the word.

He chatted with Cassie a while longer about her plans, then he told her he loved her and hung up.

Then he went back to the shit show that was his mother's life.

"Why didn't you tell me?" he asked Lisa again when he'd tucked his phone back into his pocket and had gone back into the sitting area of her loft, where she was slumped on the sofa looking at a blank brick wall.

"Tell you? What was I supposed to tell you? That I lost the Art Basel show to some pretentious fake and Lorenzo left me the moment I wasn't the big, happening thing anymore?"

"Well … yes." He sat down next to her, peering at her with concern. She looked tired and sad. And too thin, as though she hadn't been eating. He was pretty sure she wasn't sleeping, either, based on the dark circles under her eyes.

"You know, Mom, that Lorenzo guy … you're probably better off. I don't think—"

"Oh, for God's sake." Lisa rubbed her eyes with her fingertips and leaned forward over her knees as though she might retch. He was grateful when she didn't. "I'm not better off in any conceivable way. Am I better off now that I'm a nobody? Am I, Brian? Am I better off now that Lorenzo … now that's he's …" She let out a heaving sob, which alarmed Brian. He'd assumed that Lorenzo was just someone Lisa was using for pleasure, which was worrisome enough. But now, he wondered if maybe she'd really felt something for him.

"He just left!" Lisa threw her hands into the air as tears streamed down her face. "I got the call that Ernest Hedley was given the show instead of me the day before you and Cassie visited. Then, as soon as you were gone, Lorenzo said some happy shit about how I was going to be okay, how I was going to bounce back, and then he started packing."

"I knew he was an asshole," Brian said. Right now, if he could have found the asshole in question, he'd have pummeled him into a pile of quivering, bleeding pulp. Too bad that was unlikely.

"He didn't even care! There I was, at the lowest point in my life, and he didn't even pretend that he'd been with me for anything other than my connections, my fame. Good God, how could I have been that stupid?"

Brian might have thought that the lowest time in Lisa's life was the day she'd decided to leave him and his father, but apparently not.

"But … how did you lose the Art Basel show? I thought that was a done deal."

Lisa waved a hand in dismissal. "Oh, grow up, Brian. This kind of thing happens all the time. Ernest Hedley is in the news right now after that ridiculous stunt in Venice. Now, they think he'll pull in more collectors, more wealthy patrons, than I would. It's the way of the world, I suppose."

Brian had no idea what the ridiculous stunt in Venice had been, and he thought it imprudent to ask—especially because he didn't care.

"Lorenzo didn't want to let us see you. He didn't want to let us talk to you."

"Well, that was my doing." Lisa sighed. "I didn't want you to see me in that state. I was devastated. I asked him to hold you off because I couldn't face you. I couldn't face anyone. He knew that! He knew I needed him, but apparently, he didn't care."

"Mom? What did he say when he left?"

"He said, 'Ciao, darling.' For fuck's sake, he was born in Iowa."

Lisa dissolved into tears, her head buried in the crook of her arm. Brian had no idea what to say to her, what to do to make any of this better.

"Did you … Mom? Did you really care about him?"

"Of course I did!" Lisa plucked some tissues out of a box on the table next to her and blew her nose, then wiped her eyes. "What did you think, that I was with him because he looked good on my arm?"

"Well …" It was exactly what he'd thought, but again, not prudent to say it out loud.

"I'm not nearly as shallow as you think, it seems." She got up, began to walk to her bedroom, then paused, bracing herself on the edge of the sofa, one hand pressed to her forehead.

"Are you all right?"

She looked like she might faint, but Brian supposed that might be because she hadn't eaten anything in a while.

"You didn't eat lunch," he said. "Can I make you something?"

"I'm a little dizzy, that's all. I'm just … my head. I have a splitting headache. And I couldn't possibly eat anything."

"I'll bring you some Tylenol. And let me get you some tea, at least."

"Fine. Thank you, dear."

He went to get the medication and the tea, worrying that there was more going on here than heartbreak over Lorenzo.

CASSIE GOT the keys to the Moonstone Mocha building—now Cassie's Cakery—and spent all of her time when she wasn't at Central Coast Escapes working on the place and making her plan for her grand opening.

For the most part, the building had everything she needed. But she was going to have to make a few changes. She needed to have a refrigerated display case built for her baked goods, for one thing. And she also had to do something about the Moonstone Mocha sign out front.

She called around to find a contractor to build the case, and she was near despair when she had a hard time getting any of them to call her back. It was building season, apparently, and demand was high. When she did get through to someone, she was told that he had a three-month waiting list.

She couldn't wait that long.

She called Ryan Delaney, since that had worked so well before.

"Ryan? I'm having a hard time getting a contractor, and I wondered ..."

"My brother-in-law's a contractor," Ryan said. "Let me call him."

The same day, Jake Travis, who was married to Ryan's sister, Breanna, called her and said he could come out to look at the space and give her an estimate that afternoon.

"Really? That soon?"

"I had to push some things, but you know how family is. If I don't do this, I'm never gonna hear the end of it," he said.

WITH THAT PROBLEM out of the way, she Googled sign makers to find out what it would cost to have a Cassie's Cakery sign made and put up on her building.

The price for what she had in mind made her gasp.

Still, she needed that visibility so drivers and pedestrians on Main Street would see her business at a glance. She compared options and designs, then chose a sign maker on the Central Coast and called to inquire about seeing samples and placing an order.

The wait for the completed sign was going to be longer than she wanted, so she looked into window painters as a stopgap. Maybe someone could paint the name of the bakery in decorative script on her front window while she was waiting for her permanent sign to be completed.

In the meantime, the place needed cleaning. After her time at Central Coast Escapes, that was hardly a new job for her.

She scoured the floors, the windows, the tiny bathroom, and every surface of the kitchen. She put her head inside the oven, rubber gloves on her hands and a scrubber clutched in her fingers, going over every inch until the surfaces gleamed. She polished stainless steel, sanitized countertops, wiped down the shelves in the storage spaces, and gave attention to the walk-in refrigerator.

She was going to need furniture, of course, so she looked online at cafe tables and chairs, light fixtures, and a desk and chair for the little room off the kitchen that would be her office.

Her office. At her business.

Lacy came over to see the place a couple of days later while Jake was measuring and taking notes.

"I was in this place a few times when it was Moonstone Mocha," Lacy said, looking over the front room, then the kitchen. "It's a great space. I love the fireplace."

"Me too. And the garden is so pretty. Which reminds me, I'll need a gardener, because I won't have time to keep up with that myself once things get going. And I have to buy outdoor furniture! Jeez. There's so much to think about."

"You'll do it," Lacy said. "You've come this far, you can do the rest."

"I can. I really can."

She and Lacy walked through the building, their shoes making the aged wooden floors squeak as they moved.

"I don't suppose you'd consider working here," Cassie said. She'd been thinking it for a while, but she'd hesitated to bring it up. Now seemed like as good a time as any. "I'll need a barista for the coffee bar, and you've got experience. Plus, it would be so much fun."

"Oh. Wow. Trevor's still little, and the other kids ..."

"I know. I know. There are a thousand reasons you shouldn't. But still, will you consider it?"

Lacy grinned. "It really would be fun."

Cassie was so happy and so busy that she almost didn't have time to think about Brian.

Almost.

"You miss him, too, don't you?" She rubbed Thor's fur that night in her trailer as they both lay on her bed, her exhausted from a day managing both her jobs, him tired out after a long run at the dog park.

"Let's call him. What do you think? Should we call him?" Cassie had lapsed into the kind of sing-song talk one used with small children.

When she found herself actually waiting for Thor's answer, she told herself to pull it together, and she called.

"When are you coming home?" She hadn't meant to lead with that, as it seemed both pushy and needy, but that's what had come out. She covered it up by pretending it was about Thor. "Your dog misses you. I think he's sad." Cassie was the one who was sad about Brian's absence, but it seemed too girly to say so.

"I'm not sure."

She didn't like that answer—or the grim tone of his voice.

"Why? What's going on?"

She listened while he told her about Lisa's despair, her dizziness, her headaches. Lisa had also been complaining of stomach pain, and he was starting to worry that something was really wrong with her. "I can't leave until I know she's okay."

"Has she seen a doctor?"

"She says she has."

"Well, what did he say?"

The thing was, Lisa had been vague about that. Either she hadn't gotten a firm diagnosis, or she had and she didn't want to tell her son what it was.

"I just want to hang around until I know what's going on," he told Cassie. "I hope it's okay, with Thor and all ..."

"Of course it's okay. Don't worry about Thor. He's fine." In fact, she was beginning to rely on the dog's steady, warm presence. "Just take care of your mom."

CHAPTER 33

It was four more days before Brian came back, and when he did, it was just to check in, spend the night with Cassie, and pick up Thor to take the dog down to LA with him.

"I don't know how long I'll be there, and it's not fair to you to ask you to keep taking care of him," Brian told her. He'd just arrived in San Luis Obispo and was tired from the drive north. Cassie had come to his house with Thor to meet him.

"I didn't mind."

"Well, still. I kind of miss him."

When Brian and Thor had first reunited, the dog had squealed, jumped in the air, and wagged his tail so hard it seemed like he might sprain his butt. Brian had gotten down on the floor with him, vigorously rubbing his fur and talking baby talk to him.

"I kind of hoped you'd be staying," Cassie said.

Brian wanted that—God, how he wanted that—but things with his mother were … weird. Too weird for him to turn his back on her.

"She's depressed. And I think she's sick, Cass. I can't leave her alone until I know what's going on."

Not that it would be easy to leave Cassie, either.

He'd thought she was beautiful before, but making progress with her business had made her positively glow. People said that—that somebody glowed—but Cassie seemed to have a light within her that brightened everything in her vicinity.

He wanted to be one of those things—one of those lucky people in her orbit who were bathed in that light. But he also wanted to be able to look at himself in a mirror. He didn't want to abandon his mother the way she had abandoned him.

But going back down south tomorrow was going to be one of the hardest things he'd ever done, especially with Cassie looking the way she looked, and with her skin feeling the way it felt under his hands....

They took each other's clothes off and fell into bed for a long and glorious time, then they showered and dressed and went out to dinner. Then they came back to his place and undressed and fell into bed again.

"Is she still talking about you moving down there?" Cassie asked when they were lying in his bed in each other's arms, both of them satisfied and damp with sweat.

"Yeah. She is. She started out by saying I could be closer to Ike. Then, when that didn't work, she talked about the entertainment industry and my career."

"You've built your career living in San Luis Obispo this whole time," Cassie pointed out. "You're self-contained. It's not like you need a producer and a Hollywood studio."

"I told her that." He stroked Cassie's shoulder with one hand while he talked. "But ... it's not really about that. I think she's sick, and she knows it, and she doesn't want to be alone."

Listening to him, Cassie started to feel a little sick herself. Was this how it was going to end? Was Brian going to move away from the Central Coast just as Cassie was building something substantial for herself here?

"She doesn't have a diagnosis?" she asked.

Brian shrugged. "If she does, she won't tell me what it is. But she's got severe headaches. Dizziness. Nausea and stomach pain. And she's so tired. She barely gets out of bed anymore."

"Was she like that when you got there? It seems like the first couple of times you called, you didn't mention anything about her being sick."

Brian considered Cassie's question. Had Lisa seemed sick when Brian had first shown up? She'd seemed angry. Sad. Dispirited. She hadn't had much appetite, and she'd already been complaining of headaches and dizziness. But things had grown worse over the course of his stay.

It was possible that whatever was wrong with her had more to do with stress and heartbreak than with physical illness.

"I don't know what's going on with her."

"Maybe you should talk to Lorenzo," Cassie suggested.

Brian had a visceral reaction to the idea of talking to that asshole, but the more he thought about it, the more he thought Cassie might be right. After all, Lorenzo and Lisa had been living together, and he'd been handling all of her personal business. Who better to know if she really did have a significant health problem?

Brian called Lorenzo the next morning while he was out walking Thor around the neighborhood. Cassie had already left for work, and Brian was planning to make the drive down south later that morning.

Brian had Lorenzo's cell phone number from when they'd all been staying at Otter Bluff together. Now he dialed it, and Lorenzo picked up on the second ring.

"*Pronto.*"

Lorenzo's pretentious Italian way of answering the phone made Brian grit his teeth as he willed his head not to explode.

"Lorenzo, it's Brian. Cavanaugh. Lisa's son."

"Ah. Brian. If Lisa told you to call …"

"She didn't. And, to be honest, I'd rather be talking to pretty much anybody else in the world right now. But I have to ask you something."

He told Lorenzo about Lisa's health issues and asked if Lorenzo knew anything about it. Had Lisa been to a doctor lately? Had she been diagnosed with anything worrisome? Had he observed her symptoms before he'd left?

Lorenzo let out a scoff. "You're her son. Surely you know this act by now, no?"

"What are you talking about?"

"I'm talking about how she's not just a visual artist. She dabbles in performance as well."

"If you could stop talking around it and just tell me—"

"She might be sick, Brian. What do I know? It's possible. But it's also possible that her ailments only show up when she wants some-body to do something for her."

Apparently, Brian still retained some loyalty to his mother despite everything, because the statement outraged him, made him want to reach through the phone and pull out the asshole's lungs.

"Hey, you know what? Fuck you, Lorenzo."

Lorenzo laughed. "I thought there was no resemblance between you and your mother, but now I think I was wrong. Ciao, Brian."

"Fuck your ciao. You're not even fucking Italian." But he was talking to no one—Lorenzo had already hung up.

LATER THAT DAY, Brian drove to Los Angeles resolving to get to the bottom of whatever was going on with his mom.

"You're going to see your doctor, and I'm going with you," he told her shortly after he arrived. Lisa had been up and around when he'd gotten here—she was even working on a new painting—but now she was in bed, though it was only two p.m.

"I've already seen my doctor."

"Okay. When?"

"While you were gone. I told her it was urgent, and she made time for me."

"Well, I want to talk to her. What's her name?"

"I'm not going to tell you her name." Lisa was lying on top of the covers, one forearm covering her eyes as though the light hurt her.

"But I need to know what's going on."

"And I need you to understand that some things are private, Brian."

Despite what Lorenzo had said, Brian's deepest fear wasn't that Lisa was making things up. It was that she was truly sick—maybe dying—and he'd been too insensitive to see it.

"Please, Mom." He sat down on the edge of the bed, his weight causing the mattress to shift. "I need to know what's going on so I can know how to help you."

"You're helping me just by being here." She patted his hand. "You don't know how much."

He sighed. "Can I get you anything?"

"No thank you, dear. I just need to lie here until the pain passes."

CASSIE FOCUSED on work now that Brian was gone again. She finished her last days at Central Coast Escapes, supervised the building of her display cases, acquired and arranged furniture, and had her health department inspection. She applied for and received a business license and made plans for her grand opening.

She spoke to Brian on the phone every night, and she tried not to be pissy about the fact that he was still gone and had no concrete plan for when he might return.

But not being pissy was starting to get hard.

"You're going to miss my grand opening." She tried to keep any hint of a whine out of her voice.

"I can drive up there for it."

"I've worked really hard, Brian, and this is a big deal for me."

"That's why I'll drive up for it. Why are you angry, Cassie?"

So much for keeping the pissiness out of her voice. Clearly, she'd failed at that, and now she had to defend her attitude.

"It's just … I miss you." She said it in as matter-of-fact a tone of voice as she could muster.

"I miss you, too."

"Well, you wouldn't if you were here." Okay, that was maybe a little petulant. She was big enough to admit that.

"Cassie, we've talked about this. You know why I—"

"Yes. I know."

The thing was, Cassie was more and more certain that Lisa wasn't sick and that she was simply manipulating Brian to stay in Los Angeles. Part of that might be because Lisa didn't want Brian and Cassie together, and part of it was undoubtedly that Lisa simply had decided she wanted Brian in her life right now. She hadn't wanted him around before, but now that Lorenzo had left her without a man at her beck and call, it was suddenly important for Brian to be near her.

Cassie didn't have hard evidence to back her claim. But Lisa's symptoms were all things that could not be observed, either by an onlooker or by a physician.

How could you verify that someone had stomach pain? How could you test for a headache? Was there any instrument, any visual clue that could tell you whether someone was dizzy? Or tired?

To Cassie, Lisa's list of ailments sounded like something you'd hear from a kid who wanted to play hooky from school. Especially when you considered that Lisa wouldn't tell Brian anything about who her doctor was or what that person had said.

Lisa was playing him, Cassie knew it. But what if she was wrong? She didn't want to be that person who insisted that her boyfriend abandon his sick mother.

What if Lisa really was ill?

What if Cassie convinced Brian to come back north, then Lisa ended up in the hospital, or worse?

He would never forgive her, and she would never forgive herself.

~

"HONESTLY, you're right. It's hinky," Lacy said one day when she and Cassie were at the bakery working on the dine-in seating and the decor. "I mean, yes, it's possible that she's sick. Sometimes emotional trauma shows up in the form of physical symptoms, and she's had some emotional trauma with the lost show and her boyfriend leaving her."

"But," Cassie said, continuing her sister's train of thought, "she's already proven that she's willing to manipulate him to try to get him to move down there. That whole thing with the bakery? That was a lot of trouble—and potential expense—just to get your son to come to you."

The two of them were hanging some botanical prints on the walls, and Cassie held a framed print up to the wall while Lacy stood back and looked at it. "A little higher," she said. "Okay, there. Now a little to the left."

Once the print was hung, they went back to their conversation.

"And," Cassie said, "this is going to be petty, but … he said he would help me with marketing. He's got a degree in it. And now I need marketing, because my grand opening is coming up. And where is he?"

"It's not the marketing that's bothering you," Lacy said.

"No. It isn't."

"It's that you think she might win."

Cassie had to admit that her sister knew her very well. Of course that was what was bothering her. What if Lisa got her way? There was no way Cassie was going to move to Los Angeles with Brian now that the bakery was about to be up and running. Would she and Brian have a long-distance relationship? How would that work?

She had to speculate that it wouldn't work at all, with Lisa whispering in his ear about how Cassie wasn't good enough for him.

"It's just … I'm in love with him. I love him." Cassie felt tears fill her eyes, and she wiped them away with her fingertips. "After all these years of looking, I've finally found someone to love, and now …" She gestured around her at the lack of Brian. "Where is he?"

"Oh, Cass." Lacy rubbed her sister's shoulder in sympathy. "Be patient. He's going to have to figure out this thing with his mother on his own. You don't want him to come back because you forced his hand. You want him to come back because it's his choice."

"I know. you're right." She sniffled a little and drew in a shaky breath.

"And ..." Lacy said.

Cassie looked at her, waiting.

"You don't want to get too serious until things with Lisa are resolved one way or the other," Lacy went on. "I mean, imagine if you marry him, and you've got the mother-in-law from hell breathing down your neck."

"I haven't thought about marriage. I'm not there yet," Cassie lied.

"Well, you don't want to go there until you know who's coming along for the ride."

CHAPTER 34

*B*rian was feeling increasingly frustrated with the direction things had taken. The two women in his life wanted two different things from him, and the two things weren't compatible.

How was he supposed to choose between his girlfriend and his mother?

"So, what's the plan?" Ike asked him when they met for lunch one day at a burger place in Westwood. "Are you here full-time now?"

"What? No." Brian had a half-eaten burger and a plate of fries in front of him, and he picked up a fry and toyed with it. "Of course not."

Ike shrugged. "It kind of seems that way. You've been here a few weeks now. Not that I'm complaining. I like having you around. Still, you haven't put out a video since you've gotten here. You know you can't do that. You can't go silent this long without losing views."

"What are you, my mother? I already have one of those." Brian sullenly slurped his Coke.

"I'm just saying. You had a good thing in San Luis Obispo. The show was going well, ad revenue was up. You had Cassie. And now you're here. What's up with that?"

"I still have Cassie. You put it in the past tense. It's not past tense. It's present tense."

"Okay." Ike nodded and chewed a bite of his burger. Then he put the burger down and wiped his mouth with a napkin from the dispenser on the table. "Fair enough. But how long is that going to last if you don't go back? She's not moving down here to be with you, man. She's about to open her bakery."

"I know. Shit. I know that."

"So what's going on?"

Brian sat back in the booth and folded his arms across his chest. "Cassie thinks my mother is faking being sick to keep me down here."

Ike let out a soft laugh.

"What's that supposed to mean? That laugh?" Brian was indignant.

"The laugh means, Cassie's not the only one who thinks that's possible."

"Wait. What?"

Ike leaned forward and gave Brian an intense look that meant he was about to say something that mattered. "Look. I've known you since we were in first grade. You've been my best friend all that time. I was there when your mother left, and I was there when she played you over and over, decade after decade. I'm not new to this situation. I've seen it all."

"What's your point?"

"My point is, Lisa messing with you to get her way would not be unprecedented."

Brian crumpled his napkin and threw it onto the table. "You know what? Fuck you, man."

"Yeah, okay."

There wasn't much heat in the exchange—they'd known each other too long and too well for either one of them to be truly offended.

"I'll tell you something else," Ike said.

"I wish you wouldn't."

"You might just consider that there's another reason you're staying down here other than your mother's health."

"And what's that, Dr. Freud?"

"I think this thing with Cassie is getting serious, and you're scared shitless. And maybe you're more comfortable with your dysfunctional relationship with your mother than you are with the idea of something real."

Brian showed Ike his middle finger.

"Very mature," Ike said.

CASSIE HAD to hire someone before her grand opening, and she held interviews at the bakery over the course of a week. She'd advertised on Craigslist and in the local paper, and she'd gotten a fair number of responses. The problem was, a lot of the applicants either had no experience with baking or they arrived at the interview so unprepared that Cassie wondered if they were stoned, drunk, pranking her, or all three.

"This just isn't working," she told her mother at dinner one night in the Jordan kitchen after two dismal interviews. "I get that I might not find everything I want in a job candidate. But is it too much to ask that they at least be lucid?"

"You'll find someone." Nancy patted the back of Cassie's hand and offered her more pot roast.

"You're gonna have to offer more than minimum wage if you want a quality candidate." Vince propped his elbows on the table, folded his hands together, and rested his chin atop them. "I know you're on a budget, sweetie, but you get what you pay for."

She was offering more than minimum wage—just not much more. She wanted to be responsible with her money, and she didn't want Ryan Delaney to think she was spending freely just because she had a deep-pockets investor backing her.

Still, she could see her father's point.

The next day, Cassie changed the per-hour wage in the ad, raising it by two dollars, and she got a promising e-mail from an applicant within the hour.

They arranged to meet that afternoon at Cassie's Cakery.

~

"So, why did you leave your last job?" Cassie scanned Dylan Broderick's resume in her office at the bakery as her applicant sat in the newly purchased visitor chair, one foot resting casually on the opposite knee.

"The owner was a dick."

Cassie looked up sharply, and the guy shrugged and gave her a half grin.

He had attitude, but that wasn't necessarily a deal-breaker. Red hair, freckles, a mischievous, fuck-off look in his eye, and a right arm with a full sleeve of tattoos. But he had experience at one of the best bakeries on the Central Coast.

"Was he?" She kept her voice casual. "How so?"

"Woman I worked with had a baby, and he wouldn't give her maternity leave. He said either she showed up at work when her sick days ran out or he'd find someone else."

"But the Family and Medical Leave Act—"

"Yeah. He told her to sue if she didn't like it. He knew she wouldn't, with a new baby and all. Like I said. Dick."

"Oh. Well, I'd have to agree with you, then."

They talked about his experience—exactly what he'd done, for whom, and for how long—then moved on to the topic of Cassie's business and her vision for it.

"I'm new at this," she said, putting her metaphorical cards on the table. "I'll make mistakes. But then I'll learn from them. And I hope to learn from you, since you've been around in this business more than I have."

He looked at her with cool blue eyes. "You increased the pay in your ad."

"I did."

"Still not enough for me to have to teach you your job."

"You're absolutely right. It's not. And I don't expect you to teach me my job." Cassie leaned forward at her desk and rested her forearms on the surface. "But if you'll bear with me while I learn it through trial and error, we can talk about a raise in three months when we see how things are going." She had an inkling that Dylan's arrogance might be well-earned and that he might have the skills to back it up. She hoped she was right.

He narrowed his eyes at her, and she wasn't sure whether he was going to accept her offer or tell her to go screw herself.

He leaned forward and offered her his hand. "Deal. When do I start?"

WITH DYLAN ON BOARD, the next couple of weeks were an all-out rush in the run-up to the grand opening. The two of them worked on menus for what the bakery would offer routinely and what they'd be doing for the grand opening in particular.

Cassie's specialty was cakes—as the business name indicated—and Dylan's strength was bread, so that worked out. Lacy had agreed to work the coffee bar in the mornings while Nancy watched the kids. In fact, she seemed excited as hell to be getting out of the house and back to work.

Fortunately, Cassie didn't have to spend a lot of money on equipment to make specialty coffees, as much of what she needed had been left behind by Moonstone Mocha.

The week before the grand opening, Brian came up for a quick visit. Cassie found that vigorous and imaginative sex relaxed her at a time when she greatly needed relaxation. So that was good. But she was too busy to spend much time with Brian outside of bed.

She'd thought he would understand the reasons for that, but apparently he didn't, because he kept badgering her to slow down and be with him when she simply didn't have time for that.

"I thought we could just hang out, see a movie or something," he said as she rushed around his bedroom, gathering up her clothes from the floor on her way to the shower.

"Just hang out?" She stared at him in disbelief. "My grand opening is in less than a week, and I'm nowhere near ready."

"I know, but it's Sunday. Can't you just—"

"No, I can't, Brian. I have to test recipes, get in the rest of my supplies, work on marketing for the opening …"

"I can help you with the marketing," he said. "After I get back to LA, I can put together some ideas for you."

She was silent, standing there naked except for the ball of clothing clutched to her chest.

"What?" he asked.

"It's just … the marketing. That's okay. You don't have to help."

"Why not? We'd talked about it. I thought you wanted me to." He got up from where he'd been lying on the bed and put on some pants. Cassie wished she were wearing pants—fighting felt so much easier when you were properly panted.

"I did want you to."

"And now?"

"Now, it's getting close to the day, and you're …"

"I'm what?"

"You're not really available, that's all. You're busy. And I get that. But I can't wait until you're ready, because I have to get things moving. I'm running out of time."

He nodded, bobbing his head up and down, his face grim as he avoided her gaze. "You don't have time to wait for me to help you, and you don't have time to hang out with me."

"What's that supposed to mean?"

"It just means that I barely see you, and now that I'm here—"

"Whose fault is it that you barely see me?" She'd raised her voice— that meant they were going to get into it. And if they were going to get into it, she needed pants. Cassie quickly put down her clothes, slipped on her panties, and fastened her bra. She pulled on her jeans and slipped her T-shirt over her head as though donning armor for the coming fight.

"Now we're talking fault? It's nobody's fault," he said. "People's mothers need them sometimes. How is that my fault?"

"It's not!" Cassie threw her hands up. "It's not. And it's nice that you want to be there for your mom. But you can't just show up when you've got a spare minute and you want to get laid, and expect me to drop everything to watch movies with you!"

Brian was standing with his hands tucked into his armpits. "Okay. Right. Fine. But now I'm offering to help you with some of what you need to get done, and you don't want my help."

"I *do* want your help. I do! But I can't wait around until you're ready to give it!"

He raked a hand through his hair and blew out a breath. "Cassie …"

"It's fine. Look, Brian, it's fine. I can do this on my own, and I will. I am. I just can't get distracted right now."

"So now I'm a distraction?"

Cassie felt the pull of quicksand under her feet, as though anything she said to try to extricate herself would simply pull her in further until she couldn't move, couldn't breathe.

"Let's talk about this later," she said.

"I won't be here later. I'm going back to LA tonight."

She felt the sting of heat behind her eyes and willed herself not to cry. She bit her bottom lip and nodded. "Okay. I guess I'll see you, then." She picked up her purse from a table in the corner and headed for the door.

"You'll see me? That's all? Just, you'll see me?"

"What else is there?" She shrugged. "It's hard to have a relationship with someone who isn't here."

"And it's hard to think or move or do anything when everybody wants something from me. My mother, you. Everybody needs something, and everybody's pulling at me, and I don't have anything left, okay?"

"Okay." Cassie nodded. Now the tears did start to come, and she did nothing to stop them. "Well, I'll make it easy for you, then. I won't ask you for a damned thing. I'll just go, and you can focus on your mother."

"Cassie, that's manipulative. That's—"

She laughed. She couldn't help it—she laughed. "You're being manipulated here, Brian, but not by me. I'm the one woman in your life right now who's giving it to you straight. I can't play on your mother's level, and I don't want to. So, I guess she wins."

She walked out the door while he was still calling after her, still protesting.

CHAPTER 35

*C*assie cried on the drive back to Cambria, snuffling and wiping her eyes as she made her way north on Highway 1. She still hadn't had her shower—the fight had prevented it—so she went back to her trailer and got cleaned up there.

Then she dried her hair, got dressed, and resolved that she was done crying about it.

She didn't have time for crying.

When she got to the bakery, Dylan was already there, working on his recipe for sourdough bread with garlic and rosemary for the grand opening. He was wearing a bandanna around his head and a long apron over jeans and a T-shirt, and he was blasting rock music from a speaker hooked up to his iPhone. When she walked in, he was vigorously kneading dough, working it with the heels of his hands.

"Oh. Hey. Thought I'd get in early and do this. The music bothering you? I can turn it down." He seemed perky, even happy. And that pissed Cassie off. She didn't want to see someone acting perky and happy right now.

She stormed past him without answering, then went into her office and threw her purse onto the desk. Then she came back out into the kitchen, accidentally bumped into a cooling rack that was hanging from a hook on the wall, and sent it clattering to the floor.

"Damn it!" She picked up the rack and hurled it across the room.

"Oh. Hey, now." Dylan turned off the music. "Are you gonna be a dick like my last boss? Because it's better to know now, if you get what I'm saying."

"No. No." Cassie forced herself to take a deep breath, then picked up the rack and put it in the sink to be washed. "I'm sorry. I'm not a dick. I promise."

"Good to know." He put the dough in a bowl, covered it with a cotton towel, and set it aside to rise. Then he washed the flour off his hands at the sink.

"I suppose I owe you an explanation for my mood," Cassie said.

"No, you don't." He dried his hands on a towel tucked into his apron and went about cleaning his work surface.

"It's just … I had a really shitty morning."

"Understood. We're good."

"I think … I think my boyfriend and I broke up." As strongly as she'd admonished herself not to cry, here she was, crying.

"Ah, shit. That sucks. You want me to call your sister?" He patted her shoulder awkwardly.

"No." It came out elongated and shaky, a kind of *no-o-o-o*.

"Look. I'm just gonna go … somewhere … while my dough is rising. Give you some privacy."

"Okay." Cassie sat down on a stool at the work table and sobbed into her hands.

"Shit. Shit." Dylan hesitated, then pulled up a stool next to her. "I can't believe I'm asking this, but … you want to talk about it?"

"And then," Cassie said, wrapping up the story, "I told him that she wins. That his mother wins. And I left. And … I'm pretty sure that's it, right? It's over? It really seemed like it's over." She dissolved into fresh tears while Dylan sat there looking as comfortable as if his stool had been covered in spikes.

"That sucks ass," Dylan pronounced after hearing the whole story. "Competing with a dude's mother … you're never gonna win. She gave birth to him. She's got him by the balls. I mean, she made them, so."

"Right. Right. I know that." Cassie wiped her eyes with a tissue, then blew her nose. "And I don't even want to compete! Why can't he just love her, and love me, and live up here where his house is, and visit her regularly, the way people do? Why?"

"Dude's got issues."

"He does! And I just … I don't have time. Not now, not when I'm this close to having what I've always wanted. I don't have time to deal with his issues."

"Makes sense."

"But that doesn't make this any less awful." Cassie crumpled up her tissue and tossed it into a trash can, taking in a deep, shuddering breath.

"I guess not."

She stood up, smoothed her hair with her hands, and ran her fingertips under her eyes to get any last hints of smeared mascara. "I guess it's hopeless."

Dylan tilted his head in a maybe-not, maybe-so gesture. "Not necessarily."

"How is it not hopeless?"

He shrugged. "Dude's gonna get sick of his mother's shit, and he'll come around. But he has to do it on his own, not because you tell him to. Not because you issue an ultimatum."

"Okay. I get that. You think he will?"

"Maybe. Unless …"

She waited.

"He could be using his mother as an excuse," Dylan went on. "Like, this thing is moving too fast, and he's scared shitless, and his mother is a convenient way to get out of this before he's in too deep."

"Well … damn it."

~

BRIAN HADN'T INTENDED to have a fight with Cassie, and he certainly hadn't intended to have a relationship-ending blowout. All he'd wanted was to come to the Central Coast, spend some time with Cassie, and go back to LA feeling like a new man.

Instead, he was going back to LA feeling like a flaming pile of garbage.

How had that happened?

He could acknowledge that some of it had been his fault. He wasn't going to be around to help Cassie get ready for her grand opening, and that sucked. He didn't blame her for being annoyed.

And yes, he'd offered to help with marketing, and then he'd been too preoccupied to do it. So she had some valid cause to be pissed at him.

But what kind of person got angry at a guy for taking care of his sick mother? For Christ's sake. What kind of person did that?

He loved both of them, and one of them was in one place while the other was somewhere else.

How was he supposed to choose between them?

"This is bullshit, Thor," he said as he drove with the dog in the passenger seat beside him. "This is total bullshit."

Thor whined a little and curled up on the upholstery.

It wasn't like staying at his mother's place and worrying about her was fun. It wasn't like he was enjoying it. Did Cassie think he was down there partying with movie stars, taking up surfing, shopping on Rodeo Drive, and hanging out at clubs every night? Did she think he was having the time of his goddamned life?

He wasn't. He was spending his time watching his mother for signs of terminal illness, bringing her herbal tea and begging her to eat something. He was trying to make up reasons for her to get out of bed. He was doing the grocery shopping and fielding the phone calls, cleaning the loft and doing all of the things she'd hired Lorenzo to do before the fake-Italian douche had taken off for God knew where.

He wanted out of this as badly as Cassie wanted him out of it, but how? He couldn't just turn his back on his mother when she might really be in trouble.

And Cassie should understand that, shouldn't she?

What would she do if it were her own mother?

He ran through all of it in his mind as he drove. By the time he got to his mother's loft that afternoon, he was certain that he was the one being wronged here, and he'd resolved not to call Cassie, not to apologize.

She was the one who needed to apologize to him.

～

"MOM?" Brian called as he came into the loft, letting Thor off his leash.

He was relieved to find his mother in her studio space, working on a painting. She looked up and saw it was him, and she seemed almost … normal. Her color was good, her expression was upbeat, and she looked like herself for a change.

The weird thing was, that expression changed the moment she saw him. Everything just sort of fell, and her voice turned breathy and weak.

"Oh. Brian. I'm so glad you're back."

"How are you feeling?" He put Thor's dog bed on the floor, and Thor promptly curled up in it.

"Oh … you know." She sagged a little, as though half the air had been let out of her.

"No, I don't know. That's why I asked."

"It's the same," she said. "I don't want to bother you with it. Headaches. Nausea. I can barely stand without worrying that I'll collapse."

"Have you eaten anything today?"

She waved a hand dismissively. "I can't eat. I simply can't." Lisa abandoned her painting, pleading exhaustion, and went into her room to lie down.

Brian fed Thor, unpacked his bag, then decided to tidy up Lisa's loft, which had become a little disorderly in his absence. He put some glasses in the dishwasher, then found a tea bag stuck to the side of the sink. He took it to the kitchen trash can, stepping on the pedal to make the lid rise.

Inside the trash can, he found a takeout box from a local Thai restaurant. He picked it out of the trash and opened it. There was nothing left in the container except residue of sauce clinging to the sides and a few random noodles. A receipt had been taped to the side of the container, and Brian looked at it. Time: twelve-thirty that afternoon. The customer name on the receipt: Lisa. The single item that had been ordered was his mother's favorite.

So, maybe she hadn't lost her appetite after all.

BRIAN DIDN'T WANT to talk to his mother about what happened with Cassie. He hadn't intended to, and he'd told himself numerous times on the drive here that he wouldn't.

And yet, the whole debacle was pressing so hard on his mind and his emotions that he somehow ended up doing it anyway.

"I suppose you saw Cassie," Lisa said later that afternoon when she'd dragged herself out of bed long enough to make a cup of tea.

"I don't want to talk about Cassie."

"I didn't ask you to recount your every shared breath," Lisa said. "I simply asked if you saw her."

"I did. Yes. I saw her."

"Well. I'd expect you to be in a better mood than this, given the fact that you probably got laid."

"Mom!"

She shrugged. "I'm simply making a reasonable supposition, Brian."

And despite his better judgment, he did it. He told her. Was it so wrong that he wanted comfort from his mother?

"We ... ah ... had a fight. I think we broke up."

She perked up like Thor did at the sound of a can opener. "Broke up? What happened?"

He didn't want to interpret her reaction as glee that his relationship had flamed out and died. He wanted to interpret it simply as interest in the events of his life. But he knew better. And still, he told her what happened.

He edited the facts a bit, leaving out the part of the fight that involved her. Instead, he focused on the fact that he was here and Cassie was there, and how hard the separation had been on their budding relationship.

"She's mad that I haven't been there to help her get the bakery up and running. And that's fair. I haven't been there. I said I would help, and I didn't."

Lisa looked at him with the same laser-like intensity she'd used when he was little and he'd done something she'd explicitly told him not to. It was the look that usually preceded him being called by his first, middle, and last names.

"You're leaving out the most important part," she observed.

"Which part am I leaving out?"

"The part where your little girlfriend resents me."

He didn't confirm it, exactly, but he didn't deny it, either. "And you resent her, or you wouldn't be calling her my *little girlfriend.*"

"But don't you see, Brian, this is wonderful news! Now there's nothing to keep you on the Central Coast. Ike is here. I'm here. If you and Cassie are no longer together, there's nothing to stop you from relocating."

"Mom—"

"In fact, I've made an appointment for you with Avery Farrell."

He blinked at her. "Who's Avery Farrell?"

She waved him off. "Oh, you remember Avery, dear. He and I dated for a few months years ago. He's a producer for Netflix now."

Brian noted that Lisa's energy seemed to have fully returned.

"I don't remember him, Mom. We never met. I assume that was during the time you and I weren't in touch." The period of time when they weren't in touch had spanned years, beginning when Brian was a junior in high school and continuing until after he'd graduated college.

"Oh. I suppose that's right," she said, utterly without shame for having abandoned her son for more than six years. "Anyway, I told him about you, and he's dying to meet you."

"What for?"

"Why, so you can get a real job, of course. I told him about your YouTube activities, and he said he might be able to find you a job as a writer for a show they've got in pre-production. He wasn't able to promise you anything, of course, but if you'd just have lunch with him …"

"I don't want to have lunch with him."

"Fine. Drinks, then. You've gotten a slow start as far as building a career, but that's not important now. What matters is what you do from here. I'll call him and tell him you—"

"No." Suddenly, everything was clear: His mother wasn't sick. Cassie had been right—he was being played. Lisa had never supported his relationship with Cassie, and she'd lured him down here to separate them. And why? Because she was between boyfriends and she needed a man to pay attention to her?

And, of course, Lisa didn't respect his career, or his talent, or his passion for what he did. She saw him as a failure. She saw him as someone she had to save if he were to become anyone of consequence.

He felt like such an idiot.

"It almost worked," he said, his voice soft, as though he were talking to himself more than to her.

"What almost worked, dear? Speak up, I can barely hear you."

"Your plan. It almost worked."

Her smile faltered. "If you mean my plan to get you on at Netflix—"

"I don't. I mean your plan to come between me and Cassie and get me here to be at your beck and call. And you know what's the worst part of it? As soon as you find yourself another Lorenzo you won't even be interested in me anymore. The minute somebody starts fawning over you, you'll forget you have a son. Again."

"Oh, Brian, don't be ridiculous."

"Right. I'm being ridiculous. Any time I call you out on your bull-shit—your absolute, self-serving, narcissistic bullshit—I'm being ridiculous. Because my feelings couldn't possibly be legitimate."

She compressed her lips into a thin, harsh line. "This again."

"Yes, this again."

"I've told you, I left your father because I needed to pursue my career. I couldn't stay in a bad marriage, baking cookies and mopping the floor! I'd have died, Brian! Is that what you wanted? Is that what you still want?"

"No." He shook his head, shrugged. "No. I don't want anything from you. Except for you to admit that I became a good person without you. That I'm somebody of worth, and I became that because of Dad and because of Ike and his family. And none of it had anything to do with you."

He went into the spare bedroom, repacked the things he'd unpacked, snapped Thor's leash on, and headed toward the door.

"Brian, don't do this. Don't. I—"

"You love me? Is that what you were going to say?"

"I … I was going to say I need you."

Right. Of course she was. It had never been about love for her. It had always been about need. Hers, not his.

He left without saying another word.

CHAPTER 36

*B*rian showed up at Ike's apartment without announcing himself, leading Thor on his leash and looking like a man whose life had been upended by a woman. Which wasn't strictly accurate. His life had been upended by *two* women.

Ike wasn't there—he was in class—but his fiancée answered the door acting like she was glad to see him.

At least one woman he knew wasn't playing him or pissed at him.

"Brian! Hi. Come on in. Hi, Thor. Who's a good boy? Who's the best boy?" Benny rubbed Thor's fur vigorously, cooing into his ear and smooshing his face.

"Something tells me it isn't me," Brian said.

Benny cocked a fist on one hip and regarded him. "From the look of you, I'm thinking no. Ike's not here, but I've got beer. You want to come in and tell me about it?"

Brian had hoped to tell Ike everything and get his valuable perspective on what he should do. But Ike wasn't here, and Benny was a willing listener. Anyway, it might be nice to get a woman's view on things.

He laid it all out—Lisa's elaborate act of being sick; the fight he'd gotten into with Cassie over the fact that he was never there; Lisa's miraculous recovery when she learned that Cassie and Brian had broken up; and Brian's sense that he'd fucked up everything good in his life and had no hope of ever repairing things.

"Okay, a lot happened since the last time I talked to you," Benny said in what could only be described as understatement.

"Yeah. You could say that."

"So, what are you going to do?"

That was the question, wasn't it?

"Die lonely and wretched with nobody to love, and with nobody even knowing I'm dead until the smell coming from my house prompts them to alert the police?"

Benny gave him a wry smile. "Well, that's one option, I suppose. Or, you could apologize to Cassie."

They were sitting in the apartment's small living room, each of them with a cold longneck bottle of craft beer. Brian took a long swig of his, then shook his head.

"I can't."

"Why not?"

"Because it's embarrassing. She told me my mother was yanking my chain, and she was right. I told her she was being unreasonable. I told her she was being too needy. How do I walk that back? How do I admit that she was right about everything and I was wrong? It's too humiliating."

Benny leaned forward in her seat, her elbows resting on her knees, and looked at him. "Brian, you know I love you. It's in that spirit of love that I'm about to tell you something I really think you need to hear."

"What's that?"

"You need to pull your head out of your ass."

He frowned. "Now, wait. That's—"

"True. That's what it is. It's true."

Thor leaned against Brian's leg, and Brian gave him a rub. At least somebody still thought he was perfect.

"Cassie accused your mother of something, and it turned out she was right," Benny said. "And she accused you of neglecting her, and she was right about that, too. Stop me if I come to anything that's not factually correct."

Brian said nothing.

"Okay. So, it's time to grovel."

"You're not taking everything into account," he protested. "Cassie could have been way more understanding. Okay, it's true that my mother wasn't sick. But I really thought she was! And Cassie wanted me to do, what? Just ignore that? Just walk away and hope for the best? Lisa's my mother! You don't just walk away when you think your mother's in crisis."

"Sure," Benny said. "And if she's a stand-up person, she'll admit that. But she can't do that until you two have the conversation. Which you should be doing right now instead of sitting here drinking beer with me."

Brian's shoulders sagged as he shook his head. "It's not that simple."

"It is. It really is that simple."

Was it? Brian would have liked to think so, but he doubted it. He'd told Cassie he would help her with her bakery, and he hadn't done it. He'd proven to her that he was easy to manipulate and starved for his mother's love and approval. And, probably worst of all, he'd talked about his relationship with Cassie as though she were a burden—just another problem woman pulling at him and demanding things from him. How did a relationship, especially a new one, come back from that?

He wanted to turn back time to before the argument with Cassie, but that wasn't possible. He couldn't undo what had been done, couldn't unsay what he'd said.

The bottom line, really, was that he'd shown Cassie his greatest weakness, and now he doubted she would ever see him the same way again.

How could she ever see him as anything other than a mama's boy who was willing to jump through flaming hoops for the scheming, narcissistic woman who'd borne him?

Didn't that make him the exact kind of guy Cassie's own mother had probably warned her against?

"I just don't think groveling is going to do it," he told Benny.

"Maybe not," she said. "But you're certainly not going to get anywhere if you don't."

FEELING SAD AND DISPIRITED, Brian hung around long enough to see Ike. He got the same advice from Ike as he had from Benny—he had to beg for Cassie's forgiveness even if it meant annihilating his own male pride.

Then, with no further reason to stay in Los Angeles, he made the drive north. He arrived at his house in San Luis Obispo late, after the bars were closed and the streets were virtually deserted.

He took Thor around the block to pee, then brought him back inside and let him off the leash. Then he thought about unpacking, but instead, he just sank down onto his bed, fully clothed, and stared at the ceiling.

Surely there was a way he could get Cassie back without groveling. Surely there was some angle he could work, some approach he hadn't considered that would make this whole mess go away, so he and Cassie could proceed into their future together.

On the other hand, to be a man in a relationship with a woman meant the occasional plea for forgiveness. He knew that from experience. So, he might as well get used to it.

Or, he could decide this thing with Cassie was never meant to be, and he could move on.

Love was just the fucking worst.

BRIAN NEITHER CALLED nor texted Cassie for the next week. At first, it was because he hadn't decided what to say. Then he'd waited too long and the delay made things even more awkward than they had already been. Eventually his feelings evolved, and he didn't call her because he was angry that she hadn't called him.

He filled the time with activity so he wouldn't have to think about her: He planned and then shot another YouTube video; he worked on the marketing for his show; he took Thor for more walks than even the dog felt was prudent; he cleaned out his refrigerator and then his sock drawer; he watched movies and played video games.

While he did all of that, the same thought played on an infinite loop in his head: *Cassie Cassie Cassie Cassie.*

"Have you called her yet?" Ike asked on the phone on Thursday, several days after the fight.

"No."

"Why the hell not?"

Brian was lying on his sofa with Thor sprawled heavily over his lower legs. The afternoon sun was slanting in through the windows, creating elongated shadows.

"Why should I call her? Why hasn't she called me? That's the question, Ike. That's the real question."

Ike was silent for a long beat.

"What?" Brian prompted him.

"You know that thing you said to Benny about dying alone and being discovered by the smell? Yeah, well, that's starting to look more and more likely."

On Friday, he almost cracked. He was lying in bed at about eight a.m., thinking about getting up but not wanting to do it. He stared at the ceiling and thought about the fact that Cassie's grand opening was the following day. He thought about all she'd be doing today, her nervousness, her frantic activity. And he almost texted her to say good luck.

He even composed the text before deleting it.

He had so many reasons for staying silent: She'd wanted him to neglect his mother, who wasn't actually sick but who might have been.

She'd been impatient with him during his time in Los Angeles. And now, she was acting as though he didn't exist.

Those were the reasons he could freely admit. Other reasons were tucked into the back of his mind, behind some big boxes and crates so he wouldn't have to look at them: He was embarrassed. He didn't know how to admit he'd been wrong. He was scared that if he did admit it, she wouldn't want him anymore. He felt so beaten down by his damaged relationship with his mother that he wasn't sure he was capable of sustaining anything healthy and positive with a woman.

All of that rose up in front of him like an impenetrable wall, and he didn't know how to go around it or scale it.

"Don't eat me when I die at home alone," Brian said to Thor. "Then again, I won't be able to feed you, so do what you have to do, I guess."

Thor let out a high whine and rested his chin on Brian's thigh.

ON SATURDAY, Brian told himself he was not going to see Cassie. He was absolutely not interested in her grand opening, or her bakery, or anything that had to do with her.

Yes, he wished her well. He was happy for her that she finally had what she wanted. But that wasn't the same as him wanting to be a part of it.

Because he definitely did not.

The only reason he drove to Cambria at all was to get a piece of Linn's olallieberry pie. And why shouldn't he? It was really good pie.

As he made his way up Highway 1 and toward Cambria, he said to himself, *Pie. That's all I want. Just pie.*

If he overshot Linn's as he drove down Main Street, it was only because he was distracted. He hadn't intended to go as far as Cassie's Cakery, and if he had, it was only by mistake.

At ten a.m., the place was jumping with activity. The tiny parking lot was decorated with balloons and a banner declaring the bakery's official opening. All of the spots were taken, and a line extended out the front door. People were chatting and milling around in the front garden, some with muffins or scones, some with take-out coffee cups.

"Wow." Brian said the single word to no one as he cruised past the bakery. His feelings clutched at his chest. She was inside the building somewhere. She was having the biggest day of her life.

Without him.

Suddenly, he didn't want pie anymore. He wanted a scone, or maybe a muffin.

A latte wouldn't be so bad, either.

CHAPTER 37

*H*e had to wait in line for fifteen minutes before he got into the building and up to the cash register. Inside, the glass display case was full of baked goods: rolls, bagels, scones, cookies, and sumptuously decorated cakes. Lacy—who hadn't seen him yet, thankfully—was rushing around making espresso drinks and pouring coffee.

A red-haired guy with a sleeve of tattoos was working the register, taking orders and making change.

When Brian got to the front of the line, he asked for a latte and a scone, since those seemed to be the most popular items. At the sound of his voice, Lacy turned around, saw him—and froze, her mouth open in surprise.

"Oh." She was holding a stainless steel pitcher of steamed milk in her hand, a white cotton apron wrapped around her waist.

At that moment, Cassie came out of the kitchen carrying a platter of cookies. "Lacy, these are ready to go out. Could you—" Like her sister, Cassie froze when she saw Brian. The plate she was holding tipped, and a cookie slid off and fell to the floor before she noticed and leveled it.

"Brian," she said.

"Hi, Cass." He tried on a smile, but it didn't seem to fit right. "Congratulations. It looks like the opening is going great."

"I … thank you." She nodded a few times. "Thanks." The plate began to tilt again, and Lacy grabbed it from Cassie before more cookies could fall overboard.

"I'll just get this," Lacy said.

Dylan looked from Cassie to Lacy to Brian and back again. "Who's the stiff?" He motioned toward Brian.

"If you're done ordering, could I maybe …" The guy in line behind Brian gestured hopefully toward the front spot.

"Oh. Right." Brian paid for his order and stepped aside, trying to look nonchalant.

"I have to … do things." Cassie gestured vaguely around her and retreated to the kitchen.

WHILE BRIAN WAITED for his latte and his scone, he mingled with the crowd. Cassie's and Lacy's parents were there, along with her other sisters, her brother, her brothers-in-law, and a few nieces and nephews. Brian recognized a few of the Delaneys, including Ryan and Gen.

In addition, it seemed like half the town had come out to see what Cassie had done with the old Moonstone Mocha place. People stood around eating, drinking coffee, and chatting, musing about this piece of decor and the enticing flakiness of this or that baked good.

In the front and back gardens, people sat at tables or in Adirondack chairs in the shade of oaks and pines, eating and talking. The atmosphere was festive and fun.

Brian was genuinely impressed.

"You did it. You really did it," he said when Cassie brought him his drink and his scone out in the back garden. He was standing near a burbling fountain while birds chirped in the trees overhead. The morning was perfect—clear and bright—as though Cassie had special-ordered it.

"I did it," she agreed.

"Listen," he began.

Cassie wiped her hands on her apron and cut him off. "I don't have time for a fight," she said. "I don't know if that's what we're about to do—if we're about to fight—but if it is, I can't do it right now. I mean, I'm willing, but it'll have to be later, because—"

"I didn't come to fight."

She nodded. "Okay. That's good."

"I came to congratulate you on your place. It's really great. And I came to tell you that I'm back on the Central Coast for good." He wanted to tell her she'd been right about his mother, right about everything, but it all stuck in his throat and he couldn't manage to get the words out.

"You are? Really?"

"Yes. Really."

"How's your mother feeling?" She said it without rancor or sarcasm, and without any hint of judgment in her voice. And that had to have been hard, had to have taken some effort. He loved her for it.

"She's …" He shrugged. "She seems to have improved significantly." And then he thought, *fuck it.* "She made a miraculous comeback when I told her we'd had a fight and we might have broken up."

CASSIE HAD THOUGHT that when this moment came, when Brian told her she'd been right about Lisa, Cassie would relish saying she'd told him so. She'd thought her victory would feel good.

Instead, she saw the hurt in his eyes, heard him valiantly try to keep the pain out of his voice, and she felt like shit.

This wasn't the time to gloat. This wasn't the time for *I told you so.*

Instead, she put her hand on his arm and squeezed it a little. "Oh, Brian. Are you okay?"

He bobbed his head. "Yeah. Of course."

But he wasn't—she could see that.

"I want to talk about all of this," she said. "I do. But right now …" She gestured toward the customers, toward the activity around her.

"I should have helped you. I said I would, but I didn't."

She tilted her head a little as she regarded him. "Right now I need someone to circulate with a plate of samples. Are you up for it?"

CASSIE WASN'T ready to act like nothing bad had happened between herself and Brian. She wasn't ready to pretend everything was okay.

But neither her compassion nor her practical side would allow her to make an issue of it right now.

He'd wanted to believe in his mother, and she'd hurt him—again. Cassie couldn't bring herself to tear into him when the pain of that was still so raw.

And even if she had been inclined to tear into him, this was not the time. The grand opening was succeeding beyond her expectations, and she needed to give her attention and emotional energy to that.

"Are you okay? Is everything okay?" Lacy stage-whispered to Cassie in the kitchen as soon as they had a moment of semi-privacy.

"I'm fine," Cassie assured her. "Are we out of the lemon–poppy seed muffins?"

"Yes, we're out of them. And don't change the subject."

"I wasn't changing the subject. Or, I was, but only because I really needed to know about the lemon–poppy seed muffins."

"Cassie—"

"He had a thing happen with his mother, and now he knows she was playing him, and he's sad, and … he and I have a lot to talk about, but I can't do it now, so he's passing around samples."

Lacy tilted her head as she considered that. "Well, I can tell you that he's not passing out any lemon–poppy seed muffins. Those things moved faster than the Space Shuttle."

THAT NIGHT, Cassie went to Brian's place so they could talk things out. But by the time she got there, she was too tired to talk. She stretched out on his sofa with her feet in his lap while he rubbed them.

Thor lay stretched out on the floor beside her, and she absently rubbed his head with her hand.

"Ooh, right there. That's the spot." She moaned with pleasure as Brian applied pressure to her right arch, moving his thumb in firm circles.

"You were on your feet a lot today," he observed.

"I'm used to that, mostly, because of all the house-cleaning for Central Coast Escapes. And I spend a lot of time standing when I do an elaborate cake. But today I was at the bakery at four a.m. and I stayed until two hours after closing. I'm wrecked."

"You starting to regret your career choices?"

"Oh, hell no. Today was the most fun I've had in a long time. Did you see how many people were there? I mean, I know a lot of it was curiosity—people wanted to see what was going on—but everybody seemed to love the food. A lot of them will come back."

"They will." He turned his attention to the ball of her foot, kneading and rubbing.

After a while, she brought up the thing they both knew they had to address.

"I didn't think you were going to come."

"I didn't think I was, either," he admitted.

"We both said things...."

"We did."

And just when she could have called him on the hurtful things he'd said to her and all of the ways he'd been wrong, she decided instead to let him keep that essential part of himself that was so at risk right now. She let him hold onto his pride.

"I'm glad you came," she said. She sat up, reached out, and squeezed his arm. "It meant a lot for you to be there."

"I'm glad I did, too." He let go of her foot, leaned forward, took her face in his hands, and kissed her, his mouth caressing hers.

He shifted on the sofa to align his body with hers, and he lowered himself onto her, exploring the feel and the taste of her.

After that, they didn't do any talking at all.

∼

BRIAN KNEW he couldn't avoid saying the words forever. They were festering inside him, and he needed to get them out.

When they were lying in his bed later, bathed in the moonlight slanting in through the window, he finally said them.

"My relationship with my mother is so dysfunctional, I wonder sometimes if I'm too fucked up to make things work with any woman. I wanted to think it was different with Lisa this time. Then, when I finally saw that she'd been lying to me—again—I just …"

"It hurt your confidence," she said.

"Yeah. It did."

"It's not your fault." She rolled onto her side to look at him. "I don't know if anyone's told you that, but her leaving when you were little? And then staying away and only coming around when she needs or wants something? None of that is your fault, Brian."

He nodded. He cleared his throat and rubbed his eyes, and she knew he was trying not to cry. Her heart hurt for him.

"I know," he said after a while. "And yeah, people have told me that. Ike. Ike's mother. My father. But it still hurts like hell."

She held him close and let him feel that she was strong enough, solid enough, for both of them.

"When you think about it," she said, "you've got two chances to have a good family life. First with the one you're born into. And then with the one you choose for yourself."

"But the only example I've had is one that didn't work. What if I can't do any better than that? What if I'm like her?"

"You did have better examples. You had your father, who loved you and was there for you. And you had Ike's family. You saw what a solid home life looked like. You can do it if you really want to."

He ran one hand over her hair, smoothing it. "You really think so?"

"I really do."

267

She hadn't expected to be the first one to say it post-crisis, but he needed to hear it right now. And anyway, it was true.

"Brian?"

"*Hmm?*"

"I love you."

"Cassie, I'm sorry I didn't—"

She put a finger over his mouth to quiet him. "That's not what you're supposed to say right now."

He grinned and kissed her deeply. "I love you too, Cassie."

CHAPTER 38

*B*rian made up for lost time by creating a marketing plan for Cassie's Cakery that was both comprehensive and inventive.

"Social media—that's a no-brainer," he told her late one afternoon after the bakery's four p.m. closing time. "You've got to be on Facebook and Twitter, yeah. But Instagram and Pinterest are going to be your key media."

"Why?" she asked.

"Because of the visuals. You need to put up something beautiful—could be a baked good, could be a scene from your garden—every day, or at least three times a week."

Cassie saw the point of that, of course, but she was already swamped with work. When would she find the time?

"Anything else?" she asked.

"Of course. You need a website with online ordering. I can help you with that. And Cambria's very community-oriented. You need to be involved. Sponsor the community fund-raisers. Offer desserts at cost for the Greenspace auction or the high school boosters annual reverse draw. That kind of thing. Not only is it good PR, it also gets everyone tasting your products."

"Okay." She nodded. "I can do that."

"You need to get in touch with the local hotels," he went on. "How many of them offer a free breakfast? Almost all of them, right? Your muffins and croissants need to be the centerpiece of every continental breakfast in town. And," he said, "we need to do more videos. People on social media are more likely to watch a video than they are to read a static ad. But that's just a small part of it. If we make you a YouTube personality, people are going to travel to Cambria just to visit your bakery."

"They will?"

"Sure they will. And as far as the locals go, how many wedding cake orders did you get from the videos we did?"

"Four. And I'm still getting inquiries."

"Well, there you go."

They were sitting at the kitchen table in Cassie's parents' house, each of them with a cold beer. Nancy was puttering around the kitchen humming happily, excited that Cassie had started bringing her boyfriend around.

Nancy put a basket of tortilla chips and a bowl of salsa on the table. "Here you go, you two." She squeezed Brian's shoulder—she actually squeezed his shoulder.

Cassie imagined that Nancy was already counting the new grand-children she might have.

"Thanks, Mom," Cassie said.

They ate and drank as Cassie pondered her future.

"The grand opening was huge," she said. "I mean, I thought it might go okay, but ... I had no idea. I'm going to have to hire at least two more people, especially for the summer tourist season. Three, if I get orders from hotels, like you mentioned."

"You're going to need even more than that if you want to spend the bulk of your time on wedding cakes," Nancy said.

"She's right," Brian put in.

"I knew I liked you," Nancy quipped.

Cassie sat back in her chair and sighed happily. "This thing really might work."

"Of course it's going to work," Brian said.

"Now if I only had several more hours in a day," Cassie added.

"Listen." Brian set his beer down on the table and leaned forward. "Now that the repairs on my house are done, I'm putting it on the market. You think you could use some of those limited hours to look at real estate with me? I'd like your perspective."

Cassie blinked a few times in surprise. "You're selling your house? When did that happen?"

He shrugged. "I've been planning it for a while. I mentioned it when we met, remember? That's how I found out about the termites and the mold—I was getting it ready to sell. It's an old house, and it's a money pit. I need something more up to date."

"Okay." Cassie nodded. "Were you going to look in San Luis Obispo?"

"I was thinking Cambria."

"You were?"

"Sure. Why not?"

Nancy hummed a little louder, and the song was slightly more jaunty than before Brian's announcement.

"I'd love to help you look, but I'm pretty busy," Cassie said.

"You'll make time," Nancy told her.

THEY TOOK A MONDAY—A day when the bakery was closed—and toured properties with Brian's Realtor. Cassie noted, with some puzzlement, that Brian seemed to be interested in houses larger than the one he currently had, even though it was just him and Thor.

"Do you like the kitchen in this one?" he asked, walking around amid the granite countertops and the sleek maple cabinetry.

"It's nice. Spacious. Good appliances. But you don't cook."

"Maybe you'll want to use it sometimes," he said. "Like you did at Otter Bluff."

Maybe she would. After all, she still lived in the Airstream, and the kitchen there was still more suited to a Barbie Dreamhouse.

"I guess I might," she acknowledged.

"And how about the rest of the place?"

Cassie considered it. Three bedrooms. A big, open-concept great room with a stone fireplace. Two-car garage, three bathrooms, all recently renovated. A sliver of ocean view through the treetops.

It was a lovely house—one that, if she were being perfectly honest, made her heart hum.

"I love it," she told him. "But isn't it a little big for one person and a dog?"

"What if it were more than one person?" He raised his eyebrows in question.

"Are you planning to get a roommate?" Cassie, God help her, still didn't see where he was going with this, even though she should have.

"Well … I was kind of hoping you'd be my roommate. And my bedmate. And my … you know. Life mate. If you're up for it."

Her jaw dropped, and she gaped at him.

"Are you … Brian, are you asking me to marry you?"

"Would you say yes to that?"

"I … Oh, God. I don't know." Her heart hammered in her chest, and her knees were suddenly weak.

"If you don't know, then that doesn't have to be what I'm asking. We could just move in together. And then … we'll see."

"We'll see," she repeated.

"Yes."

She stepped away from him to clear her head, and she wandered through the house with him trailing behind. Suddenly, she could see it. She could see herself and Brian in this house, sharing a bed, sharing a life. She could see her big family gathering in the great room at Christmas or Thanksgiving, with Ike and Benny there, too. She could see Thor running around in the yard, chasing squirrels.

She could see all of it, and she wanted it.

"Okay." She turned to him.

"Okay, what?"

"Okay, I'll be your roommate. And your bedmate. And then … we'll see."

He pulled her into his arms and kissed her just as the Realtor walked in from outside. She'd stepped out to give them privacy, but it hadn't turned out to be quite enough privacy.

"Oh. Ha, ha. Sorry," she said.

"You want to help me write up an offer?" Brian asked her.

EPILOGUE

*I*ke and Benny got married in spring, and of course, Cassie made their wedding cake.

The cake was a four-tiered rustic design with a semi-naked application of frosting that showed hints of the layers underneath. Buttercream cabbage roses in a dusky pink cascaded down the front and pooled at the base.

Cassie had baked the cake not at Cassie's Cakery, but in the kitchen of the house she shared with Brian in the Top of the World neighborhood. This cake wasn't business, it was personal, so that seemed more appropriate.

The ceremony was held in the garden at Cambria Pines Lodge, with Ike and Benny exchanging vows in a gazebo beneath a canopy of climbing vines. They'd talked about doing it in Los Angeles, but Benny's family was here, and so were many of Ike's friends. Ike's family had to travel north from San Diego, but most of them relished the opportunity to spend a long weekend in Cambria.

Brian was the best man, of course, and Benny had three maids of honor: her three sisters. She'd been unable to choose among them.

Cassie couldn't take her eyes off Brian during the ceremony, even though she was supposed to be focusing on the bride and groom.

Brian looked good in a tux, but that wasn't what she found so compelling. It was the way he glowed with happiness for his best friend, the way he couldn't seem to wipe the big, goofy smile off his face.

Before the vows were exchanged, he looked out at the crowd, saw Cassie, and winked.

Just a wink, so quick she might have missed it.

It said everything. That wink encompassed all of his plans for both of them, for their future, their lives stretching out into eternity together.

When he'd asked what she would say if he proposed—back when they'd looked at their house for the first time—she'd said she didn't know.

But she knew now. She wanted this—wanted all of it. She wanted him, now and forever.

AT THE RECEPTION in the lodge's ballroom, there were toasts and speeches, the bride and groom's first dance, the drinking of champagne, the cutting of the cake.

All of them rode a gentle wave of happiness and goodwill.

Brian took Cassie's champagne flute out of her hand, put it on a table, and drew her onto the dance floor as the swell of music began.

"Ike and Benny look really happy," Cassie said as Brian pulled her into his arms and they both began to sway.

"They are," he agreed. "They really are."

"They're a great couple," she said. "I think they're going to last."

"We are, too." He said it matter-of-factly, as though it were a simple truth.

They danced together amid the scent of roses and the music of a string quartet. Cassie felt like she was floating, like she never wanted to stop.

"You know when we looked at the house, and I said there was a thing I didn't know?"

"Yeah."

"Well, now I know. It's yes. If you asked, it would be yes."

"Really?" His face lit up, and he spun her around so fast she felt dizzy.

She laughed. "Yes, really. I want it all. I want you, and I want to be Thor's mom."

"Speaking of being someone's mom, we do have those two spare bedrooms...."

"Let's not get ahead of ourselves."

And that was okay. There was no need to rush. She wanted it all, and so did he.

There was plenty of time to enjoy getting there together.

**

To read Ike and Benny's story, purchase Loving Benny, a stand-alone romance in the Russo Sisters series. Learn about it at www. lindaseed.com.

www.ingramcontent.com/pod-product-compliance
Lightning Source LLC
Chambersburg PA
CBHW020418260626
47156CB00007B/2454